LYSANDER'S LADY

Lysander's Lady

· ELIZABETH HAWKSLEY ·

St. Martin's Press 📖 New York

Library of Congress Cataloging-in-Publication Data

Hawksley, Elizabeth.
Lysander's lady / by Elizabeth Hawksley.
p.   cm.
ISBN 0-312-14008-8
I. Title.
PR6058.A8965L97   1996
823'.914—dc20   95-26048   CIP

First published in Great Britain by Robert Hale Limited

First U.S. Edition: March 1996
10 9 8 7 6 5 4 3 2 1

To my mother,
with love.

One

There was a sudden commotion outside the little rose-covered cottage where Miss Clemency Hastings was sitting quietly talking to her old governess, the clatter of dancing hooves, the whinny of a frightened horse, then a heavy thump and silence. Clemency ran to the parlour window which overlooked Richmond Park and peered out. In the distance a riderless horse, reins hanging, was disappearing among the trees.

'Biddy! There's a man hurt, I think!' she cried.

Miss Biddenham clutched at the arms of her chair and made as if to rise. 'This wretched arthritis!'

'No! I'll go.'

There was a low groan as she reached the garden gate. A man was lying against the wall, white-faced and with a graze on his forehead where he must have struck the wall on his fall. His eyes were closed. Clemency, after a moment's hesitation, took hold of one strong, brown hand and felt for the pulse. It was there, erratic and unsteady, but it was beating. At that moment the man's eyes opened and stared, first hazily, then with increasing intelligence at her. The hand in her lap turned and grasped her wrist and he whispered, with the ghost of a smile, 'Am I in Heaven?'

Clemency blushed and tried to pull her hand away. 'Hush, sir. You have had a riding accident. You must have taken a nasty fall.'

The gentleman frowned, wincing slightly as he did so. 'I remember. The damned horse shied at something: only half-broken.'

'Then you were foolish to ride it,' said Clemency severely. 'From the state of your forehead you must have hit Miss Biddenham's wall as you came down. It's a wonder you didn't

7

break your neck.'

He let go of her hand and dragged himself up to a sitting position and felt gingerly at his forehead. 'A graze, nothing more.'

'You are probably concussed,' observed Clemency.

'Nonsense, girl!' He tried to rise, turned pale and fell back heavily against the wall. He managed a weak laugh. 'When my guardian angel says I am concussed, it must be so! I have some brandy in my jacket pocket.'

Clemency took out the flask, unscrewed it and handed it to him. He drank deeply, sighed and handed it back to her. She was pleased to see that some colour had come back into those lean cheeks. He was sitting with his eyes closed once again and she surveyed him covertly. He was tall, loose-limbed and very dark. His black hair was wild and unruly and his face, with its thin Roman nose and high cheekbones was harshly lined. He wouldn't have looked out of place, thought Clemency, (whose leisure hours were spent reading – to the despair of her mama,) wreaking mayhem with the hordes of Genghis Khan.

'Oh!'

For his sloe-black eyes had opened and he had caught her staring at him. Swiftly she looked away. The gentleman obviously felt no such inhibitions about looking his fill: Clemency was very conscious of his gaze wandering over her face and then down over her neck and breasts. She felt her colour rise.

'So, even angels can blush?' He sounded amused.

'You ... you are looking at me,' she managed to whisper, and one part of her was wondering why she did not leave at once in the face of such ungentlemanly scrutiny.

'You are very beautiful. Hair like pale gold and eyes like cornflowers. And a figure....' He laughed. 'No, the figure cannot be that of an angel, only that of a very desirable woman!'

'Sir!' This time Clemency did attempt to rise. But his hand shot out and imprisoned hers and then the other reached out and, cupping her head, drew her gently but insistently down to him.

'N ... no!' she whispered; but it was too late. He kissed her, at first softly, his lips just brushing hers, and then with a groan he pulled her into his arms.

Clemency felt her senses reel; she had never, it seemed, been kissed before: the clumsy embraces of her father's clerks at

Christmas time, or old Mr Dodderidge's bristly kisses were simply not the same thing. Coolly, deliberately, this unknown man had sought out her mouth and plundered its treasures, and in taking he had demanded, for Clemency found her own hands slipping round his neck, her own heartbeat echoing the thud of his.

Then his hands were pulling out the tortoiseshell combs that held her hair and burying themselves in the silken tresses.

'So soft, so sweet!' he murmured against her mouth.

There was a thud of hooves in the distance and shouts. Clemency broke free and began with trembling fingers to pick up the combs and straighten her disordered hair. Dimly she was aware of people approaching. She rose to her feet, blushing, and stood awkwardly against the gate.

A man and a woman cantered up. The man jumped down.

'Strawberry returned without you,' he cried. 'What happened?'

The man shook his head vaguely. 'Heavenly intervention.'

'Very likely! I warned you she was half-broken!'

The lady, slim and immaculate in a green velvet riding-dress, now slid off her horse and, brushing past Clemency said, 'Come, we must get you home. This girl' – indicating Clemency disdainfully – 'will doubtless send a message to Dr Burnley.'

The man assisted the other to rise, brushed him down and picked up his fallen hat and riding crop. He turned to Clemency. 'Yes, there's a good girl. Stoneleigh Manor. Be a pet!' He reached in his pocket and flicked her half a guinea.

'Here, Oriana, take his things while I help him on to my horse. Well,' to Clemency, 'don't just stand there wench, be off!'

That evening, as the carriage left Richmond Park and took her home to Russell Square, Clemency carefully took out the events of the day and examined them. What had happened, after all? She had helped an injured man, guest, so Biddy told her, of the Baverstocks at Stoneleigh Manor, who had kissed her. Doubtless, like his friend, he had assumed that she was some village wench whom he had kissed idly, carelessly, as he had probably done many times before.

She could not deny that the kiss, so casually bestowed had

meant something to her; but it would be ridiculous to assume that it meant anything to him. He was suffering from pain and shock and plainly not himself. What was she hoping for? That, like Prince Charming, he would scour all the houses in the village to find out who she was?

And even if he did, what then? Would such a gentleman, guest of the elegant Oriana, be willing to pursue the acquaintance when he knew who *she* was? She might have eyes like cornflowers – here she smiled reminiscently – but she was not of his world.

She was rich, it was true, for her father, a self-made man, had worked his way up to being one of the City's most prosperous merchants. When he had died two years ago he had left her a fortune of £100,000 and her mother £5,000 a year. Mrs Hastings had promptly attached her maiden name on to her surname and become (so she hoped) the vastly more genteel Mrs Hastings-Whinborough, and once her mourning was over, set herself by every means possible to enter the select world of fashionable society.

Alas, her efforts had so far met with little success. She and her daughter were Trade, that small word that damned them for ever from entering the portals of the well born. Not that Clemency had ever particularly wished for it, for her tastes were simple, not to say bookish, and she disliked the idea of fashionable routs and parties. And that was the world to which her unknown gentleman undoubtedly belonged.

No, Clemency told herself sternly, she must forget him. It was an isolated incident. It would not recur.

Lysander Candover, 5th Marquess of Storrington by the death of his father the 3rd Marquess some six months earlier and the subsequent demise of his elder brother, Alexander, in a drunken brawl a few months later, sat in the book-room of his town house and scowled at his lawyer.

'Why the devil wasn't I told earlier of the appalling mess we're in?' he demanded, one lean, brown hand idly twisting the stem of a brandy glass. 'Good God, man, we're mortgaged up to the hilt, the rents are falling, we've no money to make even the most minimal improvements to the land, let alone the house!' He glanced up at the ceiling, one corner of which was stained with damp.

'The marquess, your noble father, always thought ...' the lawyer began unhappily.

Lysander flung up a hand. 'Don't tell me, I can guess! A certainty at Newmarket, a lucky run of the dice.'

'He was not, alas, a fortunate gambler.' Mr Thornhill shook his head sadly.

'I suppose Alex ...' began Lysander and stopped.

Lord Alexander, a dissolute and expensive young man, had always flung money around like water. Vicious and extravagant, his death had aroused no feelings amongst his nearest and dearest other than those of profound relief. In fact, thought Lysander, it was probable that his brother's dissipations had contributed as much to the ruinous state of the family finances as his father's unlucky gambling. At least the marquess played fair: Lord Alexander was quite capable of cheating.

Lysander himself, a suddenly-sobered twenty-six, had been as wild as the rest of them. But he had had only a younger son's portion; otherwise he lived by his wits. Fortunately these were keen, and a cool head and steady judgement usually enabled him to indulge his expensive tastes in horseflesh and women without too much trouble.

'And Arabella?' he enquired. Arabella was his sister, sixteen, hot-headed, wilful and as pretty as a picture. She had had six governesses in as many months.

Mr Thornhill sighed and shook his head. 'Your father always thought there was time enough to provide for your sister.'

Lysander reached over to the decanter and poured himself another glass of brandy. 'So, on a shrinking rent roll of about £900 a year, I have to pay off these mountainous debts, support my sister and pull the place together,' he said grimly. 'It can't be done, Thornhill.'

The lawyer said nothing, only shuffled some papers on the desk in front of him.

'What about my aunt?'

'Lady Helena has some money of her own. She paid the late marquess about a hundred a year for her keep. She has further said that she will pay for Lady Arabella's governess – if she has the choosing of her.'

Lysander looked up at that. 'What happened before?'

Mr Thornhill coughed. 'I understand that Lord Alexander chose the ladies – somewhat unsuitable choices, I believe.'

'I can imagine,' said Lysander grimly. He remembered coming down shortly after his father's funeral and finding some simpering creature in the post, forever making sheep's eyes at his brother over the dining-table. God knows what effect it had had on Arabella's morals.

He was silent for a moment, staring down into his glass, seeing suddenly, not the problems in front of him, but the bluest of blue eyes and a trembling little mouth. He put the glass down abruptly.

'Well?' he said harshly. 'Is there anything left to sell?'

The lawyer hesitated for a moment, cleared his throat and looked apprehensively at the marquess's unyielding features.

'Well?'

'My lord,' stammered Thornhill, 'you might consider it a liberty, but ... I have served your noble family for many years, and my father before me.'

Lysander leaned forward. 'Go on!'

'I wonder if ... of course, I shouldn't venture to suggest it if the situation weren't desperate, but ...' he paused, uncertain of how to continue.

'Never mind that,' interrupted Lysander. 'What have you in mind?'

'A suitable marriage, my lord.'

'Marriage!' echoed Lysander blankly. 'Good God, Thornhill, you must be out of your mind! Who on earth would marry a man with an uncertain £900 a year and a mountain of debts?'

'You're a marquess,' the lawyer reminded him.

'I doubt if even the pleasure of being a marchioness is worth the £50,000 it's going to take to pull us out of debt! Let alone the money that needs putting into the place. It's very flattering, Thornhill, but I cannot possibly imagine my title to be worth as much.'

'I'm not so sure, my lord.'

'Well I am! I have already been hinted away by several prudent mamas.'

'Your lordship is thinking, naturally, of members of Society. But....'

'Are you suggesting I should marry some *cit's* daughter?' Lysander's lean face tightened. His hooded dark eyes looked disdainfully down over his patrician nose.

'There are plenty of agreeable and very wealthy daughters in the City,' said Mr Thornhill steadily. 'Some of them have been educated at select Bath seminaries. I do not think you need find them either gauche or ill-mannered.'

'A Candover to marry some jumped-up tradesman's daughter!' exclaimed Lysander. 'No! There must be an alternative.'

'There is no alternative, my lord.'

Lady Helena Candover, sister of the 3rd Marquess, felt that her position as chatelaine of Candover Court, chaperone of her niece Arabella, and the only member of her family to be living within her means, fully entitled her to interfere in her nephew's affairs. She was a tall, thin lady with angular features, a harsh voice and much given to striding down the draughty corridors of Candover Court followed by various yapping small dogs. As a young girl her brusqueness had terrified the local gentry, the male members of whom dreaded having to ask her to dance and be on the receiving end of her forcefully expressed opinions. Now, in her fifties, she was deemed merely eccentric. But underneath that unprepossessing exterior she was genuinely kind-hearted, and, moreover, had the distinction of being the only person the Lady Arabella ever heeded.

She had regarded her brother's ruinous course with concern, and Lord Alexander's with despair. When the news of Lord Alexander's untimely death reached Candover Court, Lady Helena's first reaction was, 'Thank God! Now we'll have Lysander; down Pongo, down, sir!' Not that she set much store by Lysander, but he did at least play fair, and, for all his gaming and women, seemed to be able to finance them himself. At least, he had never applied to her for money, unlike his father and brother.

She watched, her acerbity masking a very real concern, as Lysander spent the first few weeks closeted with Thornhill, his face becoming haggard and drawn as he struggled to make sense of the incoming flood of final demands. To his credit he was at least attempting to tackle the problems rather than plunging headlong into further dissipation. Lysander went back to London to see what needed to be done there and, after a few days' thought, Lady Helena pushed the dogs from her with the air of one engaging upon a forlorn hope and summoned the coachman. For the sake of the Family, she must Speak!

She bade a strict farewell to Arabella, climbed into the ancient travelling coach and set off for London and her nephew's town house.

After a long and tiresome journey being laughed at by toll-keepers and post-boys (for the coach had been in the stables at Candover Court for over fifty years) she arrived in Berkeley Square.

She was too late to see her nephew that evening, and indeed welcomed the chance for a rest. 'I must be getting old, Timson,' she said to the butler on her arrival. 'It is not fifty miles, but my bones feel all shaken to pieces. I shall see the marquess in the morning.'

'I am delighted to see you, Aunt Helena,' said Lysander over breakfast the following morning, not entirely truthfully, 'but I do not know how I may entertain you. I am busy all the time with these damned bills.'

'Don't be a fool,' responded his aunt shortly. 'I have come, Storrington, because I wish to talk to you on a matter of some importance.'

Lysander raised his eyebrows.

'Thornhill has explained the situation, Storrington. Now don't look down your nose at me, I pray. He deals with my financial affairs as well as yours, you know.'

Lysander bowed non-committally.

'It seems to me that you have a choice: either you sell Candover and Arabella and I remove ourselves to Bath or some such dreary spa, *or* you do the sensible thing and marry money.'

'I have already made my views on the second option perfectly clear,' said Lysander in tones of ice. 'If I sell Candover I can afford to house us all in reasonable comfort in London.'

'Unlikely,' snapped Lady Helena impatiently. 'The place isn't worth a penny. The house is falling down, the land in disrepair;

I doubt whether even the best purchase price would do more than clear your debts. If you were lucky you might have a thousand or so for Arabella. And you'll never get Candover back, Nephew. Once it's gone, it's gone forever.'

Lysander rubbed his hand wearily across his brow, saying in a milder tone, 'I know, Aunt Helena. Do you think I haven't thought? But to marry some jumped-up tradesman's daughter!'

'Now you are being foolish. Look at Lord Yelverton. His wife came from an East India merchant's family. I hear she is a very agreeable woman.'

'He was fortunate then.'

'Not at all, Nephew. Merely prudent.'

Lysander sighed. Lady Helena looked at him hopefully. Mr Thornhill had told her of his initial reaction. Well, perhaps her efforts would be more successful. She opened her reticule.

'I have three names here. Doubtless there are many more. But these three seem to Mr Thornhill and myself to be the most promising; not necessarily the most wealthy, but the most suitable: one would certainly not wish to see some female of the vulgar mushroom sort installed as mistress of Candover!

'Here is the list, Storrington. I consider any of the ladies mentioned to have the manners and taste to fit a high position.'

'How the devil am I to decide, Aunt Helena?' said Lysander irritably. 'Damnation, it's not like looking at the form on the racecourse!'

'Nonsense, it's very similar. First of all there is Miss Grubb, only child of Mr Thomas Grubb – I believe he made his money during the late wars. Highly respected in the City. Miss Grubb was educated at the Milsom Academy in Bath and is a friend of Lady Anne Hope. She has an exceptionally well-informed mind with serious principles.'

'My mind is anything but well informed,' muttered Lysander, 'and it is well known that I have no principles at all. I know the sort of female: she'll go around in dreary bonnets and visit the deserving poor.'

'Very suitable,' said Lady Helena dampeningly. 'She can visit the villagers in Abbots Candover.'

'Go on. Who else?'

'Then there is Mrs Meddick, relict of the old nabob.'

'Good God, but how old is she? He was in his seventies, surely?'

'Mrs Meddick was his second wife, and much younger. She may be a year or so older than you but nothing to signify. Mrs Meddick,' she paused significantly, 'is worth a quarter of a million pounds!'

'I doubt then whether she'd be interested in a bankrupt marquess. With that money she could buy a perfectly solvent one!'

'Don't be sarcastic, I pray. Mr Thornhill thinks she would be interested.'

'Who's the third lady?'

'A Miss Hastings-Whinborough. £100,000 from her father, a provision merchant. She has a tiresome mother I'm told. But apparently the girl herself is accounted beautiful and sweet natured.' She suppressed the fact that the lady in question was also held to be something of a blue-stocking, though it must be admitted that to Lady Helena anybody whose reading was more than the Court Circular or perhaps turning over the pages of the *Spectator* (though, of course, not actually *reading* them) might be accounted alarmingly clever.

There was a pause, then the marquess gave a short laugh.

'What am I to say, Aunt Helena? I have a prejudice in favour of a wife younger than myself and I don't care for widows, so that rules out Mrs Meddick. And I really cannot marry a lady whose name is Grubb – besides finding uniform virtue a dead bore! So that leaves us with the pretty Miss Harding-Whortleberry, or whatever her name is.'

'Now you are being sensible,' said Lady Helena approvingly.

'If I am to marry for money then I must at least see for myself that the wench is presentable. How the devil am I to look her over without committing myself?'

'Leave it to me!' pronounced her ladyship. 'Let me see; Hastings-Whinborough ... doubtless her mother is on some charitable committee or other. I shall make enquiries!'

A week or so later the unsuspecting Clemency Hastings (for she would not call herself Hastings-Whinborough, which she found both affected and unnecessary) went to spend the morning with two friends, Mary and Eleanor Ramsgate. She was relieved to get out of the house, for though she tried to be a dutiful daughter, she could not be an affectionate one. Mrs Hastings-Whinborough's mind was of too narrow and jealous an order for her to be anything of a companion to her daughter. The first year after her father's death had passed amicably enough, for Clemency was too grieved to take in the difficulties of her new position and her mother observed the strictest mourning, for besides having the idea that black suited her blonde colouring, she was also a woman of rigid convention and the observances must be kept.

The following year her mother (now stunningly attired in lavender and pearl grey) had done her best to attach Alderman Henry Baker, for she was convinced that it would be best for Alderman Baker if she married him. Her pursuit of the gentleman occupied all of her attention and Clemency was allowed to be quiet and visit only the friends she loved best. Alderman Baker had successfully remained a bachelor for more than fifty years; his views on matrimony were well known in the City. Bets were laid as to which should prove more successful, the Alderman's misogyny or the widow's insistence. If she had known of the betting Clemency would have unhesitatingly backed her mama whose ability to get her own way had frequently worn down both her father and herself. Then, by accident or design, Alderman Baker died of an apoplexy and Mrs Hastings-Whinborough turned her attentions to her daughter.

She did not exactly say that the presence of a younger, more attractive, more intelligent female was unwelcome to her, but nevertheless her hints were enough to make Clemency uneasy and she welcomed the chance to get out of the house and visit Mary and Eleanor.

Mary and Eleanor were both lively, unaffected girls, fashionably brunette, Mary with laughing dark eyes and Eleanor with grey ones. Besides Mary and Eleanor there were three sons and another, much younger daughter, and the house was always a hive of cheerful noise and comings and goings. Clemency had always been welcome there, Mrs Ramsgate regarding her as a steadying influence on her more volatile daughters.

As soon as she arrived Mary and Eleanor pounced on her

and unceremoniously dragged her into the drawing-room.

'Come on!' Eleanor squeezed her hand affectionately. '*Tell* us! We are quite consumed with curiosity.'

'Tell you what?' asked Clemency quite bewildered.

'The marquess, of course,' said Mary, taking her friend's cloak and bonnet and pushing her down into the nearest armchair.

'What marquess?'

'Clemmie! Don't be obtuse, I pray.'

'No, truly, Mary, I don't know what you are talking of.'

'The marquess you are going to marry.'

'Marry!'

Clemency turned so white and her hands trembled so much that Eleanor said quickly, 'Mary, some water.' She patted Clemency's hand. 'You do look pale. I'm sorry if we alarmed you. We really thought you knew.'

'I think you'd better tell me,' said Clemency faintly, taking the glass from Mary and sipping it gratefully. 'Who says so? For Mama has mentioned nothing to me.'

Eleanor plumped herself down next to Clemency and said, 'You know your mama and ours are on the same committee for St Peter's?'

Clemency nodded.

'Last Wednesday, who should come in but Mrs Durham with another lady who turned out to be the Marquess of Storrington's aunt! I can't remember her name, but anyhow she engaged your mama in some private conversation, and guess what it was about, you lucky girl?'

'No!'

'Yes!'

'B ... but why me? I ... I've never even met him. Why not one of you?'

'Of course it must be you!' cried Mary affectionately, jumping up and kissing Clemency. 'You're certainly the most beautiful girl *I* know!'

'It's money, I suppose,' said Clemency with a sigh.

'Clemmie! How can you!' cried Mary. 'Of course he needs money. Is that so disgraceful? He's only recently inherited and I gather his father was quite ruinously expensive. Mama told us that he once lost £20,000 in an evening. But that is not the present Marquess's fault.'

'No,' hesitated Clemency, 'but these things often run in families.'

'What's the matter with you?' cried Eleanor. 'You'll be a marchioness!'

'I don't see what that signifies if he runs through *my* money as well as his own!' retorted Clemency, the colour returning to her cheeks.

'Your solicitor will tie it all up safely for you, I feel sure.'

Clemency sighed. 'What's his name, this marquess?'

Eleanor ran to the bookcase and took out a fat tome. 'Let's see,' she said. 'This is last year's, so the new marquess will be the eldest son. Ah, here we are! Storrington. Yes, his name is Alexander d'Eynecourt Ludovic Theobald.'

'What a name!'

'I declare I could shake you, Clemency Hastings! Here's a brilliant match offered you and you are quite lukewarm about it.'

'Perhaps some other beau has captured her heart,' teased Mary.

Clemency blushed. 'N ... no.'

'You don't seem too sure,' remarked Eleanor, closing the book and looking at her closely.

Clemency smiled more firmly. Dearly though she loved them, Mary and Eleanor were incorrigible gossips. Let one word of her encounter in Richmond Park get about and she'd never hear the end of it. 'How did you come to hear all this?' she asked brightly.

'Your mama told ours, in the strictest confidence, of course,' Mary giggled, 'but Eleanor and I were in the hall.'

'Arranging flowers,' put in Eleanor.

'So we couldn't help overhearing, could we, Nell?'

'When was this?'

'Tuesday.'

It was now Thursday. So Mama was not meaning to tell her, thought Clemency, for she'd had had ample opportunity to do so. Clemency thought she understood her mother's motives. They were a mixture of jealousy, resentment and social ambition. She had always disapproved of her father's saying, 'So long as he is a hard-working and honest man and loves my daughter, I don't mind where he comes from.'

'Nonsense, Mr Hastings,' she used to say. 'Surely you want to show your daughter off to the best advantage?'

'Clemency is not a prize porker, my dear,' had retorted Mr Hastings, looking at her over the top of his spectacles.

Clemency could not see any reverence for her father's memory holding her mother back from marrying her off, splendidly, as soon as possible.

Clemency left the Ramsgates thoughtfully. Dear Papa, he had been so good to them. He would never have countenanced such a match – certainly not without her full knowledge and informed consent.

Mrs Hastings-Whinborough was a faded blonde in her early forties, whose hair now owed more to the arts of her hairdresser than any natural colouring. She had once been a very pretty girl, but a petulant, discontented expression had marred her once beautiful features and she lacked the intelligence to realize that a more mature style of dressing would be more suitable to her present age and situation. She dressed, having come thankfully out of mourning, in girlish pinks and blues and cultivated what she fondly hoped was a youthful winsomeness. She liked to be told that she was mistaken for Clemency's elder sister.

'Poor Clemency is so bookish and quiet,' she trilled to one of her husband's friends, 'that sometimes I think that I derive more pleasure out of parties and dancing than she does!'

'Dear madam,' responded the elderly admirer, as he knew he must, 'you positively outshine her, 'pon my word you do!'

Lady Helena had been introduced to Mrs Hastings-Whinborough through the offices of Mrs Durham and found her a silly woman, but enquiries had confirmed the beauty of her daughter and the amount of her fortune. If Miss Hastings-Whinborough should prove to be as foolish as her mother, then perhaps it would all come to nothing. On the other hand, perhaps the girl's beauty would make her nephew (a noted connoisseur of female charms) more enthusiastic. In any case, so long as Lysander could be persuaded to get the girl to the altar and do his duty by the succession, it didn't much matter if he then left her at Candover. It might, indeed, be very much better than throwing a beauty, unused to Society ways, into the heart of the *ton* where she might be the prey of every gallant in Town.

Thus reasoned Lady Helena as Mrs Durham showed her and Mrs Hastings-Whinborough to a small room off the parish hall and tactfully left them alone. She watched Mrs Hastings-Whinborough's posturings with grim amusement as she tweaked at her hair and self-consciously rearranged the frills on her dress, her hands fluttering to display a variety of extremely fine diamond rings and bracelets.

'La!' she said. 'I vow and declare Lady Helena I do not know why your ladyship wishes to talk to me!' Her mind ran swiftly down her mental list of dukes, marquesses and earls and came to rest rather reluctantly on a stray viscount who had somehow crept into her list. Lady Helena Candover, she could not immediately place....

'Let us not waste time,' said Lady Helena brusquely, wishing that the whole tiresome business could be over and that she could get back to Candover before Millie had her pups. 'I understand that you have a very beautiful daughter?'

'Oh, yes indeed, your ladyship! Just nineteen and so sweet-natured you wouldn't credit it!'

Probably not, thought Lady Helena.

'My nephew, Mrs Hastings-Whinborough, is looking for a bride. At least,' she added scrupulously, 'he is the last Marquess of Storrington, and that comes to much the same thing.'

Mrs Hastings-Whinborough raised her eyes to the ceiling. 'Naughty young men will always be reluctant to commit themselves in wedlock,' she simpered, wagging her finger archly. 'But my daughter, besides being beautiful (very much like *I* was at her age, I'm told) has a fortune of £100,000. Of course she does not get control of it until she is twenty-five, unless she marries before that date with my and my lawyer, Mr Jameson's, approval.'

Lady Helena raised her eyebrows. 'I trust that any proposed marriage between your daughter and the marquess would have your full approval?'

Mrs Hastings-Whinborough floundered in a morass of half-sentences, 'Oh, my lady, I wasn't for the world meaning to suggest ... it was only ... of course my daughter would be greatly honoured if his lordship's choice should happen to light on her. A marchioness....'

'Unfortunately,' continued Lady Helena, satisfied that Mrs Hastings-Whinborough was now put properly in her place, 'my nephew inherited his father's debts along with the title. He, himself, I hasten to add is not a spendthrift.' She did not feel it necessary to add that his luck at cards was held to be phenomenal. 'Very properly he wishes to save his family home, provide for his young sister and run his estates profitably and efficiently. He is in no position, Mrs Hastings-Whinborough, to choose a bride from among his own order in Society. If he were, this conversation would not be taking place!'

'I understand, your ladyship,' said Mrs Hastings-Whinborough deferentially, feeling obscurely that to be thought unworthy of a marquess was somehow a social cachet in itself.

Lady Helena smiled kindly at her. So long as it was made absolutely clear just who was honouring whom in this proposed alliance. 'As you so rightly observe, Mrs Hastings-Whinborough,' she added graciously, 'young men are often somewhat reluctant when it comes to matrimony. I propose, therefore, that the meeting should be entirely informal. If it is agreeable to you I shall bring my nephew to tea on Friday. He may make the acquaintance of your daughter without any obligations being incurred.

'I trust that such easy informality will mean that they may like each other.' She hesitated a moment. 'My nephew is a law unto himself; I think it would be best if Miss Hastings-Whinborough had no idea of the purpose of the call. I would not wish to put her to any embarrassment if his lordship does not wish for the match. And even I, Mrs Hastings-Whinborough, cannot force him to the altar!'

Mrs Hastings-Whinborough pursed her lips. She had no intention of complying with Lady Helena's request. Clemency must be chastened into suitable submission. Left to herself she was quite likely to come down in some plain cambric gown, her hair tied up in a simple ribbon and uttering God knows what intelligent and bookish comments! Nothing put a man off quicker than female intelligence.

No, Clemency must be told. Her hair must be properly crimped and dressed, she must wear her new pink silk, and above all she must be schooled into a becoming deference to the marquess's opinions.

Mrs Hastings-Whinborough curtseyed to acknowledge Lady Helena's condescension as she rose to go and said that she need have no fear, her darling was all unspoilt.

Lady Helena suppressed her inevitable forbodings.

Clemency's worst fears were realized: she sat in the drawing-room on Wednesday evening, head down, staring unseeing at her embroidery, and tried to stop her hands from trembling.

It was all fixed – her mother had said so. She was to have her hair properly done, Mama would send her own Adèle in to her; she was to wear that horrid over-dressed pink silk. Even the marquess's aunt approved and she, Clemency, was to be grateful to her mama and deferential towards the marquess. And if, went on Mrs Hastings-Whinborough, sensing her daughter's hostility but not allowing her to speak, she did not do as her mama bid her she would shortly be very sorry, for her mother would have nothing more to do with so undutiful a daughter. She would be sent off to Aunt Whinborough in Barnet to recover her senses.

Clemency looked up at that and Mrs Hastings-Whinborough smiled triumphantly. Aunt Whinborough lived a life of self-righteous piety which was both uncomfortable and rigid. Clemency had never forgotten her only meeting with Aunt Whinborough when she found the orphan girl who was her one servant, crouched in a corner of the kitchen, her arms black and blue from the beatings she had received for some trivial fault. On that occasion her father had intervened, threatening to stop the allowance he paid her unless she treated her servants with more consideration.

Aunt Whinborough had never forgiven Clemency's interference. And her mother knew it.

'Are you listening, Clemency?'

'Yes, Mama,' said Clemency dully.

'I expect your full co-operation.'

She undressed that night feeling as if some awful trap was

closing around her. There was no escape. Wild thoughts of throwing herself on the mercy of this marquess's unknown aunt swept through her, only to be swiftly rejected. When her maid, Sally, came in, it was to find her mistress sitting, white-faced, on the edge of her bed, staring hopelessly into space.

Sally, a lively girl with dancing brown curls that were the despair of the second footman, had been previously employed by a parsimonious duchess and had often regaled Clemency with scurrilous stories of the aristocracy. She was fond of Clemency, who was generous where the duchess had been mean, and ten times prettier into the bargain.

'I suppose you've heard,' said Clemency listlessly, allowing Sally to usher her to the dressing-table where Sally brushed her hair until it shone gold in the candlelight.

'Yes, miss.'

'And I'm to go to Miss Whinborough if I don't agree.'

'Oh no, miss!'

'That is what Mama has said.'

Sally hesitated and then said, 'But this marquess, miss. It's not my place I know, but....'

'You've heard something about the marquess?'

Sally looked at the pale reflection in the glass and burst into tears. 'Oh, miss!' she sobbed. 'I wouldn't marry him if he were ten times a marquess! The duchess used to say that the marquess, Lord Alexander as he was then, was a devil.'

'W ... what did she mean by that?'

'There were stories, miss ... of young girls. They said he ... mistreated them, you know. He beat his valet once so he nearly died.'

'How horrible!'

'It was hushed up, of course.'

'How could Mama ...' began Clemency, and then stopped. She could see all too well how it might happen. A marquess was a marquess after all – she would not enquire too closely into his character or disposition.

Long after Sally had gone Clemency sat and thought. There was nobody she could appeal to. Mr Jameson, her father's lawyer and the man who looked after her fortune, was a meek little man in his personal dealings: she doubted whether he would be able, let alone willing, to encourage her in her opposition to her mother's wishes. As for Miss Whinborough, she might disapprove of marquesses on principle as indulging in ungodly luxury, but Clemency did not think that this would triumph over her pleasure at having her niece to dominate and bully.

It was then that she thought of her father's cousin, Mrs Stoneham, recently widowed and living somewhere out near Berkhamsted. When her father was alive she had several times stayed with Cousin Anne in her pleasant rectory (for her husband had been in holy orders) and had liked her sense and intelligence. She had not seen Cousin Anne for a couple of years, but Mrs Stoneham had written her a very understanding letter on her father's death and invited her to stay any time. It was an invitation that her mother had not allowed her to accept, for she didn't care for Mrs Stoneham. But Clemency and Cousin Anne, unknown to Mrs Hastings-Whinborough, had kept in touch, even if only at Christmas and birthdays.

Clemency had her new address, and she didn't think her mother knew it, for Mrs Stoneham had not moved long. Would Cousin Anne take her in if she turned up suddenly, or would she send her straight back to her mama? Either way, thought Clemency desperately, it would end any possibility of this obnoxious marriage.

With her mother's ultimatum she no longer had any choice in the matter. She would have to run away. And she would have to do it fast.

Two

Mrs Stoneham, an agreeable-looking woman in her fifties with fair hair now lightly touched with grey, was sitting sewing in her pleasant parlour in the little village of Abbots Candover when there was a loud knock at her front door. She went to the window and peeped out and, there to her astonishment, was the carrier's cart and stepping down from it, dishevelled and dirty, carrying nothing but a small travelling basket, was Clemency Hastings!

Mrs Stoneham's maid poked her head round the door. 'Please, mum, it's Miss Clemency, mum.'

Clemency, looking pale and apprehensive, entered. 'Cousin Anne?' she said hesitantly.

'Oh! My dear Clemency.' Mrs Stoneham stepped forward and embraced her tenderly. Clemency burst into overwrought tears and for a while nothing but a few muffled sobs and some unintelligible words could be heard.

'Bessy, some tea please for Miss Clemency and some of your little rock cakes.' Mrs Stoneham gave Clemency's shoulder a last pat and stood back to look at her. 'Clemency, dearest, why you're half-frozen. Come and sit down and take off your bonnet and tell me what it is. Nothing has happened to your mama, I trust?'

Clemency shook her head and gulped. It was some time before Mrs Stoneham had the whole story and even then she could scarcely credit it.

'You came the whole way in the carrier's cart?' she exclaimed, apparently more concerned by the discomfort of such a mode of travel than by the discomforts of what had preceded such a course of action.

'Yes. I feared I would be traced if I went by stage or mail. To take something humbler seemed more prudent. My maid's uncle has a small carrier service and he agreed to bring me here. It was cheaper too,' she finished practically. 'I hadn't got much of my quarter's allowance left and I didn't want to raise suspicions by asking Mama for more.'

Mrs Stoneham, whose thoughts before Clemency's arrival were full of her recent sad loss, began to look more animated. 'And you came quite unaccompanied?'

'Yes, Cousin Anne. I didn't want to get my maid, Sally, into trouble. Of course, I left a note for my mother but I told nobody where I was going. At least, Sally knows, but I am sure she will not tell.'

'Wild horses wouldn't drag it from me, miss,' promised Sally when Clemency begged her silence and gave her two guineas, which was all she could spare. She didn't care for Mrs Hastings-Whinborough, who had all the parvenu inability to combine wealth with courtesy towards her servants. Clemency had given her a good reference in case she found herself out of a job and promised to keep in touch via Sally's uncle.

Mrs Stoneham began, unwillingly, to laugh. Underneath those beautiful blue and golden looks, Clemency was both intelligent and resourceful. She had even removed her father's address book and it was very doubtful whether Mrs Hastings-Whinborough would ever trace her daughter here, even if she remembered that she, Mrs Stoneham, had moved.

Bessy brought in the tea and Mrs Stoneham was pleased to see that some of Clemency's colour returned as she ate and drank.

'No, I shan't send you back, my dear,' she said. 'Something of the sort happened to me about your age before I met my darling Robert.' She sighed and looked down at her black dress for a moment before continuing more cheerfully, 'I have not forgotten my feelings of impotence and outrage at being disposed of like a parcel! Fortunately the man died before the wedding plans came to anything. I doubt whether I should have had your courage.'

Clemency relaxed and took another rock cake.

'But, did you realize, dear Clemency, that in one respect you've stepped out of the frying-pan into the fire?'

'How is that?' asked Clemency, suddenly alarmed and

looking fearfully around her as if her cousin was concealing yet another reprobate member of the aristocracy behind the sofa.

'The Storrington family name is Candover. This is Abbots Candover. Their family seat is not two miles away!'

'Then they are unlikely to look for me here!'

'I trust you may be right. I, myself, have only been here a few months. Few people know yet who I am. Being in mourning, of course, I have only gone out to go to church.'

It was settled between them that Clemency was an impoverished cousin staying with her to support her spirits.

But they had underestimated the curiosity of the villagers, the industry of Mr Jameson and the determination of Mrs Hastings-Whinborough. The small cottage in Abbots Candover was not as isolated as they had hoped.

Lysander, grim-lipped and silent, escorted a stiff-backed Lady Helena out of the Hastings house in Russell Square and into their waiting carriage.

They left Mrs Hastings-Whinborough in hysterics in her drawing-room, her maid Adèle and her housekeeper in attendance, the one waving hartshorn, the other a glass of brandy.

'I knew she'd disgrace me one day,' wailed the lady. 'To have exposed her own mother to such humiliation!'

Adèle looked across at the housekeeper expressively. Below stairs was full of the gossip relayed by an irrepressible Sally. Miss Clemency's proposed husband might be a lord, but he was an ugly customer if ever there was one. Everybody knew what went on in some of the worst bordellos in Covent Garden that his lordship frequented and there wasn't one servant who didn't heartily pity Clemency.

'This marquess,' began the housekeeper tentatively, 'there've been some very unsavoury rumours, madam....'

'Nonsense!' Mrs Hastings-Whinborough sat up and pushed away her hartshorn in favour of the brandy. 'I have heard none. In any case, what young man does not sow some wild oats before he settles down? You shan't excuse her, Briggs. Miss Clemency has been wicked and undutiful. And when I find her, which I shall, she will be very sorry. Send Sally to me!'

Back in the carriage Lady Helena allowed herself to sink back against the squabs. 'What can the girl have heard?' she said, at last.

Lysander looked down at the crumpled piece of paper in his hand and laughed harshly. 'Nothing!' he said. 'Nothing! Just a puritanical miss's prudery. Good God, Aunt Helena, I may have been unsteady, but it scarcely merits *this*!' He smoothed out the letter and looked at it again.

Dear Mama, he read,
I cannot marry this marquess. You do not know what he is like. I have heard terrible things of him, and all hushed up by his family. I shall never marry such a man, nor shall I go to Aunt Whinborough, who beats and bullies her slaveys in a way I cannot bear. So I am going away. I shall be quite safe, so you need not be concerned. And Papa would never have countenanced my marriage to this Monster.
                                          C.H.

'I may be a rake,' said Lysander, 'but scarcely a monster.'

'No, indeed,' said Lady Helena indignantly.

'The girl's missish. She's probably seen me at the theatre with some prime article and damned me. She's as foolish as her mother and there's an end of it.' He scrumpled up the letter again and threw it disdainfully on the floor.

Lady Helena frowned. She had distinctly told Mrs Hastings-Whinborough not to tell her daughter. But she supposed that the lure of a possible marquess had been too much for her discretion.

'And don't offer me Miss Grubb,' said Lysander wearily, 'or the nabob's widow. I've courted enough humiliation. I've got to talk to Thornhill and then I'll come down to Candover and try and get it into some sort of order before I put it on the market. I'm afraid, Aunt Helena, you and Arabella will have to make up your minds to Bath.'

Clemency and Mrs Stoneham sat in the parlour a few days later with a branch of working candles between them. Mrs Stoneham was hemming some sheets while Clemency darned a small hole in one of the pillow cases. A pile of mended linen on a nearby chair attested to their industry.

'Five days!' said Clemency. 'Do you think I am safe now, Cousin Anne?'

Mrs Stoneham looked up from her sewing. 'I don't know, my dear. Your mother must make *some* enquiries. And, Clemency, you surely do not wish to disappear entirely? You are always welcome here, of course, but we must also consider what is best for your future. I live a very quiet life, you know. There is only Bessy to help me in the house and Mrs Wills's Simon from the village to come and do the garden. It is not at all what you are used to.'

'What I am used to,' said Clemency bitterly, 'is being both ignored and bullied, constantly told what to wear, what I may or may not think, who to marry! I cannot recall one instance since dear Papa died of Mama even *listening* to me, let alone taking me seriously.'

'I know. And that is why I agreed to allow you to stay. Amelia was never meant to be a mother, I fear. But dear Clemency, you are nineteen. The world surely holds more for you than sewing pillow cases for your poor relations! You are not a trouble to me, my love, never think that, but all the same, you need a proper future.'

'It seems to me that my future is either a vicious marquess or my Aunt Whinborough. My fortune comes under my control when I am twenty-five, but I can't spend six years with Aunt Whinborough, Cousin Anne, I just can't.'

Privately Mrs Stoneham thought it was unlikely that so beautiful a girl would spend anything like six years in the situation she described without some eligible young man being eager to come to her rescue. She would not push Clemency just yet, but perhaps in a month or so it might be possible to negotiate a more satisfactory return home.

The next day was Sunday and in the morning they both set out to walk the half mile to church. They arrived early and sat near the back in the pew belonging to Mrs Stoneham's landlord.

'We may see Lady Arabella Candover,' whispered Mrs Stoneham, 'but I doubt if other members of the family will come. I believe the marquess and Lady Helena to be still in London.'

Clemency nervously pulled at her bonnet so that it shaded her face more completely.

There was a bustle behind them and the Candover party

arrived. 'Lady Arabella,' whispered Mrs Stoneham as a petite, vivacious brunette tripped down the aisle. She was dressed, as befitted her youth in white-spotted cambric, her hair tied back simply under a demure white straw bonnet. But there the schoolgirl ended. Nothing could disguise Arabella's well-formed figure nor the bold glances she shot at the handsome farmer's son. Arabella, plainly, was a handful and the presence of an elderly chaperone clucking anxiously behind her seemed to have no effect on her behaviour whatsoever.

'Oh, stop fussing, Laney,' she was heard to say as she passed Clemency's pew. Then she saw Clemency, stared for a moment, then waved one small, gloved hand at Mrs Stoneham and moved on.

'Good Heavens!' Mrs Stoneham had turned. 'Here's Lady Helena!'

'She mustn't see me!' whispered Clemency urgently.

'Don't be silly. Why should she not? You are my young cousin, staying with me. What could possibly be wrong with that?'

'My name! She might ask my name.'

'I doubt whether she will speak to us,' said Mrs Stoneham dampeningly. 'She rarely stops.'

The church bell stopped, the latecomers settled themselves and an imperious nod from Lady Helena allowed the service to begin. The service was short; a previous incumbent who had taken it upon himself to lengthen his sermon from the fifteen minutes Lady Helena thought sufficient to forty-five minutes, had found the latter part of his discourse quite obscured by barks and shrill yappings from the dogs tethered outside. Lady Helena never brought fewer than six to church, tying them to a suitable tree in the churchyard in charge of the groom. On that occasion one of the boarhounds had inadvertently stepped on the yappiest of the Pekinese and the resulting noise – in which half the village dogs joined – made the service quite inaudible. The Reverend Josiah Browne, a man with evangelical tendencies, had attempted to reprove Lady Helena and got a sharp reprimand from his bishop and a swift removal to another living.

Happily, the present incumbent, Mr Lamb, was as meek as his name and observed the proper order of things. He finished his sermon with commendable promptitude.

Clemency, who was used to the long-winded vicar of St Peter's, glanced at her cousin and raised her eyebrows.

'So that her ladyship's dogs may have their morning run,' whispered Mrs Stoneham.

'You mean that the dogs are more important than our spiritual welfare?' whispered back Clemency, slightly scandalized.

'Sh! Here she comes!'

Lady Helena gathered up her various shawls and prayer books, poked the depressed-looking companion at her side and bade her follow. Lady Arabella, after one last smile at the farmer's son, slid out of the pew and tripped after them.

Clemency had hoped that she and Mrs Stoneham would be able to slip away quietly and unremarked, but she reckoned without Arabella's curiosity and the effect of Lady Helena's well-meaning efforts to turn her into a well-brought-up young lady. Arabella's brief canter through half-a-dozen unsuitable governesses, whose conversation had been far from ladylike, had left her with a taste for headier excitements than poor dowdy Miss Lane could offer. She was bored and ripe for mischief.

But Lady Helena too had spotted them.

'Ah, Mrs Stoneham.'

'Good morning, Lady Helena,' replied Mrs Stoneham, with an anxious glance at Clemency.

'I see you have a young friend with you this morning. Pray introduce me.'

There was no help for it.

'This is a young cousin of my late husband's, Lady Helena, come to spend a brief visit.'

'Miss Stoneham.' Lady Helena crunched Clemency's hand for a moment.

Clemency curtseyed and said, 'Your ladyship,' but did not correct her.

Lady Helena's methods of interrogation would have done credit to a Spanish inquisitor and, in a short space of time, she had elicited the information that Miss Stoneham was nineteen, an orphan, coming from an unfortunate experience of her first position as a governess – gross attentions from the father of her charge were hinted at – and was now staying with her dear

Cousin Anne to recover from this distressing business and in due course find a more suitable place.

Further probing revealed that Miss Stoneham spoke French and Italian and had mastered water-colours, the pianoforte and the use of the globes.

'Alas, my abilities with my needle are sadly inferior,' finished Clemency, quite awestruck by the facility with which the untruths had bubbled out and the vivid picture of the fictitious employer which had sprung into her mind. Perhaps, she thought, if all else fails, I could write lurid novels like Mrs Radcliffe?

Miss Lane was introduced and Clemency won a good point from Lady Helena for her friendly handshake and comment on the beauty of the church; so often governesses felt their position to be insecure and snubbed other dependents. Furthermore, Arabella liked her, she saw.

At this point, an idea came into Lady Helena's head. She turned to Mrs Stoneham. 'Could I persuade you to allow Miss Stoneham to come to tea this afternoon? She is just the young companion my niece needs. I shall see that she is taken home in the carriage.'

There could be nothing but polite agreement.

'But *why*, Cousin Anne?' demanded Clemency over luncheon. 'Seriously, I am very worried. However shall I carry off such an imposture?'

'You seemed to be managing very well this morning!' said her cousin, dryly.

'I know,' Clemency laughed. 'I could actually see the erring father of my charge in my mind's eye! Perhaps I should become an actress!'

'An actress!' echoed Mrs Stoneham, horrified. 'My dear Clemency....'

'I was only funning.' She took an encouraging sip of her soup and went on, 'Well, I cannot see it doing much harm. And I own that I am curious about the family.'

'I am not happy about it,' said Mrs Stoneham after a few moments' thought, 'If this deception should ever come to light....'

'I know.' Clemency was silent. 'I wouldn't for the world place you in a difficult position, Cousin Anne. I shall be extremely discreet.'

Mr Jameson, the Hastings' lawyer, sat at his desk pondering a curious piece of information that had come to hand. He had been with Mrs Hastings when Sally was cross-questioned, he had questioned the other servants himself and later had made enquiries at the posting-houses out of London.

First of all, the escape appeared to have been unpremeditated. If Miss Clemency really had not known until the day before that the marquess was paying a visit then that meant a vastly reduced time-scale. That was certainly an advantage. On the other hand she had not been reported on either the stage or the mail, nor had she hired a post-chaise so far as he could ascertain.

One thing, however, that did strike him as significant was that the late Mr Hastings' address book was missing. Now why? Mrs Hastings had been no help.

'How should *I* know?' she cried, dabbing carefully at her blackened eyelashes with a wisp of lace. 'It was Mr Hastings' business address book, I cannot think she would have fled to anybody in it.'

'What about any old school friends, ma'am?'

'I have already spoken to the Ramsgate girls,' Mrs Hastings reminded him, fretfully. And very humiliating it had been too. Mrs Ramsgate so over-solicitous but secretly gloating, she felt. She would not soon forgive Clemency that.

'Was there nobody at her seminary with whom she has kept in touch?'

Mrs Hastings shook her head. In fact this had been a bone of contention with her daughter that she did nothing to promote the acquaintance of those girls of good family who were at the Wilton Academy with her. There had been the Honourable Agnes Cartwright, for example, with whom Clemency had shared a room. Mrs Hastings was sure that an honourable must be charming, but no, Miss Know-it-all had decided that she did not like Agnes. 'She cheats at cards,' she'd said. Well, what if she did? She was an honourable, wasn't she? Everybody knew their morals were more elastic. Surely it would be worth losing a little pin money to be invited to the Cartwrights' seat? But Clemency would not even try.

'Did your husband have any relations to whom she might have gone?' asked Mr Jameson next.

'Not that I know of. Though there was old Cousin Robert.'

'Oh?'

'A man of the cloth.'

'Would Miss Clemency have gone to him?'

'He died a year or so ago and his widow moved.'

'Ah. Now where to?'

But Mrs Hastings could not remember. She was not even sure where the Revd. Robert Stoneham's living had been.

'Was he fond of your daughter?'

Mrs Hastings considered. 'When she was little they both spoiled her. They had no children of their own, that was why. But Clemency hasn't seen them for three or four years. And I doubt whether she's in touch with Mrs Stoneham. She has certainly never mentioned her to me.'

Mr Jameson sighed. It was a slim chance, but all he had. There were clerical directories he could look up for Mr Stoneham's living and then he would make enquiries. He doubted whether anything would come of it, but he intended to charge very handsomely for his time and did not begrudge the effort.

'Did Miss Clemency have any young man in her eye?' he asked tentatively. A beautiful girl in his opinion; he would not be surprised if she'd fled to Gretna with some lover.

Two spots of red flew in Mrs Hastings' cheeks. 'Certainly not!' she said. 'I wouldn't countenance it.'

Mr Jameson had kept his inevitable reflections to himself.

It was as well for Clemency that she didn't realize as she set out to walk the mile or so to Candover Court later that afternoon that the marquess was at that very moment driving through the fourteenth-century gateway that led to the house.

He had had an unpleasant few days in London with Thornhill trying to draw up a list of his late brother's creditors and seeing what disposable assets could be found to pay off the more pressing debts. Lord Alexander's horses had been put up for sale and had gone for a song, but at least it had relieved him of the cost of their upkeep. The only bright spot had been the advantageous selling of the hunting lodge in Leicestershire, which enabled Thornhill to pay off the outstanding debts on the mortgage of Candover Court which had been threatened with foreclosure.

'At least Lady Helena and Lady Arabella won't be homeless now, my lord,' said Thornhill.

'For the moment,' replied Lysander grimly. 'What can have possessed my father to take such a step?'

'I believe it was Lord Alexander's gaming debts, my lord.'

Lysander pushed back his chair. 'I shall go up to Candover tomorrow,' he said, 'and talk to Frome.' Frome was the agent of the Candover estate. 'We'll see what sort of order we can put the place into.'

'At least you have a breathing space now, my lord,' said Thornhill, looking at him with concern. The two brothers had looked not unlike each other, but family resemblances could be misleading. In his view Lysander was worth ten of the late marquess and it was a thousand pities that Alexander had not come to a bad end years ago.

The following afternoon saw Lysander's curricle turn up the drive of Candover Court. The afternoon sun caught the old stone of the house and turned it to gold. Never had his birthplace looked more lovely. It was a Tudor building with mullioned windows. The Candover who built it had used the stones from the abbey given him by Henry VIII in gratitude for his support over the marriage to Anne Boleyn. Lysander's ancestor had developed quite a taste for political intrigue but fortunately for both his newly acquired lands – and his head – a bad fall from his horse forced him to retire from court and settle for arranging suitable marriages for his offspring rather than His Majesty.

Lysander had rarely visited his home of late years. As a boy he had fished every stream, climbed every tree. But it was not his and never would be his, so on coming down from Oxford he had turned his thoughts to the delights of London. Now, unexpectedly, he was the owner of this beautiful place, and he was going to lose it. Even after all the disposable assets had been sold, they would still be £20,000 in debt. If it wasn't for that ... the land was good enough. With money put into it and more up-to-date farming methods the estate could be worth ten times the paltry £900 a year its dwindling rents brought in. He

could, at least, have tried. But the debt was overwhelming.
Candover would have to go.

To a girl strictly brought up within the confines of her London
home, to be able to walk in the country was both a pleasure and
held a slight frisson of adventure. In fact, Candover Court was
less than two miles outside the village and the trees from the
Home Wood could be seen clearly from Mrs Stoneham's
garden, but to Clemency it was a small voyage of discovery.
The flowers in the hedgerows, the swallows twittering on the
roof-tops, even the rustle of the trees, some now with a faint
touch of yellow, all made her forget her troubles and she
walked along quite happily, pleased to be unchaperoned and
to enjoy the day at her leisure.

As a child she had spent her summers in the country while
her Grandmother Hastings was alive and although this was
more rounded country than she remembered her grandmother's to have been, there were the same pleasures of fresh
air and birdsong.

She turned into the gateway of Candover Court and stopped
in surprise. She had expected to see a modern building with
classical pillars and a portico perhaps, but this was different. It
was low, only two storeys high, with small, heavy windows
and tall chimneys. At one end was the remains of what had
once been an abbey. Most of the stones had plainly been used
in building the Court, for here and there Clemency could see
the remains of tracery and vaulting incongruously bedded in
the walls of the house.

But, like the abbey, the house was now decayed. A small
bush grew out of a chimney stack and the guttering was broken
in places. The gardens, too, were overgrown and neglected. No
wonder the marquess needed to marry money, thought
Clemency. Well, it wasn't going to be hers!

Inside was much the same. The hall was large and vaulted,
with the Candover coat of arms engraved in stone over a vast
fireplace. Threadbare banners hung out from the walls and
rusty suits of armour stood in the corners. Clemency was
irresistibly reminded of one of Mrs Radcliffe's novels and felt it
needed only a headless monk to complete it. There were
certainly enough cobwebs.

Arabella, who had been on the watch, came running down as soon as she heard the door knocker. She waved the butler away and said, 'Come upstairs, Miss Stoneham. We are in the yellow drawing-room.' Arabella gestured to the rooms leading off the hall. 'These are scarcely habitable.'

'It is a pity,' replied Clemency sympathetically; 'such a beautiful house.'

'Oh, do you think so? Antiquated, I call it. I prefer something more modern.'

'Something more modern would hardly have this atmosphere,' said Clemency as they climbed the staircase. She noticed that the oak treads were worn and the banisters had not seen polish for some time. It was hard to imagine that she might have been mistress of all this decayed grandeur.

'Draughts and damp,' retorted Arabella.

'It could be lovely though.'

Arabella paused at the top of the stairs and looked carefully at her guest. 'You don't seem much like a governess to me,' she remarked at last.

Clemency's heart missed a beat. 'Oh, why not?' she managed to say.

'For one thing you are far too pretty and for another you don't *talk* like a governess.'

Clemency managed a laugh. 'And how do governesses talk, pray?' She must be careful.

'Well, Miss Lane is always apologetic if she wants to contradict me. "But you must remember, Lady Arabella, that this house has historic associations for your family". And governesses always go on and on at you to remember your *position*. Position? What position?' She gestured at the peeling walls and cracked surfaces. 'And they always try to *improve* me!'

Clemency couldn't help laughing. After a minute Arabella joined in and it was two smiling faces Lady Helena saw as she looked up from her embroidery.

Instantly six dogs started yapping and for a few moments nothing could be heard at all.

It was just as well that the dogs had created a diversion for it enabled Clemency to hide her shock and dismay at seeing a dark, loose-limbed man rise lazily from his seat as they entered.

It must be the marquess: it could be nobody else. Somehow she managed to come forward, shake hands with Lady Helena, say what was proper.

'Down Pongo, down Muffin,' said Lady Helena. 'Pay them no heed, Miss Stoneham. They will soon settle down.' She turned to her nephew. 'Storrington, allow me to introduce Miss Stoneham to you. I don't know if you recall her cousin who has recently come to live in the village? The rector's widow.'

Clemency endeavoured to stiffen her unruly knees and held out her hand blindly. Dear God, was this some nightmare?

Lysander's eyes had narrowed. 'Miss Stoneham.' He barely touched her hand. 'Have I had the pleasure of meeting you before?'

'Hardly, my lord.' Clemency had taken a grip on herself and was pleased to hear her voice sounded calm. 'I have been a governess up in Yorkshire until recently.'

Lysander bowed. There was an elusive memory somewhere. What was it? But Arabella was claiming his attention.

Clemency sank down nervelessly on to the nearest chair and accepted a cup of tea. Could it be ... was it possible? That voice, those same harsh features, those strong brown hands – was this the man who had kissed her outside Biddy's house? The vicious, depraved Marquess of Storrington? It was impossible.

She stole a look at him from under her lashes. He was turned towards Lady Helena and on his forehead Clemency could see plainly the remains of a graze.

Could she have run away from the very man who had haunted her dreams since their meeting?

But she must remember her manners. With an effort she forced herself to concentrate.

But it was easier said than done. Clemency found that her mind was a tangle of shame and confusion. Shame at having relived that kiss so many times in her mind, and worse, with having given its author every virtue. She had turned him into a hero and set him up as the epitome of the desirable. How was this to be reconciled with the degenerate and vicious young man whom Sally had described, one whom every female should shun? Clemency was not one of those women who find violence towards their own sex by the other attractive. It disgusted her and she would never consider giving her heart to a brute.

She looked covertly at the marquess. That harsh, swarthy face – were those really lines of dissolute dissipation? He was talking to Lady Helena in a quiet, gentleman-like way, fondling the ears of a spaniel whose head was resting trustingly on his knee. Could this be the man who, rumour had it, had beaten his valet so severely that he'd nearly died?

But Lady Helena was speaking to her.

'How long will you be staying with your cousin, Miss Stoneham?'

'I ... I hardly know, ma'am.'

'You are looking for another situation, I understand?'

'In due course I shall be. But Cousin Anne has kindly suggested that I take a holiday with her for a few months and I own that that will be very pleasant.'

'I don't know how you stand being a governess,' cried Arabella, mentally casting an eye over her own governesses – and especially Miss Lane, now suffering from one of her frequent headaches upstairs.

'Let us hope that Miss Stoneham's charges are better behaved than you, miss,' said Lysander, reaching out and tweaking one of her ringlets.

'It is not my *charges* that worry me,' said Clemency. 'Too often employers seem to think that they have bought more than your teaching abilities.'

Lysander raised his eyebrows, revising his first favourable opinion of her. She seemed to be damned egalitarian, like that awful Godwin woman. And who was she, after all? Some indigent cousin of a poor country vicar. It was not for her to criticize those of far better breeding than herself. Their family finances might be in an appalling state, but they were *Candovers* after all.

'Surely,' he said haughtily, 'no true lady would ever be the subject of inappropriate behaviour?'

'Nonsense,' said Clemency, roundly. Miss Biddenham had often told her that governesses were regarded as fair game.

Lady Helena looked at her with approval. She was perfectly right, of course. Alexander had all too often regarded Arabella's governesses, if young and pretty, as his especial quarry. Moreover, she was quite pleased to see that Miss Stoneham appeared to have set Lysander's back up. She had an idea in her mind with regard to Miss Stoneham and it would not do at all for Lysander to find her attractive.

Lysander bowed coldly. She was a pretty little chit, he thought, and it would not surprise him to find her making up to her employer's husband. Lady Helena had told him that it had been the other way about, but Lysander was not so green, he hoped, as to believe that. He was obscurely offended to find that she did not seem to be enticing *him*.

That evening Clemency had much to tell her cousin.

'I do not care for the marquess,' she said, firmly, repressing her treacherous heart. 'He is ill-mannered and abrupt.'

'Yet he is well liked by his tenants,' replied Cousin Anne, mildly.

'Yes, I daresay. He certainly enjoys coming the great lord over one. If they tug their forelocks and bow and scrape, I'm sure he'd be charming.'

'And *Miss Stoneham* is not going to kow-tow,' said Mrs Stoneham, slyly.

'Certainly not!' Then she laughed. 'He looked at me as though I was a *worm*, Cousin Anne. And yet I can see how much the house stands in need of repair and the grounds too. I cannot imagine what gives him so high a notion of his consequence.'

'So you don't regret your precipitate refusal?'

Clemency hesitated. 'No ... o. Of course, the house is beautiful and I am sure I should become fond of Lady Helena and Arabella. But....'

'But?'

'I could not bear to be married to a man who regarded me as the lowest of the low.'

'Do not forget, my dear, that he was talking to *Miss Stoneham* this afternoon. I am sure he would have held Miss Hastings in more respect.'

'Or her money,' said Clemency tartly.

She was beginning to see that life was more complicated than she had thought. It had been foolish to indulge in girlish daydreams about a man whose character she had not known. That might do for some trashy novel, but in real life it could only lead to disillusionment.

Before the events in Richmond and the marquess's proposal Clemency's thoughts had not turned much towards marriage. The last two years she had been grieving for her much-loved papa and before that it seemed that she was too young. Suddenly new ideas and emotions were crowding in on her and she had to find her way alone.

'Do not fret, my love,' said Mrs Stoneham. 'Lady Helena has done her duty. We may see them again in church, but I live in so small a way that normal visiting between us is not possible. I do not think the Candovers will bother us again.'

But in this she was wrong.

Three

Miss Lane, whose migraines were only equalled in severity by her determination to inculcate into her charge the principles governing French grammar, arose from her bed of sickness and decided, once more, on a fresh start. Unfortunately, she was a woman of rigid mind and four months' acquaintance with Arabella had not taught her to modify her approach. She knew how a young lady ought to behave and it was her duty to see that the Lady Arabella conformed. As this knowledge was accompanied by a fussy and diffident manner, very little of it penetrated her charge's mind and poor Miss Lane was regularly prostrated by nervous spasms and sick headaches.

She had been struggling all morning in the schoolroom with a bored Arabella beside her.

'A little more attention, Lady Arabella, if you please,' she clucked. 'What is the past participle of the verb *devoir*?'

Arabella shrugged.

'*Du*,' said Miss Lane brightly.

Arabella slammed her book shut and threw it across the room. 'I don't care,' she announced. 'I hate French!'

'Oh, my dear Lady Arabella. Pray ... every young lady must speak French.'

'I cannot see why.'

'It is the most elegant of languages. The language too of Voltaire and Racine....'

'To the devil with Voltaire and Racine!' Arabella stood up. 'It's a beautiful day and I'm not wasting it.'

Without another word she left the room, leaving Miss Lane groping for her smelling salts.

Arabella was, in fact, being deliberately obstructive.

She had managed, after church the previous Sunday, to

make an assignation with young Joshua Baldock, the farmer's son, whose father was a tenant of the Candovers. She knew that he'd be in the big hayfield on the far side of the Home Wood. It would soon be noon and the men would be having their lunch. Josh would be looking for her and they'd wander into the wood for a while and she'd tease him and perhaps allow a kiss or two.

Arabella ran up to her room, two stairs at a time, grabbed her bonnet and cloak and nipped down the back stairs.

Laney would probably report her to her aunt, but she didn't care. Candover was going to be sold, everybody knew that, although they tried to keep it from her; she wouldn't be able to have her season; she'd *die* cooped up in Bath with Aunt Helena, so she was going to grab what fun she could *now*. And nobody was going to stop her.

Clemency had not slept well. Whichever way she looked at it the events of the previous afternoon made her uncomfortable. It was definitely the same man, there could be no doubt about that, and to make matters worse, he had half-recognized her. Thank God he'd been concussed at the time! The last thing Clemency wanted was for the marquess to remember the episode as well as she did herself.

How *could* she have been so foolish as to allow that kiss, she chastized herself. She was now living within a few miles of a young man who was notorious in every brothel in Covent Garden and whose reputation was violent. At the moment Mrs Stoneham gave her a guaranteed position of respectability, but how would he behave if he recalled that incident in Richmond? He must then suppose her to be nothing better than a light woman herself.

She must be extremely circumspect, and hope that Cousin Anne was right in thinking that they would see little of the Candovers.

She came down to breakfast looking pale and heavy-eyed.

'You have been worrying,' said Mrs Stoneham the moment she saw her. 'I thought it might be so. Ring the bell, my dear, and let Bessy know you're down.'

'It is foolish, I know,' said Clemency. 'Ah, good morning, Bessy.'

'Good morning, Miss Clemency. Now, what would you fancy for breakfast, miss?'

'Nothing, thank you. I'll just have some coffee and toast.'

'You must take a nice walk this morning, Clemency,' said Mrs Stoneham. 'Get some roses back in your cheeks. Bessy will wrap you up an apple and some pie. I have Mrs Lamb, the vicar's wife you remember, calling at about noon and I think it would be wise if you were out of the way. She is a good soul, but terribly nosy.

'I understand there are some mushrooms up near the Home Wood. Take a little basket and see what you can find.'

Nothing loth, Clemency, basket and parasol in hand, set off. Cousin Anne was quite right, she thought, a quiet walk would restore the tone of her mind and help her to get things back into perspective. Accordingly, she gathered the mushrooms, sniffing them appreciatively and then retreated into the Home Wood to find a log on which to eat her luncheon.

She sat for a while, eating her apple and enjoying the dappled shade. In another month or so the blackberries would be ripe, just as they used to be at her grandmother's house when she was little. She wondered where she would be in a month.

She had just started on the pie when she realized that something was wrong. Behind her were scufflings which at first she had taken to be some blackbird in the undergrowth, but she could now hear unmistakable sobs. Clemency put down her half-eaten pie, picked up her parasol purposefully and went cautiously in the direction of the noise.

There, behind a hazel bush, lying on the bracken, was a young man, tanned and brawny and underneath him, petticoats way above her knees and with hair considerably dishevelled was the Lady Arabella Candover.

'Josh! No ... Josh!'

'But you like it,' he whispered thickly, pushing down her bodice with one brown hand and kissing as he went.

'No ...' wept Arabella. 'I didn't mean ... oh, Josh, stop!'

'I don't like teases,' the man said. 'You worked me up deliberate and now you're going to get what you asked for.' One hand was now up her thigh, caressing. He set his teeth at her throat and bit.

Arabella screamed.

Clemency started forward.

'Oh!' Arabella gave a gasp, half of shame, half of thankfulness.

Josh looked up.

He was younger, much younger than Clemency had supposed. Now she saw him she recognized him as the young farmer's son Arabella had been making eyes at in church. He didn't look more than sixteen and a sort of baffled embarrassment surged up over his face as he saw her. He sat up and roughly pulled down Arabella's dress and ran one hand over his red face.

For a moment nobody spoke. The young man looked paralyzed with horror, Arabella looked ready to cry, as much from shock as outrage, and Clemency was thinking what best to do.

Just then they heard the sound of somebody coming up the path through the wood. There, about fifty yards away was the marquess, gun in hand and game bag over his shoulder.

'I think you'd best be off,' said Clemency, nodding at Joshua.

He got up quickly. 'I'm sorry, Bella,' he said, awkwardly. 'I didn't mean to frighten you.'

'I'm sorry, too,' whispered Arabella. 'It was my fault as much as yours.'

The young man shot a quick glance at the approaching marquess and fled.

'Now, Lady Arabella, tidy yourself,' urged Clemency, pulling her to her feet and trying to brush off the bits of bracken from her dress and hair. 'Where's your bonnet?'

Arabella straightened her bodice and shook out her skirts. Then, as if it was all too much for her she sank down again and burst into tears.

'We used to play together when we were *six*,' she wailed. 'Oh, why did he have to spoil it all? He used to bring me frog-spawn and help me catch sticklebacks.'

Clemency stroked her hair.

'Last time he kissed me he was quite respectful,' said Arabella resentfully.

'So you thought you'd tease him a bit more,' suggested Clemency, but she put her arm round Arabella and gave her a hug. 'But you must know that that is a dangerous game, particularly with a very young man. I daresay he is as ashamed as you are by now.'

The marquess was now within ten yards of them and able to see that all was not well. He had, in fact, heard Arabella's scream.

'You won't tell him, will you?' whispered Arabella.

'I shan't need to,' retorted Clemency dryly.

Lysander took the situation in at a glance. His gaze travelled from his sister's dirty petticoat to rest, with increasing anger, on an all-too-obvious love-bite.

'Where's he gone?' he demanded, turning to Clemency.

'Who, my lord?'

'Don't be a fool, girl. Young Baldock.' He hitched his gun up his arm.

'I have no idea,' said Clemency coldly. 'And, if I were you, I wouldn't pursue it.'

'Not pursue it when my sister's been assaulted?'

'Your sister has not been assaulted, my lord. And I think you should stop and consider before doing something which will make the whole thing public. Have you *no* thought for Lady Arabella's reputation?'

The marquess glared at her.

'Who the hell do you think you are to tell me what I should or should not do? A jumped-up governess from God-knows where!'

'Please, Zander.' Arabella put one trembling hand on his sleeve. 'It was partly my own fault.'

There was a pause. 'Get back to the house, both of you,' he said at last, gesturing with the gun. 'I'll see what my aunt has to say.'

'But my cousin ...' began Clemency.

'The groom shall go over with a note,' said Lysander impatiently. 'I want a full account of this affair and you're staying until I have one.' He waited impatiently while Clemency collected her basket and then followed them both back to the house.

His expression was so grim that neither of the girls dared to speak.

* * *

Mrs Stoneham had just seen off a garrulous Mrs Lamb and was beginning to wonder when Clemency would return when she had a visitor. She was out in the garden, keeping half an eye open for her young cousin, the other half engaged in dead-heading the roses, when a gig drew up at the gate. A small dapper little man climbed down and the horse, which Mrs Stoneham recognized as belonging to the Crown, lowered its head and began cropping the grass on the verge. The man stuck a couple of stones under the wheels to secure the gig and came forward.

'Mrs Stoneham?'

'Yes.'

He handed her his card. Mrs Stoneham scanned it with a sinking heart. A lawyer with an address in the City. It was obvious why he was here.

'How may I help you, Mr Jameson? I do not recognize the name, I confess.'

'Could we speak in private, madam?'

'Certainly. Will you come in?' She led the way into her parlour and bade him be seated. 'A cup of tea, sir?'

'A cup of tea would be most welcome.'

Mrs Stoneham rang the bell. One swift, pregnant glance passed between her and Bessy as she gave her orders. Mrs Stoneham then allowed herself to relax. The ensuing conversation was carried on with both sides prevaricating and neither willing to admit it. Mr Jameson had heard at the Crown where he'd hired the gig that Mrs Stoneham had a beautiful golden-haired niece staying with her. The description and her time of arrival fitted Clemency and he was pretty certain that his search was over.

For her part Mrs Stoneham was giving nothing away. Yes, a young relation was staying in between governess's posts. No, she was not here at the moment, it was possible that she was over at Candover Court – Mrs Stoneham did not think anything of the sort, but saw no harm in letting it be known that her young visitor had the *entrée* there. No, she did not know when she would be back. No, she had not heard of Clemency Hastings' flight: what a shocking thing! How Amelia must feel it.

It was obviously out of the question for Mr Jameson to accuse Mrs Stoneham of deception. He could only wait and hope that the wretched girl would come in. It was hardly possible that Mrs Stoneham had two beautiful, golden-haired young relatives. But there were one or two niggles in his mind. One was that the cottage was a stone's throw from the Storrington family seat, surely the last place on earth that Miss Clemency would choose? And secondly that the young lady was apparently an invited guest there. But was it true? The doubts, however, were enough to make him hold his hand.

He accepted Mrs Stoneham's offer of a second cup of tea and wondered what he should do.

At that moment there was a tap at the door and Bessy came in with a note. 'Sent over from Candover Court, ma'am,' she said, with a triumphant glance at Mrs Stoneham. That'll cook his goose, she thought. Bessy had been with Mrs Stoneham since her marriage and there were few secrets between them. She was quite as anxious as her mistress that Mr Jameson should depart incontinent.

Mrs Stoneham, with a murmured apology to Mr Jameson, took it. It was short and to the point. The Lady Arabella had met Miss Stoneham up in the Home Wood and had invited her back. Lady Helena trusted it would be all right if Miss Stoneham stayed the afternoon and the groom would bring her home later.

Mrs Stoneham was not going to do anything so obvious as hand Mr Jameson the note, but she let it lie on the table where he could see it and, with a murmured excuse, went to fuss a little with the window blind to allow him time to read it.

When she returned she was pleased and relieved to see Mr Jameson preparing to go.

'I am sorry for the intrusion, madam,' he said. 'I shall have to continue my search elsewhere.'

Mrs Stoneham said something sympathetic. 'You may, of course, rely on my discretion,' she added. 'I am sure that Clemency, wherever she may be, given time and the assurance that she will be freely forgiven this drastic step, will wish to return home. I cannot believe that Amelia was serious in threatening to send her to Miss Whinborough, a most unsympathetic woman, in my opinion.'

'You must be right, madam,' said Mr Jameson, bleakly. Neither of them believed it for a moment, but the fiction of the distraught mother must be maintained. In any case, he understood her well enough. Whether Miss Stoneham was Clemency Hastings or not, Mrs Stoneham would not move an inch in the matter while Mrs Hastings proved so obdurate.

He bowed and soon after the gig was seen trotting back in the direction of the inn.

Mrs Stoneham mopped her brow and tried not to think what her husband, whose morals were unimpeachable, would have said.

One thing was clear, though: the little house at Abbots Candover was no longer a safe place for Clemency. Mr Jameson might have allowed himself to be fobbed off, but he knew, and she knew that he knew, that her guest *must* be Clemency Hastings. The question was, would he allow the deception to remain?

They were in Lady Helena's drawing-room: a sullen and silent Arabella, struggling with tears; a pale-faced Clemency; Lady Helena herself, who was looking concerned – though whether her concern was for her pregnant bitch, Millie, who was expecting an Interesting Event at any moment, or her niece, it was difficult to say; and a grim-faced marquess.

'If that damned Miss Lane cannot control Arabella, she must go!' he said, banging his fist on Lady Helena's work-table so that several cotton-reels fell off and some of the smaller dogs started yapping. 'I'm up to my ears in the business of trying to put the estate in some sort of order and I *cannot* concern myself with Arabella's behaviour. Look at her! She looks like a trollop! Good God, Aunt Helena, it's going to be difficult enough marrying her off with virtually no dowry as it is, and who would want damaged goods?'

'Storrington!' said Lady Helena, firmly. 'Moderate your language! And pray tell me how Miss Stoneham comes into all this? Surely young Baldock was not attempting to seduce *both* girls?'

'I found her with Arabella; I don't know why and I want to know from her what the devil was going on.'

Arabella began to sob noisily. 'I didn't mean it!' She turned her face into Clemency's shoulder. Clemency put an arm around her.

Lysander cast Clemency a look of acute dislike.

'Well, Miss Stoneham?'

'There is no need to take that tone with me, Lord Storrington,' said Clemency, nettled. 'I am neither your sister nor one of your employees to be ridden over roughshod.'

Lysander seemed to have difficulty breathing.

For a moment Clemency was frightened. The marquess's reputation was quite bad enough for the idea of him hitting her to be a possibility. She forced herself to sit calmly. Whatever he might do in a Covent Garden brothel, he would surely not attempt in his aunt's drawing-room?

'You are surely not suggesting that Miss Stoneham was party to this assignation?' said Lady Helena. She knew that Lysander was under considerable stress, but this went beyond the bounds of what was permissible.

'What were you doing there, Miss Stoneham?' he demanded.

'I was picking mushrooms.'

'*My* mushrooms!'

'Oh, for heaven's sake, Storrington,' snapped Lady Helena, 'we are not concerned with a few mushrooms! And you're upsetting Millie. Yes, Miss Stoneham. And then?'

'I heard somebody in distress and found Lady Arabella.' She paused for a moment, wondering how best to proceed. 'It was obvious that she had got herself into a difficult situation and had not considered the consequences of her liveliness and teasing on a susceptible young man, much her age and whom, I gather, she has known all her life.

'The moment I arrived he was undoubtedly as embarrassed and ashamed as Lady Arabella herself. He apologized and left. That is all.'

Lady Helena considered her. So did six dogs and the marquess.

'And what do you suggest be done?' she asked. 'You seem to hold such firm opinions for a young lady that I do not hesitate to ask.'

'I would leave well alone,' said Clemency frankly. 'Both have learnt a lesson, I trust, and I cannot see that any purpose would be served by publicizing the affair.'

'Very sensible, my dear. Now, Arabella, go upstairs and change. You are all covered in grass. I shall expect you down here for tea when you are ready.'

Arabella gave Clemency a quick, grateful kiss and left the room. Lysander watched with an expression hard to define.

'Now, Miss Stoneham,' continued Lady Helena, 'what do you suggest for the future?'

'Aunt Helena,' broke in the marquess impatiently, 'I cannot see that this unfortunate affair is any business of Miss Stoneham's. Though she seems very ready with her opinions.'

'It was you, Storrington, who insisted on bringing her here,' pointed out Lady Helena. 'Yes, my dear?'

Clemency hesitated.

'Well, Miss Stoneham?' said the marquess. 'Cat got your tongue?'

'You must forgive me, my lord, if I refer to your lordship's affairs,' said Clemency at last, 'but it is common knowledge that the estate must be sold up and Lady Arabella may well feel that her future is very limited. She may have decided to seek some excitement while she could. She has not confided in me, but so young and pretty a girl must surely have been looking forward to her come-out?'

Lysander didn't look at her. He was staring down into the fireplace.

'Might there be a relation or a god-parent, perhaps, who would be willing to undertake this duty? Even the hope of a modest season would surely turn her thoughts in a more seemly direction. And if your lordship plans to be here the rest of the summer, she might welcome some young company.'

'I have no plans for a large house party,' said Lysander, shortly. 'Since you seem to know all about my affairs I am sure you will understand that I cannot afford the entertainment.'

'We could ask the Fabians,' said Lady Helena thoughtfully.

'Damned Methodists,' snapped Lysander.

'Nonsense. Lord Fabian has been doing a lot of work with the Society for the Abolition of Slavery certainly, and I agree that Adela is tiresomely over-involved in church visiting, but Lady Fabian is charming and Diana must be about Arabella's age.' She looked at Clemency. 'Second cousins,' she said, 'and *most* suitable. Thank you, my dear.'

'Very well, Aunt. We'll invite the Fabians if we must. At least they won't expect too much laid on. But I'll invite the Baverstocks as well. I need some liveliness amid all this uniform virtue and Oriana and Mark will stop things becoming too deadly.'

'As you wish,' said Lady Helena doubtfully. She didn't care for Oriana Baverstock. She was beautiful and well born, certainly, but her disposition was calculating. She was the sort of woman who would get Lysander if she could – though her dowry was no more than moderate – and then jettison any responsibility for unwanted dependents like Arabella. She knew that Lysander hoped to salvage something for Arabella's dowry, but doubted whether this would have Miss Baverstock's blessing.

Lysander, who had been contemplating his prospective guests with distaste, gave a sudden laugh. 'We'd better ask Giles Fabian as well,' he said. 'Arabella can practise her wiles on him! A very earnest young man, my cousin Giles,' he added to Clemency. 'Last time I heard he was hoping to become a missionary.'

Clemency smiled back, wondering how it was that a laugh could so light up that harsh face. 'Your sister will enjoy being a temptation,' she said.

For a moment his eyes warmed as they looked on her, then he turned away as the butler came in to announce that Mr Frome awaited his lordship's pleasure in the estate room and Lysander left them.

'You know, you are a very sensible young woman,' said Lady Helena approvingly, when he had gone. She didn't know why it hadn't struck her before, but Lysander needed some company quite as much as Arabella. He was beginning to look quite haggard. And if Cousin Fabian was not precisely enlivening, at least he would take Lysander's mind off his problems. As for Oriana Baverstock, perhaps when she saw the true state of affairs at Candover, she would have second thoughts.

'Thank you, my lady.' Clemency bent to stroke Millie, who was curled up on the sofa next to her.

'I wonder, would you consider the post of Arabella's governess? It would only be until next year, if we can persuade Lady Fabian to bring her out with Diana.'

'But ... but ...' stammered Clemency, not knowing whether to laugh or cry. She was actually being *asked* to stay under the same roof as her erstwhile hoped-for betrothed!

'I know you must be concerned about teaching so intractable a pupil, but really, Miss Stoneham, I shall not expect miracles. If you can but keep Arabella out of the arms of the local tenantry I shall be satisfied. She needs more of a companion than a governess, I think.'

'Your nephew would not agree, madam,' said Clemency bluntly. 'He has taken me in dislike.'

And that, thought Lady Helena, was one of the benefits of the idea. In her view it was providential. A young and beautiful girl, like Miss Stoneham, was a hazard in any household where there were susceptible young men.

'Storrington is a law unto himself,' agreed Lady Helena. 'But his attitude need not concern you. It is *I* who pay for Arabella's governess.'

'Nevertheless, madam, I could not consider it without his agreement. Indeed, I must discuss it with my cousin. I did promise to be with her over the summer. She was sadly distressed at Cousin Robert's death.'

Lady Helena smiled graciously. It was inconceivable to her that a mere rector's widow's convenience would not give way before her own.

Nothing more was said on the subject. Arabella, unwontedly subdued came down for tea. The marquess remained in the estate room. After tea Lady Helena waved aside Clemency's insistence that she could walk home and ordered round the curricle.

'You shall hear from me, Miss Stoneham,' she said firmly, 'very soon.'

The drive home was all too short to allow Clemency the period of reflection she needed. She had much to think about. First of all there was the extraordinary offer from Lady Helena: how might she refuse it without giving offence? It was one thing to go over to Candover Court for tea under a false name, and quite another to take up a job there. The repercussions if she were ever found out, on Cousin Anne as much as herself, were too awful to be contemplated.

Then there was the marquess. Here, Clemency's thoughts were more tangled. There was no doubt that he was dangerously attractive when he tried, and he plainly did not like her, but all the same, they would be in a more intimate situation than either her heart or her reason found comfortable. Miss Hastings of Russell Square, heiress, had some protection: Miss Stoneham of nowhere in particular would have very little.

Lastly, she had noted with dismay the name 'Oriana'. Undoubtedly, the Baverstocks were the couple she had seen briefly on that fateful afternoon at Miss Biddenham's. She did not think that either of them had bothered to notice her, but it was not a risk that she cared to run.

The curricle arrived in Abbots Candover all too soon and the groom jumped down to let down the step for Clemency and hand her her basket, now containing, as well as the mushrooms, the brace of wood-pigeons the marquess had shot, a couple of cucumbers and an earthenware bowl full of strawberries. Lady Helena obviously considered that more than thanks was called for.

The groom touched his hat to her, turned the curricle, and left.

That night Mrs Stoneham sat at her dressing-table while Bessy brushed her hair. In fact, Mrs Stoneham was perfectly capable of brushing her own hair, but the evening ritual was pleasant to both of them and the agreeable fiction was maintained that Bessy's help was needed with unlacing stays and unbuttoning hooks which allowed them both to enjoy a comfortable chat about the day's events.

'I never realised before how exhausting deception was,' remarked Mrs Stoneham. 'When I was young I used to long for an exciting life and used to imagine myself as a smuggler – we lived near Rye as you know – outwitting the preventative officers and smuggling French brandy under their very noses. I can now think of nothing more disagreeable.

'I am constantly in a quake lest I should betray Clemency by some ill-considered word. There was Mrs Lamb this morning, and that dreadful visit from Mr Jameson this afternoon and *now*, on top of it all, Clemency is asked to become a governess at the Court! Where will it all end?'

'I think it's ever so romantic,' said Bessy wistfully, patting Mrs Stoneham's night-cap as she spoke. 'Miss Clemency is such a beautiful young lady that it seems right somehow that she should have these adventures.'

'It's not Clemency having adventures that I object to,' retorted Mrs Stoneham, 'it's *me*! I'm too old and it doesn't suit me.'

'If Miss Clemency goes up to the Court, madam, she will be off your hands.'

'Yes, but will she be safe there, Bessy? That's what is worrying me. I've never taken much notice of rumour myself, but from what Clemency says the marquess is a libertine, to put it no worse. He, surely, cannot fail to notice how very beautiful she is. And this house party! There will be several other young men who may feel that a governess is fair game. I cannot like it.'

'I shouldn't worry yourself, madam,' said Bessy soothingly. 'Miss Clemency is one to stand up for herself, never fear.'

'I shall tell Clemency to befriend the dogs,' said Mrs Stoneham, after a few moments silence. 'A young man will hesitate to attempt familiarities when surrounded by hordes of ill-trained dogs.' She allowed herself a small smile and relaxed slightly. Clemency had only to scream and there would be instant pandemonium.

'I think it would be a good thing for Miss Clemency to go, madam, if you'll pardon the liberty. You will no longer feel responsible and *that* will relieve your mind, I know. Mr Jameson will be unable to get at her and I do not think that being a governess to a wayward young girl for a short while will be a bad training for life. It will give her an understanding of those less fortunate than herself – not that I mean any disrespect to Miss Clemency, who is a very pretty-behaved young lady.'

Bessy didn't say so, but she couldn't help hoping that Miss Clemency might end up as a marchioness after all. Perhaps, when she was thrown into this young man's company she might change her mind. Perhaps he would whisk her away in a chaise and four! Bessy could picture herself assisting at a midnight elopement to Gretna Green and how romantic *that* would be!

'In any event, there's no help for it if Lady Helena wants her,' sighed Mrs Stoneham. 'I would be loath to write to Mrs Hastings and betray my trust, and Clemency plainly cannot stay here, so Candover Court it will have to be.'

* * *

Oriana Baverstock sat in the pretty breakfast-room at
Stoneleigh Manor and surveyed with gratification the letter her
brother had handed across the table. An invitation to Candover
Court! Oriana had never been there – whilst the former
marquess and Lord Alexander were alive, even her easy-going
father would never have permitted a visit – but she had seen an
engraving of it in the guide book and knew that it was of
considerable antiquity. Not that she cared much for that,
preferring modern comforts, but she very much liked the idea
of being invited there and a small house party would relieve
the tedium of country life. It would also further her aims with
regard to Lysander.

Miss Baverstock was one of those young women who are
great favourites with the opposite sex, being very pretty and
blessed with the capacity to make any male feel that he was
deeply interesting, but who are not much liked by their own.
Most of her female contemporaries found her somewhat
calculating and certainly not one to ask for a favour. If you were
ill it would be no good looking for Miss Baverstock to pay you a
visit. The general opinion among her own sex was that she was
out for what she could get, and with a very reasonable fortune
of £10,000 and all the attractions of a neat figure, large brown
eyes and dancing brown curls done à la Madonna, it was
agreed that she would probably get it.

There was, however, a snag. Much as Oriana would like to
become a marchioness, she was not sure that the sweetness of
her disposition would show to the best advantage if Lysander's
estates were as much encumbered as rumour had it. Lysander,
of course, had not discussed such things with her, but she
knew from her brother, Mark, that he was in pretty deep water
with his father's and his brother's debts.

'What do you think, Sis, eh?' said Mark. 'Should you like to
go?'

'Of course! It might be amusing.' Oriana seemed wholly
absorbed in choosing an apple.

'Lysander says not to expect much. He will be taken up with
estate business and unable to set up much entertainment.'

'Mm.' Oriana looked over the letter again. 'Our company will
be a favour to him, he says. Naturally, we must go. Poor
Lysander! What an awful business.' She bit delicately into her

apple and added nonchalantly, 'Do you know how bad things are?'

Mark shot her a comprehensive glance but said only, 'Pretty bad, I gather.'

'I shall be able to judge for myself, doubtless. Shall you tell Papa, or shall I?'

'You tell. I cannot see that he would object. Lady Helena Candover will be there as chaperone as well as these Fabians.'

'Very well.'

Sir Richard Baverstock was indolent and since the death of his wife some five years earlier had never bestirred himself about anything that didn't directly administer to his own comfort. Oriana had had to organize her own come-out some three years earlier, dragooning her grandmother into doing the necessary. To do Sir Richard justice he had not stinted on her season and stumped up without complaint to launch his daughter creditably. The truth was he was proud of her looks and perfectly ready to enjoy his mother's weekly accounts of Oriana's triumphs at a distance.

Once assured that Oriana would be properly chaperoned at Candover Court he had no further objections to make and was even persuaded to let them have the travelling carriage.

'After Storrington, are you?' he grunted. 'Well, look before you leap, girl. I hear he's under the hatches and I've no intention of bailing out an expensive son-in-law.'

Oriana didn't reply. Papa was distressingly vulgar sometimes, she thought. Besides, she knew very well that he would pay whatever was necessary for a quiet life.

'We shall leave on Friday,' was all she said.

It was a severe shock to Clemency when the housekeeper had shown her up to the attic bedroom so recently vacated by Miss Lane, and the coachman had unceremoniously dumped the small valise on the floor, to see where she was expected to sleep.

The walls were white-washed, or had been some twenty years ago, and were now flaked by the sun and stained in one corner where damp had come in. There was a thin strip of drugget on the floor by the bed, otherwise the floorboards were bare. A mottled chest of drawers stood against one wall with a speckled looking-glass above it. The bed was a half tester that had seen better days and the mattress, when Clemency gingerly felt it, was decidedly lumpy.

There were two points only in its favour: one was that it was at least clean; and secondly, it faced south and did, in fact, look down towards the gatehouse and the front drive. Now, in late August, with the afternoon sun streaming in, it had a certain old-fashioned charm.

Clemency unpacked slowly. There were some pegs behind a cotton curtain and she hung up her dresses. The housekeeper had told her that the maid would empty the slops every day and see that she had clean water in the ewer. Clemency understood that she could not expect hot water in the mornings – that was reserved for the ladies and gentlemen downstairs – cold water would have to do.

Clemency sank down on to the bed and looked at the little miniature of her papa which she had put on the small bamboo table next to the bed. Whatever would Papa say if he could see her now? Her father would never have sanctioned her marriage to so dissolute a man, be he ten times a marquess, nor would he have agreed to her being sent off to her Aunt Whinborough.

There was no use repining. She must make the best of things. She and Cousin Anne had discussed the possibility that in a few months Mrs Stoneham might contact Mr Jameson discreetly and see how the land lay. Her mother would surely find her long absence awkward and maybe a face-saving formula might be found.

For the moment though she was here. It could, she reflected, have been a lot worse. She had heard horror stories from Miss Biddenham of half-a-dozen wild and rude charges, of being treated like an upper servant. Lady Helena had, at least, been clear on that point. 'You will accompany Lady Arabella downstairs for all meals,' she wrote. 'I am anxious that she loses her hoydenish ways in preparation for her come-out next year, and shall look to you to improve her manners and deportment.'

Clemency didn't see quite how this was to be accomplished but, in any event, at least she would not get half-cold kitchen left-overs!

She touched the miniature gently and rose to go downstairs.

Just then there was an impetuous rat-tat-tat on the door and Arabella danced in.

'Famous!' she cried. 'I am so pleased you are come, Miss Stoneham. No more horrid old French!'

'If your aunt wishes you to continue your French we shall have to do so,' said Clemency with a smile. 'Perhaps we could get hold of some back copies of *La Belle Assemblée* and look at fashions in French. How about that?'

'Well, it would be better than Racine,' said Arabella grudgingly, determined not to be mollified.

Clemency laughed. After a moment Arabella smiled. 'Aunt Helena wants me to bring you downstairs the moment you're ready. It is just us. The Fabians are arriving tomorrow and the Baverstocks on Friday.'

Lady Helena greeted Clemency graciously. They shook hands.

Clemency was about to sit down when she suddenly noticed something. 'Oh! Lady Helena! Millie's had her puppies. Aren't they sweet?' There was a box in a corner of the room where Millie was jealously guarding four minute puppies.

'It is a pleasure to see you, my dear,' said Lady Helena approvingly. She couldn't think why Lysander had taken against this charming girl. Miss Stoneham knew they were in mourning, of course, and she had the tact to wear a dove-grey dress, trimmed with black velvet. Yes, thought her ladyship, she will be good for Arabella.

Lysander had risen as Clemency and Arabella came into the room. He bowed slightly, but did not offer her his hand. It was very obvious that he had not wanted her to come.

Clemency, feeling suddenly depressed, sat down. Why was he not more welcoming? Had he not forgiven her for stumbling upon Arabella and young Baldock? But that was not her fault!

Then she scolded herself. What did it matter to her if the marquess disapproved of her? She wanted nothing to do with such a man and the less she saw of him the better pleased she'd be. She tried to concentrate on what Lady Helena was saying.

She fully expected him to return to the estate room as soon as he had done the correct thing and greeted her.

Unaccountably, he stayed.

Four

Clemency and Arabella spent most of the following morning arranging flowers in the various guest bedrooms. It had, in fact, been something of a problem to find enough rooms that were habitable and beds whose mattresses were reasonable and where the hangings were not disintegrating. It had not crossed Lady Helena's mind to concern herself with the problem – what did they pay a housekeeper for? – but Mrs Marlow had only been there for the last five years during which time very few guests had stayed, the 3rd Marquess preferring drinking parties with his hunting cronies and Alexander spending most of his time in London.

On the very afternoon of her arrival Clemency noticed that the housekeeper was looking flustered, not to say harassed, and had asked Lady Helena if there was anything she could do to help.

'Of course, my dear,' said Lady Helena absent-mindedly. 'Pongo, *will* you get down!'

And Clemency interpreted that as permission. It was just as well, she found, when she descended to the kitchens, for Mrs Marlow seemed to be in hysterics and on the point of giving in her notice. Clemency did her best to soothe her. 'I have had some experience of entertaining, Mrs Marlow,' she said, 'so if I can be of any assistance do, pray, ask. I shall put myself under your direction entirely.'

Mrs Marlow brightened up and over a cup of tea in the housekeeper's room confided in Clemency that she would never have taken on the job if she'd known there was to be lots of gadding about. She added that her previous post had been looking after a retired couple in Bath where the excitements did not go beyond a small party of an evening.

At Clemency's request they went over the bedrooms.

'Good gracious!' cried Clemency. In one room there was a mouse's nest in the bed. 'We cannot put Lady Fabian in here!'

'It's at such short notice, Miss Stoneham,' wailed Mrs Marlow. 'We are so short staffed and there's all the meals to do as well. Molly and Peg are needed in the *kitchen*. I simply cannot spare them to clean out the bedrooms.'

'Of course you can't. We must get in a couple of girls from the village.'

'But his lordship....'

'You leave his lordship to me.' Clemency thought that he could surely find a few shillings for the extra help. He could hardly expect his guests to sleep on the floor, after all!

Mrs Marlow was able to summon up a couple of girls and by the time the Fabians arrived the following evening there were four bedrooms ready. True, the Misses Fabian would have to share, but Clemency felt that they must put up with it. The Honourable Giles was lodged in what had once been a dressing-room to the state bedroom. The state bed was quite unusable and riddled with woodworm. Clemency doubted whether anybody had slept in it for a hundred years. The dressing-room was very small, but at least it was clean and dry and in any case, there was no choice.

Lysander, coming out of his bedroom on the morning of the Fabians' arrival met Clemency, apron over her dress, and a pile of linen in her arms. She also had a smut on her nose and little tendrils of golden hair had escaped from the knot on the top of her head.

'Good God, Miss Stoneham! Are there no servants to do that?'

'No,' said Clemency, truthfully.

Lysander became conscious of a sudden desire to tuck those little ringlets back into their proper place, or even curl them round his finger. Abruptly, he thrust his hands into his pockets.

'Hardly a suitable occupation for my sister's companion,' he said, raising an eyebrow.

'Oh, Lady Arabella is helping as well,' said Clemency sweetly. She bobbed a curtsey and left him.

Lysander retreated in no very good order.

When they met again at lunch he expostulated to Lady Helena.

'You have employed Miss Stoneham as a governess,' he said, 'and yet I find her behaving like an upper servant and allowing Arabella to help her.' He told himself that he would be better pleased to know that she and his sister were doing French up in the schoolroom.

Lady Helena looked up from tempting Muffin with the remains of her chop bone and said, 'Nonsense, Storrington. It won't do Arabella any harm to see how a house is managed. I'm only grateful that Miss Stoneham has taken the botheration of it off my hands. She and Mrs Marlow are managing very well.'

The marquess tried another tack. 'Don't hesitate to ask if you would like *me* to do anything, Miss Stoneham,' he said sarcastically.

'Thank you, my lord,' replied Clemency promptly. 'I believe Mrs Marlow would like you to bring in some wood-pigeon. She hopes to make her broiled pigeon with mushroom sauce, which I understand is a favourite.'

'If there are any mushrooms left after your depredations!' This infuriating girl had come into his house and within less than twenty-four hours appeared to be running it!

Clemency, uncertain how to take this, looked doubtfully at him, but to her relief he was smiling. She relaxed. 'Lady Arabella and I will deal with the mushrooms,' she said demurely.

'And your French conversation? Is that to be wholly neglected now?'

'*Pas du tout. Nous parlerons français en cherchant des champignons!*'

Arabella looked alarmed, but Lysander only laughed.

'*Touché*, Miss Stoneham.' He looked at her rather more favourably. He liked a girl who stood up to him and really, he couldn't hold it against her that she'd come upon Arabella in the wood. In fact, it could be viewed as providential. She was uncommonly pretty too, though too slim for his taste. He preferred more opulent brunettes like Oriana and, in any case, Miss Stoneham was only a paid companion when all was said and done. Whatever Alexander might have got up to, it was quite against Lysander's code to trifle with a servant.

By the time the Fabians had arrived and they all sat down to dinner, Clemency felt as though she'd been at Candover Court for weeks instead of less than a day.

Lord Fabian, portly and in his fifties, had the air and breeding of a gentleman. He treated Clemency with quiet courtesy, as did his lady. Lady Fabian was dressed more fashionably than her lord, but she too seemed perfectly at home in the shabby grandeur of Candover Court. Mrs Marlow and her minions had done their best, but nothing could disguise the frayed and faded curtains or the patches of damp on the silk wallpaper. It was Lady Fabian who was a cousin of Lysander's mother, so perhaps she felt that a little shabbiness amongst relatives didn't matter.

Anyway, it was common knowledge in the family that the 3rd Marquess had run disastrously through his fortune and Alexander had been no better. She had not seen Lysander since he was a schoolboy, but by all accounts he was the pick of the bunch.

Her daughter, Adela, was rather shocked by the almost Gothic atmosphere of decay. Adela, in her mother's view, was rather too addicted to piety and good works. She had been out now for three years and so far nobody, unless you counted that dreadful curate from the East End Mission who suffered from adenoids, had shown the smallest sign of coming up to scratch. A thin-faced girl, with a flat chest, she prided herself on her worth as the daughter of a baron. Being third cousin to the Marquess of Storrington had always been a source of quiet satisfaction to her – though she had met him only once and that many years ago. It had not stopped her, however, from mentioning the relationship rather too frequently to her friends. The state of the house and grounds came as a nasty surprise, and she didn't care for her cousin Lysander's swarthy looks either.

If the house was falling into rack and ruin, thought Adela, it was clearly God's Judgement. And Arabella looked something of a minx: she hoped Diana wouldn't be drawn in.

Diana, the younger daughter, looked with envy across the dinner-table at Arabella. How pretty and lively she was! Diana, who for many years had suffered from Adela's pious homilies on the modest demeanour to be shown by a Christian gentlewoman, found herself wishing that she had something of the freedom her young cousin had. And her governess was so pretty too! Diana's governess was angular and bony and not the sort of person who would ever be enlivening company.

As for the Honourable Giles, that embryo missionary, he had taken one look at Clemency and been quite unable to think of anything else. He paid no heed at all to Adela's whispered injunction that Miss Stoneham was only the governess and to stop making a fool of himself. He continued to gaze at her throughout dinner and barely touched his pigeon and mushroom casserole. Clemency was wearing a black silk dress, delicately ruched at neck and hem, which set off her pale gold hair and slender figure to perfection.

Lysander, to his aunt's relief, looked more relaxed than she'd seen him for weeks. Timson had found a few bottles of claret left in the cellar which somehow had survived Alexander's ravages and the marquess was pleased to see that Lord Fabian was enjoying it as well. Evidently, being involved in good causes didn't stop his enjoyment of the good things in life. In fact, Lysander found his lordship surprisingly congenial and decided that he would ask his opinion on one or two of the knottier problems to do with the estate that Frome had come up with. Lady Fabian too was a sensible woman, he decided, and in her straightforward company even his Aunt Helena was behaving with less eccentricity than usual.

He had less time for the younger generation. Adela was plainly a prude with neither figure nor countenance, and Diana was still a gawky schoolgirl. He turned his head to look at Giles.

That young gentleman was staring, enraptured, at Clemency.

Lysander's look turned to a glare. If Miss Stoneham thought to entrap a callow youth with those fairy-tale looks, she would have to go. That dress she was wearing, for instance. It was black, which was perfectly suitable, but did governesses really have low-cut bodices? Miss Lane had never done so. He felt, suddenly, angry and uneasy. In spite of the fact that Clemency, very properly was confining her attention to Lord Fabian on her left and Arabella on her right, he continued to keep his eye on her and Giles throughout the rest of the meal.

Arabella was enjoying herself immensely. Even though she

was forced to sit between Clemency and her cousin, Adela, because of the shortage of men, she couldn't help relishing her first grown-up dinner-party. She had even been given a small half-glass of wine!

She had swiftly decided that Giles was of no interest to her. The outcome of her tryst with young Mr Baldock had been distressing, but at least Josh was a proper man – unlike her cousin Giles, who looked a slow-top if ever there was one! She tried to picture Giles in the bracken and failed. And there was Diana, who was gazing across the table at her with an expression very similar to her brother's at Clemency. So far they had only exchanged a few words, but Diana was so eager to be a friend that even Arabella's selfish little heart was touched. She smiled at her across the table and was rewarded with a beam which quite lit up her cousin's face.

When Lady Helena rose and took the ladies with her to the drawing-room, Lysander gestured to Lord Fabian and Giles to move and sit by him. Timson set the port between them and departed.

'Charming girl, Miss Stoneham,' said Lord Fabian reflectively. 'Talks sense too, unlike my poor Adela. Where does she come from?'

'She's a cousin of a rector's widow recently moved into the neighbourhood. My aunt thought she'd be able to keep an eye on Arabella, which a string of governesses has lamentably failed to do!'

'Pretty too,' went on Lord Fabian. 'You thought so too, didn't you, Giles?' Giles choked over his port and went scarlet. 'The only thing that puzzles me is why she's hiring herself out as a governess at all.'

'Why do you say that?' demanded Lysander, frowning.

'Governesses are usually meek and deferential. Miss Stoneham has all the assurance of a beautiful woman who has never had to count pennies.'

'She certainly doesn't scruple to inform one of her opinions.'

Giles gulped and said, 'Miss Stoneham's utterances must always command respect....'. He caught Lysander's sardonic eye and subsided.

'Miss Stoneham's utterances are frequently uncalled-for,' snapped the marquess.

Lord Fabian's eyes twinkled. Lysander had his fair share of the Candover arrogance, he thought. He didn't think a set-down or two from Miss Stoneham would come amiss. He wondered whether the marquess himself was at all taken by her remarkable beauty.

Thank God that he, himself, was of an age where he could enjoy the attentions of a pretty woman without all this hostility that the marquess was showing poor Giles. He was glad to see his son showing some interest in women at last. He and Adela were, both of them, over pious in his view.

He had regarded their stay here with some misgiving and had only consented because his wife had begged him to. Now, he thought that it might turn out to be quite amusing.

Up in the drawing-room Arabella and Diana were sitting on the window-seat. Diana was nervously twisting her hands in her skirt, making it a mass of creases. Both girls were young enough to wear white mourning, but whereas this suited Arabella's more vivid colouring, Diana, being sallow, simply looked washed out.

'Are ... are you s-still having l-lessons, Cousin?' she managed to ask.

Arabella made a face. 'I'm supposed to be, in the mornings, but now you are here, I daresay Aunt Helena won't mind if they are dropped.'

'Oh.' Diana's voice was wistful.

'Why?' demanded Arabella.

'I ... I was h-hoping to join you.'

Arabella stared at her in astonishment. *Want* to do lessons? She looked across at Clemency who was attempting a very one-sided conversation with Adela.

'Miss Stoneham!'

Clemency looked up.

'Cousin Diana wants to share my lessons. But do I have to do them while we have guests?'

'Certainly,' said Clemency. 'It's only for the mornings, after all. You may join your guests in the afternoons. And of course Miss Diana may join us, if her mama agrees.'

'Oh, *thank you* Miss Stoneham!' Diana's face lit up again.

'But why do you want to?' asked Arabella curiously.

Diana twisted a little fringe on her dress nervously. 'I ... I'm not v-very good in c-company,' she whispered. 'I'm always a-afraid of s-saying the wrong thing.' She looked imploringly at Arabella. 'You're so p-pretty and lively,' she went on, 'you d-don't *know* w-what it's like.'

'It's pure selfishness to think only of yourself in company,' put in Adela, who had been listening. 'If you thought of others more and of yourself rather less, you wouldn't *be* so stupidly shy.'

Diana retreated, crushed.

Arabella darted a furious look at Adela who had taken a small prayer-book from her pocket and was now reading it. 'What a horrid thing to say!' she exclaimed.

Adela, looking quite saintly, ignored her.

Meanwhile Lady Helena and Lady Fabian were sitting together on the sofa, Muffin between them, and talking.

'I am very pleased that you wrote, Helena,' said Lady Fabian. 'I cannot think how it comes that the idea of bringing the girls out together had never occurred to me before. I think I fancied Arabella to be about fourteen! But it is a providential arrangement. I have been at my wits' end about Diana. I was *dreading* bringing her out. All she does in company is go scarlet and stare at the floor.'

'I must warn you, Maria, that Arabella can be something of a handful,' said Lady Helena.

'But at least she isn't silent!'

'No, indeed! Rather the reverse.'

'I would far, far rather have a girl who was perhaps a little too lively than one who cannot say a word,' said Lady Fabian feelingly. 'Dear Arabella will look after Diana, I know, and give her confidence.'

Lady Helena thought briefly of Arabella's latest escapade and crossed her fingers. She hoped that nothing would occur to make Lady Fabian change her mind.

When Clemency got to bed that night she thought over the events of the day with quiet satisfaction. That the arrangements for the Fabians had gone smoothly was in large part due to her, she knew, and she couldn't help feeling pleased about that. Then, apart from Adela, she liked the Fabians: she certainly didn't foresee any problems with Giles's youthful admiration, and Lord Fabian was a gentleman. Any fears of either of them behaving like her fictitious ex-employer were laid to rest. She had great hopes, too, of Diana being a good influence on Arabella. Arabella had always been the spoilt, youngest child, the one to be looked after. Now she had found somebody who needed *her* protection and cossetting.

On a more practical level she had found a spare mattress that was infinitely more comfortable than her own. It belonged to a truckle bed in one of the spare rooms. Clemency had had no hesitation in getting it moved up to her own room. Last night it had been very difficult to find a comfortable position, tonight, she trusted, would be different.

The only thing that disturbed her slightly she admitted, as she brushed out her hair and plaited it for the night, was the marquess. She was all too aware that he was an attractive man, and all her strictures could not entirely wipe out that meeting in Richmond from her mind.

She would take care, she told herself, to keep out of his way as much as possible. The mornings, thank God, were still to be devoted to the schoolroom – she had Diana to thank for that. She must find some unexceptionable occupation for the afternoons, perhaps helping Lady Helena wash and brush the dogs, or even taking them for walks.

In any event, once the Baverstocks arrived, she would be needed far less. She retained a brief, but telling, memory of Mr Baverstock disdainfully flicking her a coin and of Oriana's contemptuous eyes. She didn't think that she had anything to worry about from them.

She was destined to be completely wrong.

The Baverstocks arrived at about four o'clock the following afternoon. Lysander, who was in the estate room with Frome with half an ear open for the sound of their carriage, went out to greet them.

The butler had opened the big oak doors. The coachman had come round from the stable block at the same time. Timson then went to open the carriage door and let down the steps. He recognized at once, as Oriana stepped down, that here was a possible future chatelaine. The look she gave the house in front of her was decidedly proprietorial. So was the look she gave its master.

Mrs Marlow was in the hall to curtsey to the new arrivals –
like Timson she seemed to have second sight where a future
mistress was concerned – and to direct one of the maids to take
Miss Baverstock's abigail and Mr Baverstock's valet downstairs. She recognized Miss Baverstock at once as being one of
those ladies who had a complete disregard for servants (she'd
not be one to be generous with vails!) and who would, in all
probability, be very fussy. So it was with some trepidation that
she led the way up the oak staircase with its worn treads and
along to the south wing where she and Clemency had decided
to put the Baverstocks.

The two girls from the village had been at work all morning
in the rooms, scrubbing and polishing, and Clemency had
brought up some flowers tastefully arranged, but even so, Mrs
Marlow knew that it was shabby and the furniture decidedly
old-fashioned.

Somehow, Oriana's disdainful glance around made her feel
she must apologize in a way she hadn't felt necessary with
Lady Fabian.

Oriana listened impatiently and thought that the first thing
she'd do as mistress of Candover Court would be to get rid of
incompetent old servants.

'Send Eliza to me, would you,' was all she said.

Her maid, too, had her complaints. 'I have to share a room
with Lady Fabian's maid, Miss Oriana. It is not at all what I am
used to.' She shuddered. The room was practically bare and the
place smelt of mice. There weren't even any curtains.

Oriana shrugged. Maids were always complaining. 'My hair
must be done again before I meet Lady Helena,' she said. She
would wear her rose-coloured satin tonight, she decided.
Everybody else in mourning would set it off admirably.

It was not actually Lady Helena she was concerned about;
she had met her several times in London and knew perfectly
well that that lady would never notice whether her hair was
done or not. It was the other, so far unknown, members of the
house-party, in particular the Honourable Adela and the
Honourable Giles. Oriana always wanted to make sure that she
outshone any marriageable female and impressed any available
male.

In fact, only Lady Fabian and Adela were in the

drawing-room with Lady Helena and one look at Adela set her mind at rest. Lysander would certainly never look twice at such a starched-up miss as the Honourable Adela!

A little later Giles, Diana and Arabella came in from the garden and Oriana was both relieved and disappointed. Diana was a nonentity like her sister, and Giles, unfortunately, too immature to appreciate her charms, Arabella, however, might be worth charming a little; she might have influence with her brother.

She was quite unprepared for Clemency.

Clemency had been in the garden with the others engaged in picking raspberries. She had worn an old dress, the one in fact that she had travelled in, in Sally's uncle's cart, so it didn't matter if the threads got pulled or if it got stained. She went upstairs to change and came down just as tea was brought in. She wore a white spotted muslin, charmingly edged with a ruff, and a black sash edged the bodice.

Her effect on the Baverstocks was considerable. Mark, who had been staring gloomily out of the window, wondering what on earth had made him come, surrounded as he was by dowds and schoolgirls, jumped to his feet. He was further encouraged to hear that this Miss Stoneham was Arabella's governess. A very pretty piece of cherry-pie, in his opinion, and the fact that she was a governess made everything so much easier: no fear of being called to book by some outraged parent.

'How do you *do*, Miss Stoneham,' he said, and gave her hand a meaningful squeeze. He was pleased to see that she coloured faintly.

He glanced across at his sister and was amused to see that she was looking decidedly put out. Poor girl, she'd hoped for a clear run, he supposed. He wondered, briefly, what Lysander's intentions were. He'd said nothing when he'd shown Mark to his room, only talked about possible fishing, so probably he wasn't interested in the beautiful little honey-pot. So much the better; Mark didn't care to poach on the preserves of his friend.

Oriana had extended two fingers to Clemency and immediately turned back to continue her conversation with Adela.

Governess, she thought. Ha! Could she be Lysander's *chère amie*? Well, she, Oriana Baverstock, would soon put Miss in her place. At that moment Clemency got up to get Lady Fabian another cup of tea and Oriana saw, with indignation, that she was wearing silk stockings! Silk! For a governess! If governess she was. Lady Helena might have allowed herself to be bamboozled into allowing such a female into the house, but she, Oriana, had no illusions as to this Miss Stoneham's true status.

Mark, too, had glimpsed the stockings. He had bought enough silk stockings for actresses temporarily living under his protection to recognize them at a glance. So Miss Stoneham wasn't quite the demure governess she seemed, then? Other lovers had paid for those expensive little articles of clothing. So much the better. It made approaching her that much easier.

Lysander had been looking forward to the Baverstocks' arrival. He had envisaged a pleasant repetition of his various visits to Stoneleigh Manor; shooting with Mark and agreeable flirtations with Oriana in the evenings or when the weather proved inclement.

He had been at Eton with Mark and they had both come on the town at the same time and indulged together in the various activities usually pursued by young men of rank and fortune, even though, in Lysander's case it was only the £500 a year he had inherited from his god-father. Light-heartedly, they'd pursued opera dancers and betted in the various gaming-houses. Lysander had a cool head for gaming and, provided he kept to games of skill rather than chance, he usually managed to bridge the gap between income and expenditure. It was just as well: for having put up his son's name for White's and warned him against cheap whores, the 3rd Marquess obviously considered that he was under no further obligation with regard to his second son (who was, after all, only a spare) and forthwith abandoned him. Not that there was a quarrel; the marquess was perfectly pleased to see his son at Candover over Christmas or to give him lunch at White's on one of his rare visits to Town, just so long as it was clearly understood that no financial help would be forthcoming.

He might have been wiser to have pursued this course with his elder son, but no, Alexander was his heir and must be granted every indulgence.

However, there were a number of country houses where

Lord Lysander Candover was a welcome guest, and in spite of straitened circumstances he contrived to live very agreeably. He was well aware, of course, that an impoverished gentleman, even the second son of a marquess, would not be considered as a proper *parti* for their daughters by match-making mamas, but as he had never seriously considered matrimony this did not worry him. At least no fair debutante could ever accuse him of trifling with her affections.

It was in this belief, that any serious intentions were out of the question, that he had invited Miss Baverstock to Candover Court as well as her brother. He had always liked Oriana, indeed admired her ability to go for what she wanted – no milk-and-water miss, she! – and found her attractive, so a month or so in her company was a pleasant prospect.

He had certainly not expected any problems.

As Lysander did not like dining at country hours – it seemed absurd to eat one's dinner at six o'clock and be ravenous again by ten – he insisted that they kept town hours and dinner was served at half past seven. On the Baverstocks' first evening he invited them after tea to step out with him and see the old cloisters, the ruins of which still stood at the east side of the house. It had been a warm day and though the sun was now sinking, Oriana hardly needed her shawl.

Lysander offered her his arm. Mark followed them. There was one subject uppermost in both brother's and sister's minds, but neither of them approached it directly. Instead Oriana said, 'What a sweet girl your sister is, Lysander. So lively and unaffected.'

'Pretty too,' added Mark.

'I'm pleased you think so,' replied Lysander, smiling. In spite of Arabella's infuriating behaviour he was fond of his sister and liked to hear her praised.

'Will Lady Helena be bringing her out this year?' asked Oriana. 'She must surely be of an age now to dispense with a governess?'

The unspoken question hung in the air.

'Cousin Maria is bringing her out with Diana,' said Lysander. 'Ah, here we are. The cloisters date from the thirteenth century, though as you can see, there is not much left of it.'

Oriana gave the cloisters a cursory glance and said lightly,

'Poor Miss Stoneham then. Out of a job. Still, that is the lot of governesses, one hears.' She looked around her and added, 'What a pretty place. It must be enchanting in June all covered in roses.' Then, 'It must be a sad wrench for her to part with the sweet girl.'

Lysander gave a short laugh. 'None of us knew of Miss Stoneham's existence a couple of weeks ago. It was my aunt who insisted that she be employed. Arabella has a knack of sending her governesses off in hysterics. Aunt Helena hopes that somebody more her age will succeed where poor Miss Lane – and so many others – failed. However, it is only until the Fabians go up to town in April.'

'You do not care for Miss Stoneham, I gather?' said Oriana, picking at a bit of moss which was growing in a crack in the wall.

Lysander found himself suddenly extraordinarily reluctant to talk about Miss Stoneham. He had no inhibitions about expressing his disapproval to Clemency herself, or even to his aunt, but he found that he did not want to do so with Oriana. He shrugged, 'I have nothing to say to the arrangement,' he said shortly. 'Aunt Helena has charge of Arabella.'

Mark, listening, was cheered up by this. He would not want to cut Lysander out with his *chère amie*, but if he was not in pursuit then he, Mark, need have no qualms. Governesses were two a penny: Lady Helena would simply have to find another. Miss Stoneham (he wondered what her first name was) was far too pretty for the role of drudge. He would install her in some pretty house in Chelsea perhaps, if she came up to expectations. He, too, looked round the cloisters and at once saw its possibilities.

'Fine trysting place,' he remarked. 'Wonder what the old monks got up to in here?'

Lysander laughed. 'Sorry to disappoint you. I understand they were noted for their piety. Abbot Walter, on whose tomb you are sitting, ended up a cardinal, I believe.'

More fool he, thought Mark.

Clemency had much to think about when she went upstairs to change for dinner. She disliked Mr Baverstock on sight: he was one of those detestable men who believed that they were irresistible to the fair sex. He was the sort of man who gazed into your eyes wanting to see his own reflection. She hadn't liked the way he'd squeezed her hand, nor the style of his conversation which was all hints and innuendo.

The problem was that, as a governess, her options were limited. She could not give him a sharp set-down, nor ask for protection: Lady Helena would obviously not notice anything and the marquess would probably not care. In any case, any complaint she made would doubtless only confirm him in his disapproval of her. For the first time in her life Clemency saw that she would have to do her own chaperoning.

She would have to be very circumspect. Perhaps she should endeavour to engage Adela in conversation: a course of action she suspected would be as much of a trial to Miss Fabian as to herself.

But a far greater shock awaited her at dinner. The table had been altered slightly because of the new guests and now it was Mark who was sitting on Lady Helena's left and thus almost opposite Clemency. She was fully aware that he was often looking at her, endeavouring to catch her eye, but she studiously confined her conversation correctly to Lord Fabian and Diana on either side of her.

However, that did not stop her hearing Oriana, who was on Lysander's left.

Clemency had seen at once that Oriana was interested in Lysander. Serve him right, she told herself, if he was saddled with a thoroughly self-centred wife (one who would put weight on in her middle years too). But somehow Clemency's attempts to dismiss Oriana from her thoughts were fruitless and she found herself listening for her conversation with the marquess.

'I understand that there are some famous beauty spots around here, Lysander,' said Oriana, very willing to demonstrate that she had the privilege of being on first-name terms. 'I hope that your estate business won't be all-engrossing. We shall rely on you to show us round, you know.'

Lysander! thought Clemency. Not Alexander?

'What a famous idea, Miss Baverstock!' cried Arabella. 'We could take a picnic. Zander, do say that we could!'

'You cannot disappoint your sister,' said Oriana, archly.

'What do you think, Aunt Helena?' asked Lysander.

Lady Fabian closed her eyes for a moment. The thought of half-a-dozen ill-trained dogs rampaging over sheep-filled fields filled her with horror. When Lady Helena demurred it enabled her to say quite truthfully, 'Helena, I should be delighted to chaperone the young people if you feel it is too much for you.'

In any case, she thought, Mark Baverstock was an eligible young man and perhaps he would take an interest in Adela. It would not hurt to promote their better acquaintance at any rate.

'Very well,' said the marquess. 'Miss Baverstock commands and it shall be so. Miss Stoneham, how will Mrs Marlow cope, do you think? We are very short-staffed,' he added to Oriana.

'I am sure it will be all right, my lord, provided that Mrs Marlow has a couple of days' notice,' said Clemency. It would serve as an excuse, too, for her to keep out of the way if she had to help Mrs Marlow.

'Miss Stoneham must not be deprived of the pleasure of the picnic if she is to oversee all the work, as I gather she will, Lysander,' said Lady Fabian, smiling kindly at her. She approved of Clemency, who was taking pains to help Diana and Arabella become acquainted and whose efforts to talk to Diana during the meal had not gone unnoticed by her fond mama.

'I hope so,' said the marquess, non-committally.

Giles gave his mother a grateful look.

Afterwards, leaning over Clemency's chair in the drawing-room, Mark whispered, 'Your presence at this picnic is indispensable, Miss Stoneham.'

'Really?' said Clemency coldly.

A put-down? How intriguing, thought Mark. He allowed himself to tweak a tendril of golden hair and added, 'For *my* enjoyment, it is.'

Across the room Lysander watched them.

It was the arrangement with Lady Helena that Clemency should spend Sunday afternoons with Mrs Stoneham and never had the sight of Cousin Anne in church been more welcome. Clemency felt as though she had been at Candover Court for weeks and the crop of problems of the last twenty-four hours were such that she longed for a period of quiet reflection. She was very glad to slip into the old pew beside Cousin Anne and to feel her world steadying about her.

It was not a welcome sight to Mark Baverstock, however. A respectable rector's widow and at the very gates of Candover Court too! The last thing he wanted. No good thinking that you could buy off that sort of woman. She would screech if she thought he had compromised her precious cousin and if he wasn't careful he would find himself leg-shackled. He would have to tread very carefully indeed.

It was not, however, the problem of Mr Baverstock that was uppermost in Clemency's mind when, at last, she was seated with Cousin Anne in the little dining-parlour. Hesitantly, she began to talk.

'Do you mean that you ran away from the wrong man?' demanded Mrs Stoneham.

'I ... I don't know. That's what I want to find out. When Eleanor and Mary Ramsgate looked him up in their book he was Alexander d'Eynecourt Ludovic Theobald. And Lady Arabella calls him "Zander", so naturally I thought....'

'Perhaps "Lysander" is a nickname,' said Mrs Stoneham doubtfully. 'It's hardly a usual name, after all.'

'You don't have a peerage, do you?'

Mrs Stoneham shook her head. 'What would I want with such a book? No, my dear, after luncheon we will take a little walk back to the church – I believe the Norman font is worth seeing if we need an excuse – and we will look at the memorials. The Candovers are buried there; you remember the Elizabethan tomb with the lord and lady lying on their sides?'

'Yes indeed. And their children kneeling round the base.'

They met Mr Lamb in the church.

'My young cousin is interested in the Candover chapel,' said Mrs Stoneham.

'Of course, of course. It will be a sad day when the family goes, Mrs Stoneham. Not that they have been very good church-goers, I fear.'

'The present marquess, is he the fourth or the fifth?' asked Mrs Stoneham next.

'The fifth. As you know his brother only held the title for a few months.'

Clemency and Mrs Stoneham looked at each other.

'Oh dear. Was it an accident? I am so newly arrived that I do not know the story.'

Mr Lamb settled himself against the lectern. 'I am sorry to say that he died in a drunken brawl. A very idle and vicious young man. He rarely came to church and no respectable village family would send their daughters to work at the Court while Lord Alexander was alive.'

'How ... how strange that the present marquess should have so singular a name,' said Clemency. 'One not unlike his brother's, too.'

'A most ungodly name,' said the vicar feelingly. 'I wonder my predecessor agreed to christen him by it.'

'Come, my dear,' said Mrs Stoneham, 'we must not keep Mr Lamb from his duties. Let us look around the chapel.'

When they got there Mrs Stoneham pointed to a small memorial tablet on the wall.

Sacred to the memory of Alexander d'Eynecourt Ludovic Theobald Candover, 4th Marquess of Storrington. Born January 15th 1786. Died March 21st, 1817.

This tablet was erected by his brother, Lysander, 5th Marquess of Storrington. 1817.

R.I.P.

'Nothing about deeply lamented, I notice,' said Clemency.

'It is obvious that this young man must be the one your maid warned you against,' said Mrs Stoneham, sinking down on to a pew.

'Yes.'

Clemency could hardly take it in. It was not Lysander, she kept thinking. He wasn't the one who had gambled and whored his patrimony away and was notorious for his cruelty. It was not Lysander! A surge of thankfulness shot through her. The man who had so tenderly kissed her that day was not the callous rake she had thought.

'S ... sorry, Cousin Anne. What did you say?'

'I asked you whether you would have declined to meet the new marquess if you had known the truth?'

'I ... I don't know.' Clemency pressed her hands to her cheeks.

If she had known that it was Lysander who came to Russell Square that day, what would she have done?

'It's too late to think of that now,' she said at last. 'He ... he must have felt grossly insulted by my refusal to meet him. And he has made it very clear now that he dislikes me. So even if he had come I doubt whether he would have been interested.' She took hold of her thoughts firmly and shook them into a proper order. 'So I had better make the best of it.'

Five

Of the three younger gentlemen of the party, two found Miss Stoneham's absence on the Sunday afternoon made the world quite flat and boring. Giles mooned about, first in the cloisters, whose romantic gloom exactly mirrored his sentiments and then, more prosaically, accepted Diana's and Arabella's invitation to join them for a walk in the wood. If *she* wasn't here, he thought, he might just as well accompany them as not.

Mark, too, found that the afternoon had its *longueurs*. Scruples forbade that he and Lysander went shooting or fishing on a Sunday and he certainly was not going to join Adela in her Bible-reading. Oriana and Lysander were plainly happily occupied amusing each other and he didn't care to play gooseberry to them.

At last he decided to take a walk. He would wander in the direction of the village and, with luck, he would meet Miss Stoneham coming back. He'd learnt that she was expected to return in time for dinner, so as long as he was on the road to Abbots Candover shortly before six he couldn't fail to meet her. If he couldn't seize the opportunity thus offered, then his name wasn't Mark Baverstock.

Lysander had detached Oriana from the group of ladies sitting under the cedar on the front lawn and taken her off to view the folly – a mock ruin built by his great-grandfather on his return from the grand tour. It stood on a small eminence behind the house and the 1st Marquess, who had been something of a classics scholar, liked to go there and compose Horatian odes. Lysander, having no turn for poetry, thought only that a little dalliance in a romantic ruin would be an agreeable way to pass a Sunday afternoon.

Oriana was wearing the thinnest of summer sandals, so this

entailed the marquess frequently taking her hand over the uneven ground.

'So stupid of me,' said Oriana, looking at him from under her lashes.

'But such a pleasure for me,' Lysander replied promptly.

Pleased with themselves and with each other they reached the folly and turned to look back.

Oriana saw a long, low, sprawling building with defective guttering and crumbling stonework. She could even see from her vantage point that some of the roof had gone on the stable block and that a small tree appeared to be growing out of one of the chimney stacks. The house was uncomfortable too and she had no doubt that in winter it would be cold and draughty and almost certainly damp. If she had her way she wouldn't hesitate: sell the place for the best price she could get and buy a snug little estate with a modern house.

'Charming,' she said.

'Damp and in a state of decay,' said the marquess, though his eye rested fondly on the stone-tiled roof and the Elizabethan chimneys, twisted like pieces of barley-sugar.

Oriana laughed. 'But so picturesque.' She was dismayed. Mark had hinted that Lysander's affairs were in trouble, but she had not imagined them to be *this* bad. Marquesses didn't lose their estates, surely? They might be in straitened circumstances, but they usually came about. Her hand had been resting lightly on his arm and she now dropped it.

Lysander sighed and turned away from the house. 'Let us go back the other way,' he said. 'Past the old abbey fish ponds.' He held out his hand to help her down the steps. 'I wonder where Mark has got to?'

'I think he was going for a walk towards Abbots Candover,' said Oriana with careful innocence.

Lysander's brows snapped together in a sudden frown. Then he shrugged. 'Not a very interesting walk.'

'I daresay my brother will find something to amuse him,' said Oriana.

Clemency left Mrs Stoneham's at about a quarter to six.

'No curricle for me *now*,' she said, laughing, as she kissed her cousin goodbye.

'I do not altogether like this,' said Mrs Stoneham. 'No, not the lack of a curricle. It's your being a governess, in so vulnerable a position. I hesitate to make a mountain out of a molehill, but I worry about what you tell me of this Mr Baverstock.'

'I don't care for him myself,' replied Clemency, 'but I cannot think that he would offer his lordship the insult of seducing one of his staff while a guest in his house!'

'I hope you may be right,' said Mrs Stoneham dubiously.

'I shall cultivate Pongo!'

Pongo was a Great Dane, of an amiable disposition and a sort of cheerful stupidity.

'Would that answer do you think?'

'Probably not.' Clemency laughed. 'He is the *most* idiotic animal. He likes to place his forepaws on your shoulders and lick your face – which would certainly dampen any ardour on Mr Baverstock's part!'

Mrs Stoneham allowed herself a small smile, but added, 'If you have the smallest problem with Mr Baverstock, Clemency, I shall have no hesitation in taking it up with Lady Helena.' She spoke sternly: having got rid of Mr Jameson she felt responsible for her young cousin's welfare.

'Don't worry, Cousin Anne. I am sure that he means nothing more than a mild flirtation.'

It was still warm when Clemency left the village and the late afternoon sun sent long shadows across the road. Butterflies danced in the hedgerows and little flocks of chaffinches flew from one hawthorn bush to another.

Clemency allowed her thoughts to drift back to the marquess. Supposing she had met him that afternoon in Russell Square? What then? She would have been wearing that over-trimmed pink silk. Mama would have made her blush by her anxiety to impress and it would have been quite impossible to have said anything sensible. Furthermore, there would have been all the shock of realizing that it was the same man she had met outside Biddy's house.

Clemency could not realistically envisage a happy ending to that meeting. She did not think that either a show of wealth or her mother's ostentatious deference to his rank would have impressed the marquess. Certainly he would have gained no very realistic impression of herself.

But now what? Now she had seen him in his home setting, had felt the force of his temper, what did she now feel? Clemency didn't know.

She was pondering on this pleasurable indecision when she rounded a corner of the road about half a mile from Candover Court and found Mr Baverstock leaning on a gate, idly watching a herd of cows. He turned to watch her approach and Clemency couldn't help feeling that he had the look of a wolf who has suddenly seen his dinner.

Mark straightened up and strolled over.

'Well, well! Miss Stoneham! What a pleasant surprise.'

'Sir,' Clemency curtseyed. She tilted her chin and took a firmer hold of her parasol.

Whatever Mark's intentions had been he now changed his mind, for he laughed quite pleasantly and said, 'What is this? Parasol at the ready? Am I a monster then, Miss Stoneham?'

'I hope not, sir.' Clemency turned to look at him, a cool, steady gaze that Mark found somewhat disconcerting.

'I am sure you could not be so cruel as to deny me the pleasure of escorting you home.'

Clemency didn't reply and after a moment Mark added, 'To tell you the truth Miss Stoneham, this afternoon has been cursed flat. M'sister and Zander took themselves off somewhere – and I was very much in the way – and I really couldn't spend a lovely afternoon talking piety with Miss Fabian, now could I?'

Clemency couldn't help smiling. Mark relaxed and said, 'That's better. Upon my word, Miss Stoneham, I mean you no harm.' He held out his arm to her and, somewhat reluctantly, Clemency took it.

He was going to have to lime the twig more carefully than he thought, he realized. This was one little bird who would not hop willingly into his hand. Well, that would add spice to the chase.

'How fortunate for you that you have so charming a lady as your cousin to visit on Sundays,' he said. 'I am sure that you deserve it after a week with that little minx, Arabella!'

Clemency laughed. He's not as bad as I thought, she said to herself. I must have misjudged him. 'Lady Arabella and I go on very well,' she said.

'I can see that Arabella must appreciate her time with *you*,' said Mark, allowing himself to pinch her fingers lightly. 'It's how you find *her* that concerns me.' Clemency blushed and disclaimed and he added, 'And this picnic, Miss Stoneham. Don't tell me that it is not *you* who are responsible for all the arrangements. I do not like to see you burdened with so much.'

There was just enough warmth in his voice to bring back Clemency's original unease. They were now nearing the gatehouse and she let go of his arm.

'Thank you so much for your escort, Mr Baverstock,' she said. 'I must not trouble you further.' She hesitated a moment and then added, 'It is kind of you to be concerned about my *burdens* as you call them, but I assure you that you have no need. I may command a home with my Cousin Anne at any time, but I choose to be independent.'

Mark raised his hat to her and allowed her to go. What the devil was she after, he thought irritably. She was certainly a very beautiful girl: did she think by these tactics to entice him into marriage?

When she got up to her room Clemency began automatically to change for dinner, but her mind was otherwise engaged. Mr Baverstock had been perfectly civil, if a trifle too warm for her liking, but all the same, she did not want to encourage him. What was she to do?

She considered confiding in Lady Helena but rejected it. What could she say after all? That she suspected Mr Baverstock's motives? What indeed had she to go on: a hint or two here, an innuendo there. Nothing that Lady Helena's straightforward mind could comprehend. Lady Fabian might be more sympathetic, but what could *she* do? In any event, Clemency suspected that Lady Fabian was hoping that Mr Baverstock might take an interest in Adela – she would hardly be pleased to know that he was making up to the governess!

She changed swiftly into her black silk, brushed her hair up into a Grecian knot, gave one last look at her reflection in the mirror and went downstairs. Was life always as complicated as this as a governess, she wondered? She wished she could write to Biddy and find out.

Dinner was not a comfortable meal for Clemency. For reasons unknown Adela seemed to regard her being downstairs as an affront, Mark's attentions were on the border between civility and intrusion and after dinner Oriana was enjoying herself by quizzing Clemency on her pleasant walk back.

Lysander was hovering by Oriana's chair, near enough to overhear. 'So you met Mr Baverstock *accidentally* did you, Miss Stoneham?' he said.

Oriana looked down to hide a satisfied smile.

'Yes, my lord.' Clemency looked straight at him. 'It was, however, quite unnecessary for Mr Baverstock to put himself to so much trouble.'

Lysander, frowning, looked at her.

'Perhaps he felt he'd received some encouragement to do so,' put in Oriana, sweetly. 'Governesses are occasionally *coming*, I believe.'

Clemency flushed at the contemptuous tone of voice. 'I cannot speak for other governesses, Miss Baverstock. I can only say that I would prefer any *gentleman* to allow me to enjoy my time off in peace.'

'Are you insinuating that my brother is anything less than a gentleman?'

'Come now, you mistake Miss Stoneham, Oriana,' put in the marquess hastily. 'You must agree, surely, that a governess is entitled to the normal courtesies between a lady and a gentleman?'

'Certainly. Provided, of course, that she *is* a lady.'

'My idea of a true gentleman,' said Clemency, ignoring Oriana and turning to the marquess, 'is your cousin, Lord Fabian. He treats every woman, down to the kitchen maids, with the same courtesy.'

She recognized, of course, that Oriana had meant to be insulting, but she declined to pick up the gauntlet. Whatever her pretensions, Miss Baverstock was a vulgarian at heart, in her opinion. She wondered, rather wistfully, what the marquess's involvement with Oriana was. She might have a sadly common mind, but she also had the opulent attractions of a Lady Hamilton. Clemency tried to tell herself that she did not care.

Her main point was gained: she had made her position with regard to Mr Baverstock quite plain. She must be content with that. She rose, curtseyed slightly and went to find Diana and Arabella.

Lysander found himself in something of a quandary. So far as he could tell Miss Stoneham's manners were above reproach and certainly this quarrel had not been of her making. But he was reluctant to criticize Oriana. He found himself feeling vexed with Miss Baverstock for putting him in this position.

Oriana had come to something of the same conclusion for she smiled and said prettily, 'Oh dear, I really didn't mean to offend Miss Stoneham. Dependents can be so touchy, I know. I am sure she didn't mean to entice my brother. Poor Mark, I shall tell him that he is quite in my black books and he must stop any little pleasantries with Miss Stoneham.' She managed to convey the impression that Clemency was making a fuss about nothing.

'I'd be grateful if you would,' said Lysander, relaxing. He raised her hand to his lips and kissed it.

The picnic was set for Tuesday and on Monday afternoon Clemency left Diana and Arabella with Lady Fabian and went to help Mrs Marlow. That poor lady was going distracted and Clemency was left to decide how many bottles of ale and ginger beer it would be proper to bring, or would the ladies prefer lemonade? It was Clemency who gave the orders to the gardener for lettuces and cucumbers and a basket of fresh fruit.

Lord Fabian, Giles and Mark had gone out fishing while Lysander was in the estate room with Frome. Thus it was that Clemency found herself taking tea and plum cake up to his lordship at four o'clock.

Frome was tidying away his papers as she entered.

'Good Heavens! Miss Stoneham.' Lysander went to take the tea-tray from her. 'What has happened to Timson?'

'He is helping Mrs Marlow with preparations for tomorrow, my lord. There are some heavy hampers to be moved.'

The marquess grunted but let it pass. 'A cup of tea, Frome?' he said. 'Miss Stoneham will pour.'

'No thank you, my lord. I must get back and I promised to call on old Bates on my way. The poor fellow's very bad.'

'Consumption, isn't it?'

'Aye, and the third of the family to go this year.' He shook his head and picked up his greatcoat.

'Is there anything we can send?' The marquess looked at Clemency.

'Mrs Marlow has sent down some beef tea, my lord.' She forbore to mention that Adela had also gone down with a religious tract.

Frome left. 'A cup of tea, my lord?' asked Clemency.

'Yes, please. And pour yourself one. You look as though you could do with it.' Those gold tendrils were escaping again, he noticed.

Clemency did so and rather warily sat down on a shabby green leather armchair facing the desk. The estate room, like all the rooms at the Court, needed painting. Its panelling was dull and cracked and the furniture heavy and worn. There was a threadbare Turkey carpet on the floor. A number of heavy ledgers lay open on the desk.

'I am sorry, my lord, that you are in so much trouble,' said Clemency impulsively. She gestured towards the ledgers.

Lysander sighed. 'The ironic thing is that there have been several opportunities in the last twenty years for radical improvements. An extra cut on the canal, for example, or an extension of the new toll road to Abbots Candover, both of which would have made a significant difference to the profitability of the estate. Frome was telling me just now that he begged my father to invest in them.'

'You must feel it very much.'

'And the village,' went on Lysander, as if it were a relief to talk to somebody sympathetic. 'I don't know whether you've had the opportunity of walking round it, but some of the cottages are in a disgraceful condition.'

'I have seen them.' One, she remembered, had moss right up the walls and the thatch was half rotten with damp.

'What *was* my father about?' Lysander demanded angrily. 'These are *our* people, neglected. There is no school for the children, nothing. I tell you, Miss Stoneham, that I have sometimes felt quite ashamed to be seen in the village.'

'They speak fondly of you,' said Clemency. It was true; one of the girls who had come up to help had told her how the marquess had ordered Mrs Marlow to give her some broth for her invalid mother. 'The old lord would never 'ave done that, miss,' she'd confided.

'It is my responsibility and there is nothing I can do,' he said sadly.

Except marry an heiress, thought Clemency. But she only said, 'What shall you do, my lord, when the place is sold?'

'I haven't considered. Probably enlist in some line regiment. I shan't be the first officer to live on his pay. In any case, it doesn't matter too much about me, I shall manage. I'm mainly concerned that Arabella shall not lose out. Which reminds me, Miss Stoneham, I have not had the opportunity to thank you for your advice there. Cousin Maria is delighted with the idea of bringing the girls out together, though whether she'll still think so after a month or so of Arabella remains to be seen!'

Clemency laughed. 'Doubtless your sister will continue to get into scrapes, but I'm sure she will do nothing to jeopardize her come-out.'

'And you, Miss Stoneham. What will *you* do after you leave here? I ask as a fellow-traveller, so to speak.'

'My position is a little different,' said Clemency carefully. 'I … I am afraid that I quarrelled with a near relation and became a governess in consequence. But I am fortunate in that I come into some money when I am twenty-five, so for me, whatever happens, there is some financial security ahead.'

'Good God! You haven't run away from home, have you? Can I expect an irate papa coming down on me?!'

'Nothing so dramatic, my lord.' She allowed herself to echo his tone.

'I know. You were being forced into marriage with a brute!' He frowned, thinking suddenly that so very beautiful a girl must have had suitors in plenty. Some clod-hopping clerk, perhaps, with clumsy hands and red face.

'Something like that.'

'So you found yourself a position, in Yorkshire was it? and were pursued by a lecherous husband. I hope, Miss Stoneham, that you are not being similarly annoyed by any of my guests?' He raised an eyebrow.

The conversation with Oriana was in the forefront of both their minds. Clemency looked at him for a moment and then said, 'I have done my best to make my respectability clear.'

'Come to me if you have any problem,' he said shortly. There was silence for a minute. The marquess had picked up a quill and was playing with it. 'I think, perhaps, that you and I got off on the wrong footing,' he said at last. 'I should like to apologize for my ill-manners towards you, Miss Stoneham.'

'It shall be forgotten,' said Clemency, simply.

'Thank you.'

After she had gone the marquess attempted to go back to his ledgers, but his thoughts were plainly elsewhere.

Oriana was bored. The visit was not altogether turning out as she had hoped, mainly because Lysander was cooped up in that wretched estate room when he should have been entertaining his guests. Lady Helena had set off on one of her brisk walks to exercise the dogs and Lady Fabian was dozing gently under the cedar tree, some embroidery on the grass beside her. The men were fishing and Diana and Arabella had gone off on their own. Oriana had no intention of offering to help Clemency with the preparations for the picnic – so that left only Adela. Normally, Oriana would not bother with such a dowd as Miss Fabian for a moment, but it did occur to her that perhaps Adela might know more of Lysander's true financial position. Accordingly, she suggested to Miss Fabian that they take a stroll together.

Adela was not above being flattered by such an attention and after each lady had put on a bonnet and found herself a parasol they set off in the direction of the Home Wood. They had to go past the kitchen garden and through its ornamental gate they caught a glimpse of Clemency in earnest conversation with the gardener. She was not wearing a bonnet and her golden hair was blowing slightly in the breeze, framing her head like a halo.

The gentlemen might have paused to admire but neither lady felt any such inclination. Adela pursed her lips. 'Surely Miss Stoneham would be better employed doing what she is paid to do,' she commented waspishly.

'Lady Helena allows her far too much licence,' agreed her companion. 'I know the marquess has found her to be too forward: he hinted so yesterday evening.'

'I own that I cannot like her,' said Adela. She had been decidedly put out to learn that Mr Baverstock had actually escorted her back from Abbots Candover.

'Nor I. In fact, Miss Fabian, between ourselves, I fear she is something of a fraud!'

'No!' Adela's eyes lit up.

'I was shocked to notice that she was wearing silk stockings! Now what governess on no more than thirty pounds a year can afford silk stockings?'

'My father says that she has plainly been used to a comfortable household,' said Adela. 'He finds her charming.'

'I expect her sort are very good at charming men,' said Oriana significantly.

'But this is dreadful! What should we do?' cried Adela. 'And my sister is being taught by the woman.'

'We can do nothing – yet,' replied Oriana. 'She has already cast out wiles for my brother and sooner or later she will overreach herself, I am sure.' Oriana had every intention of helping that process along a little, if she found the opportunity.

Adela coloured. She was not so full of piety that she hadn't noticed Mr Baverstock's attractions, though so far he had shown her only the commonest courtesy. That, she now saw, could be put down to the machinations of Miss. Adela knew herself to have breeding and a respectable dowry and what had Miss Stoneham got, after all? A pretty face and devious ways.

'She has already quarrelled with Lysander. I overheard Cousin Helena telling my mother so.'

'I don't think she is Lysander's type,' said Oriana with a touch of complacence.

'I doubt he's rich enough to tempt her,' retorted Adela with most un-Christian spitefulness.

Oriana glanced at her. 'The estate is certainly run down.'

Adela was just about to inform her companion that the estate was all to pieces and must be sold, when she stopped. She was shrewd enough to realize that something more than indifference lay behind that careful show of unconcern. Adela had become quite an astute committee member of her church's missionary society and knew that to withhold information was sometimes the more successful strategy. Miss Baverstock had, she decided, a streak of ruthlessness about her and she, Adela, would hold her peace until she saw more clearly what that lady was after.

She decided to drop a different titbit in and see what happened.

'It is a pity that the match with the nabob's pretty daughter didn't come off,' she said. 'Why, what is the matter, Miss Baverstock?'

'N ... nothing,' answered Oriana. 'I have dropped my parasol, that is all. So stupid of me.'

Adela smiled.

Diana and Arabella had spent the afternoon on Arabella's tree swing. This was the branch of an old beech tree which grew out over the brook which had once provided water for the abbey fish ponds. It was one of Arabella's favourite spots and neither girl was too grown-up to enjoy it. The branch was quite low, and if they tucked up their skirts it was easy enough to climb the tree and edge out over the brook. If you went out far enough you reached a point where the branch swayed with your weight.

In fact, of all the young guests, Diana was the only one who was thoroughly enjoying her visit. Miss Stoneham was wonderful, she thought, and the lesson that morning was such fun and so lively, and she liked her cousin Arabella. After years of being bullied by Adela, patronized by Giles, and suffering torments of shyness, she found herself beginning to blossom.

Arabella, too, was enjoying herself. She had never known anybody of her own age and sex before. In spite of, or perhaps because of, their very different characters they swiftly became very good friends. Diana admired Arabella's liveliness and pretty looks and in turn Arabella found that her cousin, though shy, had very much her own opinions – usually far more judiciously thought out than Arabella's. Arabella was, in fact, quite immature for her age in some ways, and she recognized that Diana had something she needed.

'I get into such scrapes,' she sighed, wriggling into a more comfortable position on the branch. 'But I was so bored before you came, Di, you don't know!'

'I wish I could get into scrapes,' confessed her cousin. 'I am far too cowardly though.'

'It's not so much fun,' confided Arabella, bouncing a little so that all the leaves shook, 'and last week it was nearly disastrous. If I tell you, Di, you promise that you won't be shocked?'

'How can I promise not to be shocked,' said Diana reasonably, 'when I don't know what you are going to say? But, whatever it is, I'll still be your friend, Bella.'

Arabella plainly decided that this was sufficient and in a low voice she told her cousin of the Josh Baldock affair. 'I was so frightened, Di,' she ended in a whisper, 'and afterwards I felt so ashamed too. It was awful. And I daren't think what would have happened if Miss Stoneham hadn't come.'

'Nobody has ever wanted to kiss *me*,' said Diana wistfully. Then she added, 'You are lucky having Miss Stoneham.'

'You don't think I'm too awful, then?'

'Of course not.' Diana gave her shoulder a brief pat.

'And you're not shocked?'

'Well, yes, I am a little. But I'm also a bit envious too, I must confess.'

Arabella laughed. 'Oh Di,' she cried, 'I *am* pleased you came! What fun we're going to have with our come-out!'

'I hope so,' said Diana dubiously, thinking of tongue-tied evenings she'd spent. 'I'm sure I shall be a wallflower. You know how stupid I am in company.'

'But *I'll* be with you, Di. I shan't let you be neglected.'

'I wish Miss Stoneham were coming too.' She paused and then asked, 'What is her name, Bella? Her Christian name, I mean?'

Arabella looked surprised. 'I don't know. I've never thought to ask.'

'I just wondered. I'm sure it's something pretty.'

After the sun in the kitchen garden and the heat of the kitchen, Clemency found that she had a slight but persistent headache.

'It's because you went out without a bonnet, Miss Stoneham,' said the housekeeper severely, but she was fond of Clemency and patted her hand to show that she didn't mean it. 'Fair young ladies, like yourself, always suffer worse from the sun. Now you just sit down here and Molly shall bring you some of my rose-hip tea.'

Clemency smiled rather wearily at her. 'Thank you, Mrs Marlow. Some of your tea would be most welcome.'

'I can get one of the girls to bring you up some supper on a tray, if you like, miss.'

Clemency shook her head. 'It's not that bad, Mrs Marlow. I daresay it'll go away in a while.'

'She doesn't want to be another Miss Lane,' put in Molly. She spoke feelingly, for she had been frequently kept running up and down with herbal infusions and lavender water for that lady.

'Now, don't be cheeky, Molly,' said Mrs Marlow, sternly.

Molly only grinned. Clemency smiled at her. Molly's manner and outspokenness reminded her sometimes of Sally.

'Why don't you sit in the cloisters, miss,' Molly went on. 'It's nice and cool there just now.'

'What a good idea.' It was only half past six and there was time enough before she must go up and change for dinner. Clemency finished her rose-hip tea, thanked Mrs Marlow and got up.

The sun had gone round the other side of the house and a slight breeze had sprung up. The cloisters were pleasantly shady as Molly had said. There was a faint smell of roses and a few bees and butterflies were still flitting from flower to flower. Swallows twittered and swooped through the air. Clemency sat down on Abbot Walter's tomb and breathed in deeply and gratefully, feeling the tension drain from her.

The problem with the kitchen was that it was so old-fashioned, she thought. It really needed a new close-range, which would be an economy on coals and not give off the fiercesome heat of that old open one. How the kitchen staff stood it, she couldn't imagine. No wonder Mrs Marlow occasionally took to palpitations. On a hot August day the heat was quite unbearable.

Her thoughts then turned to her tea with the marquess. She now saw that she had misjudged him when she thought he was Alexander. His position deserved her sympathy rather than reproach. He was paying the price for the folly of his father and brother. It didn't seem fair that he should be responsible for debts that weren't his. She could now understand, she thought, if he was sometimes short-tempered and abrupt.

But she couldn't help feeling a twinge of anxiety over what

she had said about her own position. Had she given anything away? She didn't think so. So far as she knew nobody but Lady Helena and the marquess himself knew of the abortive visit to Russell Square: certainly Arabella, chatterbox that she was, had never mentioned it. And there was no way that it could be linked with her.

So far as she could see she was safe from discovery.

Such was her absorption in her own thoughts that she didn't hear footfalls behind her until two hands clasped her round the waist and Mark leant over the tomb and kissed her.

Clemency screamed.

'For God's sake, be quiet, girl!' Mark's grip tightened. 'Do you want everyone down on us?'

'Let me go this minute, sir. How dare you come up on me in that way?' She wiped her mouth angrily with the back of her hand.

Mark laughed. 'Come on, sweetheart. It was only a kiss.' He bent his head to kiss her again.

Clemency screamed again, much louder this time and began to struggle.

Reluctantly, Mark let go. God, the girl was prudish after all. 'It was only a bit of fun,' he protested.

'For whom?' retorted Clemency icily.

There was a sound of hasty footsteps on the gravel and the marquess came round the corner. Clemency was standing, her face white with fury, and there was a long red graze up her arm where she had scraped it against the stone of the tomb in her struggles. Mark was nonchalantly surveying the scenery.

'Whatever is the matter?' Lysander looked from one to the other.

Mark shrugged. 'A misunderstanding.' Lysander said nothing and Mark felt impelled to add, 'Miss Stoneham didn't hear me coming and squawked, that is all.'

There was another unnerving silence and then Lysander said coolly, 'The gong will be going in twenty minutes, Baverstock. I suggest that you go up and change for dinner.'

Mark hesitated a moment and then said, 'I apologize for startling you, Miss Stoneham,' and left.

Clemency shut her eyes and sank down on the tomb. Her arm was throbbing and she could feel tears prickling behind her eyelids. 'Thank you, my lord,' she managed to whisper.

The marquess sat down beside her and took hold of her hand so that he could examine the graze.

'This must be washed,' he said in a voice that was not entirely steady, 'and I daresay Mrs Marlow will have something to put on it.'

'Yes.'

Neither of them moved. Clemency gave a small hiccup and a tear fell on to the marquess's hand, then another. 'I'm sorry, my lord. It ... it is nothing.'

'My poor girl.' Lysander put his arm round her and settled her head on his shoulder. 'Here.' He handed her his handkerchief. 'Now tell me.'

'I ... I had the headache, my lord – the kitchen is very hot – and I came out here for some cool air and quiet before dinner. I did not hear Mr Baverstock come up behind me. He ... he ... I do not wish to speak ill of a friend of yours, my lord. Let us say he acted under a false impression.'

'Damn him,' said Lysander with feeling. 'Has he no discrimination?'

Clemency blew her nose firmly and wiped her eyes. 'Not much,' she said frankly. She suddenly felt extraordinarily happy.

Lysander gave a laugh and hugged her briefly. 'No, he never had. But I'll have a word with him. We can't have him upsetting you like this.'

Clemency straightened herself. 'Thank you, my lord. I am grateful for your timely arrival. I hope it doesn't put you in too awkward a position with regard to Mr Baverstock.'

Lysander dropped his arm somewhat reluctantly. 'Oh, I can handle Mark,' he said.

Embarrassment suddenly took hold of both of them. Clemency got to her feet and said with an assumption of ease, 'I'd better go and change. Dinner will be soon.'

'Dinner will be soon,' said Lysander somewhat distractedly. 'I'd better go and change.'

Clemency, conscious of her rising colour, hastily dropped him a curtsey and left. Lysander stared unseeing at the evening swallows for some time before he, too, went back to the house.

* * *

Dinner was a quiet meal, a number of those present, including the host, finding themselves disinclined for conversation. After the ladies had withdrawn Clemency requested permission to retire.

'Of course, my dear. You look fagged to death, doesn't she, Maria? I hope all this picnic nonsense isn't too much for you?'

'Oh no! It's just that I find the heat very enervating. I shall be better after a good night's rest.'

In the dining-room the port went round with less than its usual energy. The fishermen were feeling somewhat somnolent and the marquess was unusually taciturn.

'Where's this picnic spot, Lysander?' asked Lord Fabian. 'There will be some shade, I trust. Today was really too hot for enjoyment.'

'There's a little ruined chapel by a stream where we usually go. It's quite a pleasant and shady place at the end of a small wood, so you may be comfortable under the trees, Cousin.'

'I haven't had a picnic since I don't know when,' said Lord Fabian. 'Takes me back a year or two.'

The party broke up soon after the gentlemen had joined the ladies for coffee in the drawing-room. Lysander, having escorted his female guests to the end of their corridor went down to the kitchen to check that all was in readiness for the following day.

Mrs Marlow and the maids had gone to bed. Only Timson was down there completing the locking-up for the night. Several hampers stood open on the floor and some smaller wicker boxes stood on the table. On one of them was a note and it was this that arrested the marquess's attention.

'Timson!' he called. 'What is this?'

Timson came up the cellar steps. 'I'm sorry, my lord. I didn't hear you.'

'Who wrote this note?'

Timson glanced at it. 'It's only a list of provisions for the picnic, my lord.'

'I can see that!' retorted the marquess. 'I want to know who wrote it.'

'I really couldn't say, my lord. It is not Mrs Marlow's writing.

Probably Miss Stoneham.'

The marquess picked it up and scanned it. There was something tantalizingly familiar about the writing. Where the devil had he seen it before?

Six

The day of the picnic was destined to rank as one of the high spots in Clemency's memory, though it had started off badly when she had come down to breakfast early to find that only Mr Baverstock was in the dining-room. He was helping himself to devilled kidneys and bacon from the sideboard and barely said 'Good-morning'. Whatever the marquess had said, if anything, had plainly left Mr Baverstock feeling resentful.

Clemency had not had a good night either: her arm was sore and she had not slept well. She poured herself some coffee and took a slice of toast. Mark was obviously not going to talk, so Clemency picked up yesterday's copy of the *Morning Post* and opened it. There was the usual bulletin on Princess Charlotte's health and the approaching Interesting Event and an article about the current select committee's enquiry into the practice of using small boys as chimney sweeps. Both of these would normally have excited her interest or sympathy, but this morning she barely glanced at them.

Had she bothered to glance at the Lost and Found column she might have seen a notice to interest her more. *Miss C. H-W.* it read, *Please contact Jameson. Box 240. Confidence assured.*

As soon as she had finished her breakfast she left the room and went down to the kitchen. Downstairs everything was bustle. Half-filled hampers stood on the floor and Molly and Peggy were energetically pounding and scraping for Cook. Clemency raised an eyebrow at Mrs Marlow.

'Everything's in order, Miss Stoneham. Mr Timson will see that it's all in the travelling carriage for noon prompt.'

'Thank you. That's wonderful.' Clemency sped upstairs to see how Arabella and Diana were getting on. Lessons were supposed to start at nine o'clock, but Clemency doubted whether much work would be done that morning.

However, both girls were in the schoolroom. Clemency had suggested that they set up a nature diary and they were arranging a moss-lined basket to take to the picnic and bring back specimens. Arabella, Clemency had discovered, had quite a talent for water-colours: one of the few of that young lady's abilities which could be called proper to a damsel of rank. She, therefore, would do the drawings and Diana would write them up in her best copperplate.

'Must we look for something *rare*, Miss Stoneham?' asked Diana.

'I think you and Arabella should choose,' replied Clemency.

'Oh no, Di, let's choose something interesting,' put in Arabella. 'Something with pretty leaves, like ivy. Otherwise it's so boring to paint.'

Diana looked at Arabella half-doubtfully.

Clemency smiled affectionately at Diana. 'My dear,' she said, 'it isn't morally reprehensible to prefer to draw the beautiful rather than the dull, you know. You must allow for your cousin's artistic sensibilities!'

Diana's face lightened. 'Adela wouldn't approve,' she said. Her sister, she was beginning to see, was capable of seeing Sin in everything.

'Adela isn't here,' retorted Arabella. She found Diana's moral qualms incomprehensible sometimes. 'Anyway, God made pretty flowers, as well.'

This was unanswerable and the girls set-to and collected their sketch-pads and notebooks together for the afternoon.

'Miss Stoneham,' said Arabella, suddenly, 'we were wondering – I hope you won't think it rude – what your Christian name was. Diana said she was sure that it was something pretty.'

Clemency laughed. 'There's no secret about it,' she said. 'It's something of an old-fashioned name: Clemency. I don't know whether Diana will think it pretty or not.' Then she added, more soberly, 'But, listen, girls, I do not want you to make everybody a present of it. I don't mind you two knowing, but it's to go no further.'

'Of course not. We won't tell anybody, will we, Di?'

Diana shook her head. She was rather disappointed.

'Clemency' seemed like all those tiresome virtues in her sister's religious tracts. She'd have preferred something more romantic, like Clementina.

At midday the assembled party gathered in the hall. The various hampers were to go in the old travelling carriage and Lysander's curricle was to be taken by the Fabians, Lord Fabian driving behind the carriage. The young people would walk. A footpath went alongside a stream, most of it winding through a little wood, so the company would be shaded from the midday sun and need not fear to arrive exhausted. It was hoped that they would arrive concurrently with the carriages.

Giles contrived to walk as near Clemency as possible. 'I say, Miss Stoneham,' he said, flushing slightly, 'do let me carry your basket.'

'Why, thank you, Mr Fabian.'

Arabella and Diana exchanged glances and stifled giggles.

'Why, it's got moss in it.'

'Yes. Pray be careful of your clothes, Mr Fabian. The moss is damp. We hope to collect a few flowers for our nature diary.'

Giles wanted to pay a graceful compliment about Clemency as the goddess Proserpina, but was unable to find a way of putting it without it becoming hopelessly convoluted. He was relieved to see that Mr Baverstock had gone on ahead. With all the acute perceptions of a young man in love Giles had noted Mark's attention to Clemency with a sort of angry jealousy. He mistrusted Mr Baverstock's motives – Giles did not need any moral guidance from his sister to see that Mark was up to no good – but at the same time he envied him his ease and assurance.

He would, he decided, constitute himself as Clemency's champion. He would be excessively noble and Never Speak his Love, content only to watch over her safety like a knight of old. Naturally, he thought, kicking at the brambles in a melancholy way, he would catch a malignant fever in her service (she would fall into the brook whilst attempting to escape Baverstock's dastardly clutches and he, Giles, would rescue her) and die. His deathbed would be prolonged and he would expire with her name on his writhen lips. At this point it occurred to him that he did not, in fact, *know* her name and to die uttering 'Miss Stoneham' did not have the same ring as, say, 'Mary' or even 'Cecilia'.

The villain of the piece was, meanwhile, walking beside Adela and trying not to yawn over her accounts of her church mission work. In fact, he was regretting coming to Candover, and if it hadn't been for his sister he would have ordered his valet to deliver him an urgent letter to himself ordering his immediate return home. However, Oriana plainly had her own fish to fry and Mark, in a lazy way, was an affectionate brother. If that wretched chit, Miss Stoneham, had been more forthcoming, he told himself, he would be perfectly happy here for a month or so. Daytime dalliance and nights of delicious consummation in that little top room of hers would have passed the time very pleasantly.

Unfortunately, she was prudish. Either that, or cunning. If she thought to entrap him into popping the question then she was wide of the mark; and he smiled to himself at the pun. All at once, an idea occurred to him. He would set up a flirtation with Arabella. He had no notion, naturally, of attempting to seduce his friend's sister – the fat really would be in the fire then – or of marrying her. Arabella was pretty, not entirely inexperienced, he guessed, and enough of a handful for her behaviour to be a worry to Miss Stoneham. If he dallied a little with the girl then he would be very surprised indeed if Miss Prunes and Prisms' duty did not lead her to accompany them. She would be forced to accept his attentions for fear of what he might do to her charge otherwise.

The more he thought about it, the more he liked the idea. It was really very neat.

Oriana was in something of a quandary and it stemmed from the piece of information Miss Fabian had let slip. Had Lysander really offered for some nabob's daughter? A *cit*? Surely not. She had heard him talk many times on the intolerable mushroom upstarts who made a fortune and then tried to push their way into society. Nobody was more conscious of the dignity of rank than Lysander!

Miss Fabian must have been misinformed. This satisfied her for perhaps twenty seconds and then she recollected the state of the house. Everywhere showed evidence of neglect. Oriana was not experienced in such things, but it was plain enough that there was no money to put into the most basic repairs. Then she thought: but he has only been marquess for a few months, there has been no time to put things in order.

All the same, it worried her. She had been out now for three years and felt that it was time she married. Her admirers had always been many but her suitors rather fewer. Somehow most gentlemen decided that they would rather call a halt at admiration – not that Oriana cared much for that, she felt that for the best part, her admirers were beneath her anyway. She was determined to marry well. Her fortune entitled her to a barony at least and Miss Baverstock saw no reason to stop there.

An impoverished marquess was better than no marquess at all and she found Lysander not unattractive.

Then on top of this she wanted to do something about Miss Stoneham, put a spoke in her wheels. The wretched girl had the sort of angelic looks that many men found irresistible – if you liked the insipidity of flaxen hair and blue eyes. There had been some sort of fracas the previous evening, Mark wouldn't say what, but Oriana suspected that Miss Stoneham would not be above using her looks to try to snare a husband. The fact that Oriana had every intention of trying the same thing was, naturally, beside the point. It was Miss Stoneham's duty to be content with the position in life to which Providence had appointed her: it was Miss Baverstock's duty to do the best she could for herself.

The trouble with governesses, she thought, was that they had claims to gentility. A pretty serving-maid could be dismissed as no threat; a governess was a different matter. All the same there was something about Miss Stoneham which didn't quite fit. It would be a kindness to put the marquess a little on his guard.

Accordingly she chose her prettiest muslin, a primrose colour, embroidered with knots of flowers, which set off her shining brown curls admirably, and she wore a straw gipsy hat tied with yellow ribbons and set off to charm the marquess. As she had hoped, Lysander made his way to her side and they led the little procession. The company straggled out as they entered the wood and, glancing over her shoulder, Oriana saw that she could talk without being overheard.

After having complimented her companion on the beauty of

the day, the woods, the flowers and the weather Oriana remarked, 'It is so kind in you to give Miss Stoneham, too, the pleasure of an outing.'

'She looks after the girls,' he said shortly.

At that moment a shriek of most unladylike laughter could be heard from Arabella, followed by a gentle scolding from Clemency.

'I'm sure she does her best,' Oriana slashed at a nettle with her parasol.

The marquess said nothing.

'Of course,' she went on, 'it is obvious that she has been used to far more comforts than she can command now, poor thing.'

'What do you mean?' demanded Lysander.

'Well, she wears silk stockings. Now what governess can afford that? And the shawl she was wearing last night: Lyons silk – and not cheap.'

There was a pause. Lysander's black brows had snapped together and he looked grim. Oriana looked around her and breathed in deeply. 'Ah!' she sighed, 'fresh country air! I wonder sometimes why we choose to go up to Town at all with so much beauty here.'

'You don't care for her, do you?'

'Who?' asked Oriana, putting on a bewildered air.

'Miss Stoneham.'

Oriana shrugged and laughed. 'I can't get rid of the feeling that she is not quite what she pretends to be,' she said. 'But I daresay I've been reading too many novels! I would be happier if I were sure that she had no designs on my poor brother.'

'You think she has?'

'My dear Lysander,' Oriana pressed his arm warmly, 'you have only to watch them together to see that she is attracted. Naturally, she has hopes – what governess wouldn't – however well she may attempt to hide the fact.'

'I don't believe that she has encouraged his attentions.'

Oriana smiled, 'You are too trusting, sir!' she said. 'A show of reluctance can sometimes work wonders.'

'I see.'

'I thought you might.'

They arrived at the ruined chapel to find the carriages and the

Fabians already there. The coachman had taken down the hampers and spread out several rugs on the grass and Lady Fabian was busy unpacking. Clemency immediately went to help her. Giles followed. 'Is there anything I can do to help, Miss Stoneham?'

'Thank you, Mr Fabian. What about putting the drink somewhere cool.'

'Where shall I put it?' Giles looked helplessly around. His visions of knight-errantry had not included several dozen bottles of ale, ginger beer and lemonade.

'Why not ask your cousin,' Clemency nodded to where Lysander and Mark were helping to unpole the horses. Really, she thought, he was quite hopeless. Thank God her father had had more liberal notions with her own upbringing. Clemency had been expected to learn to dress herself, make her own bed, even to cook from time to time. In vain had her mother protested that it wasn't ladylike. 'Nonsense, Amelia,' her father would say, 'I don't want our little Clem to be one of those fine misses who is lost without somebody to look after her.'

The others, Diana, Adela and Oriana, she noticed were doing nothing, though whether this was from laziness or ignorance, she wasn't sure. Arabella had followed Clemency's lead and was helping to unpack the hampers.

'Di!' she called, 'come and help me wipe these glasses.'

The glasses had been carefully wrapped in straw.

'That's right, Diana,' said Lady Fabian, bracingly, 'do something useful.'

Oriana and Adela looked at each other.

'Why don't we explore this quaint little chapel, Miss Fabian,' said Oriana. 'We cannot all be expected to unpack.'

Adela followed her.

'I have warned Lysander of Miss Stoneham's encroaching ways,' she continued, as soon as they were out of ear-shot. 'He will be keeping a close watch on her behaviour, you mark my words.'

'Mama will not see anything amiss,' replied Adela, resentfully. 'I warned her and all she said was that Miss Stoneham had very pretty manners and she was pleased to see Diana liked her. Diana! Why, what does *she* know, the little fool?'

'I am determined to expose Miss Stoneham for what she really is,' said Oriana. 'Governess, indeed! I wouldn't be surprised if she wasn't some out-of-work actress.'

'How disgusting!' Adela drew her skirts around her as if anxious to avoid any possible contamination.

'Well, she certainly doesn't act like a governess. Where is her humility, her proper deference?'

'She certainly behaves as if she were our equal!' agreed her companion.

'Exactly so, Miss Fabian.' She glanced at Adela and added, 'I noted that my brother escorted *you* through the wood, and seemed very happy with his company!'

Adela blushed. She'd never been teased about a man before and she felt a sort of pleased confusion. 'Mr Baverstock thinks just as he ought on serious subjects,' she managed to say.

Oriana turned away to hide a smile of incredulity. She didn't for one moment believe that Mark felt anything other than polite contempt for such a poor little dab of a creature. But it suited her plans very well to have Adela on her side, so she added, 'Mark rarely takes to ladies of quality.' Let Miss Fabian take that as she pleased, she thought.

Just then they heard Lady Fabian calling them and made their way back to the picnic.

Clemency was occupied in cutting slices of Cook's veal loaf and Arabella was handing round plates and cutlery. Diana was arranging the salad on a large plate.

Lysander looked up to smile at Oriana. 'Come along, lazy one,' he said, 'and you too, Cousin Adela. Arabella, some plates for our guests.'

Oriana arranged herself gracefully on the rug and took the plate and allowed Lysander to help her to ham and a slice of veal loaf.

Clemency saw out of a corner of her eye that Mark was helping Arabella to salad, picking out little radishes and popping one into her mouth. Arabella was laughing. Adela, her plate empty, was staring ahead with reddened cheeks.

'Miss Fabian,' Clemency called, 'may I offer you some of the loaf? Cook's special recipe, she tells me, so I hope you approve.'

'Thank you.' Adela, far from looking grateful, looked mortified.

'Mr Baverstock,' said Clemency, coldly, 'would you be so kind as to see that Miss Fabian has everything she wants?'

Mark chose one last radish and offered it with hand on heart to a giggling Arabella, and then turned to Adela.

Lord Fabian eyed Clemency approvingly. Pretty girl, and she had strength of character too. She had organized Giles, Diana and Arabella and was not above pointing out to Mr Baverstock where his duty lay. Giles, of course, was in love with her, but Lord Fabian saw nothing to concern him there. On the contrary, he was pleased to see his son's fancy had alighted on a young lady of excellent principles and charming manners.

He certainly didn't believe the faradiddle that Adela had supposedly told his wife, that Miss Stoneham was making up to young Baverstock. So far as *he* could see, she didn't like the fellow above half, and the boot was more likely to be on the other foot.

The only person of whose sentiments he remained somewhat in doubt was the marquess. Lysander hardly ever spoke to Miss Stoneham, he certainly didn't put himself in her way, and yet Lord Fabian could sense some undercurrent of feeling there. He had mentioned it to his wife.

'Oh dear,' that good lady had said, 'I do hope not. Poor Lysander! It would be so very unfortunate if he should have developed a *tendre* for Miss Stoneham.'

'Well, none of our business, thank goodness,' said Lord Fabian. 'I'm sorry for him if it's so, Maria. I like your cousin, my dear, but he has enough problems already on his plate.'

Lady Fabian agreed. Looking round the picnic party she remembered their conversation. Lysander was talking to Miss Baverstock, she noted, and seemed happily absorbed. But as she was watching he suddenly looked across at Clemency for a moment. It was not a lover's glance, there was nothing of tenderness in it, nothing to lend colour to her husband's assertion.

On the other hand, it was certainly not indifferent.

Luncheon was finally over. The last piece of plum cake had been eaten. Lysander leaned back against a tree trunk and ate an apple. The cherry bowl was almost empty and there were a dozen or so empty bottles lying by one of the hampers. Nobody seemed very inclined to move. Oriana rather shocked Adela and Diana by lying back on the daisy-studded grass and closing her eyes. Mark's gaze wandered from Arabella to Clemency and then he said, 'Come along, Arabella and Diana, what about this nature diary I've been hearing so much about?'

Diana sat up reluctantly, but Arabella waved him away. 'It's too hot,' she said.

'Come for a paddle, then.'

'A paddle?' Arabella sat up.

'Why not? It's hot. A paddle will cool you down.'

Clemency dragged her thoughts together. Mr Baverstock must not go paddling with Arabella, it would be most improper. She would have to rouse herself.

'A paddle,' said Lord Fabian, suddenly entering the conversation. 'Well, why not? No, you stay, Miss Stoneham. You've been on the trot all day. Yes, Mr Baverstock, take the children for a paddle. You too, Giles. You'll help look after the girls, won't you?'

Mark threw him a look of intense dislike which Lord Fabian blandly ignored.

'Will it be all right, Mama?' whispered Diana, half-horrified at the idea of taking off her stockings and letting everybody see her bare toes.

Lady Fabian correctly interpreted a look from her husband and said, 'Of course, my dear. Why don't you and Arabella take your stockings off behind a tree and leave them here. Don't go out of ear-shot, though. Thank you, Mr Baverstock, a very kind idea.'

'Would you like to join us, Miss Stoneham,' said Mark next. 'Lovely cool water. I'm sure you'll come with us, now, won't you?'

'Oh, do come, Miss Stoneham,' cried Diana.

Clemency sat up again.

'Leave Miss Stoneham alone,' put in Lysander, finishing his apple and tossing the core into a hedge. 'Let her have a well-earned rest.'

There was nothing to be done. The four paddlers left and soon shrieks of delight could be heard from Arabella with Diana's quieter echoes.

Clemency, who was indeed tired, allowed herself to lean

back against a broken column and soon fell asleep. When she awoke the sun had moved round and there was only Lysander to be seen. Clemency blinked and sat up.

'Oh!' she said. The picnic things had been cleared away save for the glasses. 'I'm sorry ... I should have helped....'

'Nonsense, you were tired. Have some lemonade. I've got a bottle or two in the brook keeping cool.'

'I'd love some. Heavens, how hot it is.'

'You could have a quick paddle, too, if you wish, Miss Stoneham. You could take off those pretty silk stockings of yours and leave them behind that bush where Arabella and Diana have left theirs. Here, pass me your glass.'

'You're the third person who has mentioned my silk stockings,' said Clemency, laughing. 'Is there some mystery about them?'

Lysander looked a little self-conscious. 'No, no, of course not.' Though Oriana's words echoed in his head.

'My papa always gave me a dozen pairs of silk stockings as a Christmas present,' she said. 'Somehow, I've never worn anything else. Though since he died....' She stopped, recollected herself and added, 'I ... I see that they are probably unsuitable for a governess. I hadn't thought.'

There was a short silence. Then Lysander said, 'Come, Miss Stoneham, why don't you and I have a quick paddle.' He leaned over to undo his shoe buckles. Clemency put down her glass and retreated behind the bush.

When she came out, somewhat self-consciously aware of her bare feet, Lysander was waiting for her. He held out his hand. 'Come on. I'll help you down the bank. Mind your skirts.'

Clemency was in a state of confusion, almost as if she were still asleep and dreaming. Part of her realized that she ought not to be paddling with him like this, but somehow, she was not quite as much in control of herself as she might be. Lysander had very nicely shaped feet, she noticed; her own seemed very small and pale beside his.

'What pretty feet you have, Miss Stoneham,' he said, with a smile.

Gingerly she dipped one foot in the water. 'Oh!' It was cold, but refreshing. She clasped his hand more tightly and stepped into the brook. 'Oh!' she said again. 'Wonderful!' She hitched her skirts up more firmly and allowed herself to be led into the stream.

'Where are you taking me?'

'You'll see.'

Hand in hand they walked slowly upstream and in a few yards it turned to the left and the picnic place was lost to view.

'Sh! Quiet.' Lysander was walking very slowly now. They were midstream and their movements made no splashes. Then he stopped and pulled her towards him. 'Look,' he whispered, 'can you see? There, on that branch sticking out.'

'Oh! Yes. What is it?'

'A kingfisher.'

'Isn't it beautiful?'

The kingfisher must have heard them, or caught a movement, for suddenly it flew off, a brilliant streak of iridescent blue. Lysander turned to smile down at her.

At that moment the world seemed to stop for Clemency. Everything froze and time itself stood still. She was aware only of that aquiline face, those dark eyes and her hand in his. Lysander too was staring. 'I've seen you before, haven't I?' he whispered at last, his other hand had come up to caress a tendril of hair that had escaped.

Clemency opened her mouth to speak.

'Coo-ee! Lysander!' It was Arabella's voice. 'Where are you?'

Reality flooded in. All the difficulties of her position came back to her. Lysander gave a deep sigh as if his mind too was similarly engaged.

'I think it would be better if we went back separately,' he said, striving for a normal tone. 'I have no wish to make things difficult for you.'

Clemency took a deep breath. If found she would be in a most unpleasant position. 'Can it be done?' she asked practically.

Lysander gave a sudden grin. 'Good girl,' he said. 'Nothing simpler. There's an easy way out a yard or so upstream. You'll come out in the field where the carriages are. Just walk downhill. I'll go back the way we came.' He escorted her to the bank, saw her safely to the top, raised her hand briefly to his lips and said, 'Off you go.'

'Thank you for showing me the kingfisher,' said Clemency, shyly.

'My pleasure.'
He was gone.

Arabella had come to find her brother partly to tell him all about the dam they had built and how she was sure they had found the remains of his and Alex's old one and used some of the stones from it, and partly because she was feeling somewhat confused about Mr Baverstock and wanted the shelter of her brother's wing. In some respects Arabella was quite astute where men were concerned: there had been enough clandestine experience to let her know when she was genuinely admired, and this was not the case with Mr Baverstock.

He teased her, he flirted, but it was almost as if he was aiming it at somebody else and Arabella wasn't at all sure that she liked it. He had, for example, mentioned the village fair the coming Saturday, and hinted that he would take her for the dancing in the evening if she wanted to go. He could provide a couple of masks; nobody would know them.

Normally, this sort of forbidden outing would have made an instant appeal. Indeed, last year she had undertaken a similar expedition with Josh Baldock and enjoyed it tremendously. She had oiled the kitchen door with a feather, sneaked out, and nobody had been a penny the wiser. But Mr Baverstock was not Josh Baldock: he must know as well as she did that he should not take her there. So what did he mean by it?

She was relieved to hear Lysander's answering call and immediately stepped down into the stream and went to meet him. She had missed the sight of Clemency who had scrambled up the bank, run swiftly down the field using the carriages as cover and darted behind the bush to retrieve her stockings and sandals.

Clemency emerged to find that Giles and Diana had returned. Diana ran up to her.

'Oh! Miss Stoneham, look! We have collected some flowers.'
She gestured to her brother who came forward with the basket.

Clemency pulled herself together with an effort. 'Well done,' she said. 'What have you got? Ah, yes, wood sorrel.'

'And look at these. We found them by the bank.'

'Kingcups. Aren't they pretty?'

The last of the picnic things were now put away and the hampers and rugs were packed into the carriage. The horses were poled up again. Lord and Lady Fabian returned from their stroll in the wood and very soon the company was re-assembled. Lysander and Arabella climbed up from the stream and went to find their shoes. If Lysander was somewhat silent nobody seemed to notice. Arabella had recovered her spirits and was chattering away and Oriana and Adela were laughing about something.

Mark was feeling pleased with himself. He had put a little plan to Arabella that he was sure she would find appealing in spite of her scruples. He wouldn't press it for the moment. Let her think about it. When she agreed, as he was sure she would, he had an idea that would put Miss Stoneham completely in his power. She was wasted as a governess, he told himself, such a beautiful piece of cherry-pie deserved pretty dresses, trinkets, even a discreet little place of her own if she came up to expectations. He stood there and contemplated Clemency's ruin as though he were doing her a favour.

Nothing must go wrong. To disarm any possible suspicions he offered his arm to Adela and prepared to submit to half an hour of boredom.

On the way back Clemency walked beside Diana and Arabella, neither of whom stopped talking, and escorted by the faithful Giles. All that was required from her was an 'oh' from time to time, which was just as well as her feelings were in such a state of turmoil that she could not have carried on a coherent conversation for long.

Her one predominant emotion was the realization that she was in love with Lysander. It was the feeling outside Miss Biddenham's house but a hundred times stronger, because now she knew him better, could understand and appreciate his character. He was a good man, she thought, smiling reminiscently. He cared what happened to his sister; he was anxious for his dependents and willing to shoulder the heavy burden of his responsibilities.

He might be a rake with Mr Baverstock in the London gaming-hells or pursuing various West End *coryphées*, she didn't know. But she was quite sure he was not a vicious man like his brother. There were many problems ahead, not the least of which was how did the marquess see her, but Clemency found she was quite unable to concentrate on any of them.

Her mind was solely engaged in the pleasurable re-examination of the short trip upstream and that precious moment standing with him in the water where they saw the kingfisher. What would have happened if Arabella hadn't called out was a question she would leave for a quieter moment.

Oriana walked back, as she had come, with the marquess. She had quite enjoyed the day even though she had been unable to further her knowledge of Lysander's financial position. But as they walked at the end of the party a new danger presented itself. Every now and then the marquess glanced at Clemency. It was no more than a look, but it assured Oriana of one thing: something was going on. Lysander was too much of a gentleman to flirt with his servants, but he was not indifferent.

For a moment fury overcame all else and she had to dig her nails into her palms to stop the utterances that sprang to her lips. So this was what the little slut had in mind! Not content with getting her claws into Mark, she now wanted a second string to her bow!

That settles it, she thought. The sooner Miss Stoneham was off the premises the better. Now, how best to go about it? The walk back was almost totally silent, but neither of them noticed. If the subject of their thoughts was the same, their cogitations thereon were completely different.

When they reached Candover Court again Oriana went over and touched her brother's arm.

'A word with you, if you please,' she said with a smile, excusing herself to Adela. She took his arm and moved away.

'What is it, Sis?'

They were soon out of ear-shot.

'I want that pretty piece you're after out of the way,' she said. 'Do you indeed?'

'I do. And you may need my help. She has friends in the Fabians, you know.'

Mark looked at her.

'Come on, Mark. We've always helped each other, haven't we?'

'You think she's after Lysander? said Mark, frowning.

Oriana shrugged. 'I'm not concerned with Miss Stoneham's

feelings. I'm sure she'll do very well in the role you have in mind.'

'Careful, Sis, what you're about. Rumour has it that the dibs are really not in tune with Lysander. Well, look at the place. Alexander must have been thousands in debt. He dropped six thou. one night at Watiers. I was there.'

'She annoys me,' said Oriana unheeding, 'so good and helpful. I can't bear that sort of sugar-and-spice miss. I shall be glad to see her take a fall.'

Mark grinned. 'All right, ' he said. 'This is what I'm going to do.' He told her.

Oriana pondered. 'Will she follow though?' she asked. 'She might just tell Lady Helena.'

'She knows that Arabella's come-out is dependent on her good behaviour. She won't want to risk it.'

Miss Baverstock thought for a moment. 'You won't be able to stay here afterwards,' she said. 'You can't.'

'Frankly, my dear, I don't want to. I've been thinking it's far too slow. A letter will arrive for me on Saturday morning, bidding me come home.'

'But you can't travel on a Sunday!'

'Watch me! It's no use, Oriana. I don't know what's happened to Lysander, but he's become a devilish dull dog. No, I'm planning a nice little jaunt to Paris with the delectable Miss Stoneham.'

'But what about me? You can't just leave me here. Only think of my position.'

'Your position will be all right so long as Miss Stoneham's disappearance isn't too closely linked with mine. They may suspect, but nobody will know for sure. And once I've removed the girl then the way will be clear for you with Lysander – if that's what you want.'

'There is that,' said Oriana, slowly. 'And what about Arabella?'

'She can find her own way home. And if she knows what's good for her she'll keep her mouth shut.'

'Very well. If you need any help, tell me.'

'I was going to leave a note for Miss Stoneham myself – drop it in her room before I went. But it would be much safer if you did it.'

* * *

Lysander arrived home to find a letter from Mr Thornhill on the hall table. He thought that he now had a full count of all the late marquess's outstanding debts, he wrote, and he proposed to come up to Candover Court, if it were convenient for his lordship, the following week. He had had several offers for the estate and wished to discuss them with the marquess.

Lysander scanned the letter briefly and was just about to toss it on to his desk when he noticed a postscript over the page.

You did me the honour of telling me the outcome of your unfortunate visit to Mrs Hastings-Whinborough, he wrote. *You may be interested to hear that the young lady is still missing – I heard from a colleague of mine, a Mr Jameson, who deals with her affairs – and there was some thought that she might have fled to Abbots Candover! Apparently, the young lady has a relative there. I told Jameson I thought it most unlikely: beautiful heiresses do not normally remain unnoticed in country villages.*

It was noticeable that though the previous page of Mr Thornhill's letter had received the most cursory attention, the marquess pulled up a chair and sat down in order to read the postscript again.

Seven

Lady Helena Candover had heard enough from her cousin Maria to be made extremely uneasy about Miss Baverstock. First of all there was the danger that that young lady was intent on becoming a marchioness and secondly, she was apparently getting her claws into Miss Stoneham. Lady Helena had no intention of allowing the one governess who appeared to be able to keep Arabella under control to be harried by an overbearing miss like Miss Baverstock. And she certainly did not want her in the family.

Why was it, she thought, that the moment you became involved with people there were problems? Frankly, she much preferred her dogs, who mated where she told them and knew their place in the order of things. Something must be done.

The following morning, over breakfast, she announced, 'Miss Baverstock, I shall be pleased to have your company this afternoon. I am going to pay a call on our vicar and his wife. I am sure you will be delighted with them.' Her tone brooked no argument.

'Certainly, Lady Helena.'

'If you care to accompany us, Miss Stoneham, I shall be pleased to drop you off at your cousin's for an hour or so. You may take her down some of his lordship's fruit.'

'Thank you, Lady Helena.'

'We shall leave at two. Storrington, will you order the carriage? You can have no other use for it this afternoon.'

'Is that a statement or a question?' muttered Mark, *sotto voce*. 'A formidable lady, your aunt.'

'My carriage and my fruit are at your disposal, Aunt Helena,' said the marquess.

But Lady Helena was impervious to irony and had already

turned her attention back to her dogs.

Arabella and Diana exchanged a speaking glance. Neither of them liked Oriana and Arabella, in particular, was alarmed at the thought of her being shown any special favour. As soon as was polite they excused themselves and dashed up to the schoolroom to discuss it.

Clemency had flushed painfully at the marquess's tone: she certainly did not want her cousin to be on the receiving end of his unwilling generosity.

Oriana gave a satisfied smile and helped herself to one of the marquess's fine nectarines.

The marquess had much to occupy his mind. Quite apart from estate business, there was the disturbing news Arabella had confided the previous afternoon that Mark had suggested a stolen trip to the village fair on Saturday night. Arabella might be a little minx, but she had often, as a child, confided small misdemeanours and problems to him and he saw no reason to doubt her veracity.

But why on earth should Mark want to do such a thing? He must know very well that it was the sort of expedition which could well ruin his sister's chances of Cousin Maria bringing her out in the spring. Lady Fabian was tolerant, but such hoydenish behaviour would hardly recommend Arabella to her if it should ever become known.

Lysander acquitted Mark of having designs on his sister's virtue, and he certainly dismissed any idea of Mark wanting to marry Arabella. So why?

The thought flashed briefly through his mind that it was Arabella herself who had teased Mark to take her. But, if so, why tell her brother? Besides, the poor child was plainly uneasy about it. All Lysander could do was to tell Arabella not to tell *anybody* and to let him know if Mark mentioned it again.

Then his thoughts turned to Oriana. He did not know why it was, but having the Baverstocks to stay was not proving the pleasure he had hoped for. Mark had already had to be warned off any dalliance with Miss Stoneham, and now apparently he was intent on a clandestine expedition with his sister. Oriana, too, was something of a disappointment. Recently, he had noticed something of the shrew in her disposition and the marquess had the uneasy feeling that there was more to her thoughts than appeared on the surface. He couldn't rid himself of the notion that there was some *calculation* there.

They did not make for comfortable guests, either of them. Perhaps, he told himself, it was just that he was under stress; he had not allowed for the sheer misery of parting with 400 years of family history. It did not occur to him that it was *he* who had changed.

Up to his brother's death, Lysander's life had been free from any but the lightest entanglements. He had had various opera dancers in keeping and enjoyed their company while it lasted, which was never very long. He shot at Menton's, went to his club, won and lost at cards or the races, in short, behaved like most young men of fashion who had financial independence and no responsibilities.

Suddenly, all that had changed. The most onerous burdens had been thrust upon him. He was now responsible for his sister's welfare and creditable establishment in the world, and to a lesser extent, that of his aunt and a host of dependents. Initially, he had been overwhelmed, not to say resentful, but gradually his feelings had changed. He didn't want to go back to his old untrammelled life, he realized. He wanted to be able to pull his family home out of the red, to run it as it should be run, even to settle down with a family of his own.

It was this last idea that unsettled him most. The moment he found himself thinking that a wife might be an agreeable addition to his life, as well as other responsibilities, he attempted to banish the notion. He must be mad! Hadn't he and Mark always agreed that a life free of emotional commitments was the most amusing? Did he really want the same face at breakfast every morning and the burden of puling brats? What could he be thinking of?

He then thought of Lady Helena's invitation to Oriana. Could his aunt be meaning to express her approval of the match? How would Oriana fit into the role of chatelaine of Candover Court? She was attractive and would be a gracious marchioness. She would certainly run the house efficiently, he was sure.

But it was nonsense to think like this. Lysander could not see Sir Richard agreeing to his daughter's dowry being used up to pay off Alexander's debts. No, the only way he could keep Candover was to marry money, as Thornhill had suggested.

He picked up Thornhill's letter again and turned it over. Strange that the girl should still be missing. He had been so angry at that meeting with Mrs Hastings-Whinborough of the tinted blonde curls and artificial manner, that he hadn't allowed himself to dwell too much on the aftermath. Like mother, like daughter, he'd thought, on reading that foolish, hysterical letter. The girl had probably fled to some lover who would be only too glad of her fortune. There was no point in thinking of it now.

All the same, he continued to think of Thornhill's postscript: he couldn't get it out of his mind that there was some connection that he was missing.

Shortly before two o'clock Clemency went down to the kitchen to see whether Mrs Marlow had any commissions for her in the village. The estate was more or less self-sufficient, but still things like cones of sugar and candles came from the village shop.

'No, thank you, Miss Stoneham. We had an order come up on Monday.'

'Very well.' Clemency had turned to go when she saw a hamper, nearly full, on the floor.

'That is for you to take with you, miss,' said Mrs Marlow, correctly interpreting her look of surprise.

'But I'm sure Lady Helena didn't mean that much!' cried Clemency. 'She was thinking of a small basket, perhaps.'

'His lordship's orders, miss. He came down personally.'

Clemency looked at the hamper in some consternation. She didn't want to have to explain it to Lady Helena, and certainly not to Miss Baverstock.

At that moment the coachman came in, touched his hat to Clemency, and strapped up the hamper.

'I'll put it on the back, miss,' he said, winking at Mrs Marlow. 'That road it won't get in your way.'

'Th ... thank you.'

'You have a nice day, Miss Stoneham,' said Mrs Marlow. 'I'm sure you deserve it.'

Clemency ran upstairs to fetch her pelisse and put on her

bonnet, and at two o'clock, she stepped into the carriage after Lady Helena, two of the Pekinese and Miss Baverstock. The journey was accomplished in the laboured exchange of commonplaces between Miss Stoneham and Miss Baverstock. Lady Helena saw no reason to speak when she had nothing to say and she was occupied with soothing her dogs, one of whom was nervous in carriages and barked incessantly. Miss Stoneham and Miss Baverstock struggled valiantly, but in the end they too gave up and stared out of the window in silence.

The coachman drew up outside Mrs Stoneham's cottage, let down the steps for Clemency and then went to get the hamper.

With the forward seat unoccupied there was now more room in the carriage and Lady Helena calmly took out a bone from her reticule and threw it on the floor. The distraught Pekinese fell silent. Oriana hastily drew back her feet and turned to face her hostess.

'Charming gel, Miss Stoneham,' said Lady Helena briskly. 'Don't you agree, Miss Baverstock?'

'She must have had glowing references,' replied Oriana, obliquely.

'References, Miss Baverstock? I don't understand you.'

'From her previous employer, Lady Helena.'

'Nonsense, do you think I cannot judge for myself?'

'I am sure your ladyship is very astute,' said Oriana carefully, 'but all the same, with such a sweet child as Arabella in question, one cannot be too careful.'

Lady Helena raised her lorgnette and looked at her companion through it. 'Do I understand that you wish to undermine Miss Stoneham's position,' she said coldly.

'Perhaps somebody her own age can see things your ladyship might miss,' suggested Oriana. 'It has escaped neither Miss Fabian nor myself that Miss Stoneham wishes to fix her interest with my brother – or even with the marquess.'

'Really, Miss Baverstock, you have been reading too many romantic novels, I fear. Miss Stoneham has no such intention. I take no account of Adela; she is plainly jealous. From my own observation I would say that it is your brother who is subjecting Miss Stoneham to some unpleasantness. If you have any influence with him, I suggest that you put a stop to it. As a guest, Mr Baverstock is expendable; Miss Stoneham is not.

'But while we are on the subject, perhaps *you* have an interest in that direction with my nephew?'

Oriana was so taken aback by this sudden attack that she was initially speechless. When she found her voice she said, too angry to be wise, 'With respect, Lady Helena, that is Lord Storrington's and my business!'

Lady Helena gave a short laugh. 'Storrington's business! Good God, girl, are you not aware of the situation? The estate will be sold by the end of the year, and even then it will barely pay off my brother's and nephew Alexander's debts.'

Sold! For a moment anger overtook all other emotions. Sold! When it was her best chance of becoming a marchioness. How *could* he? Surely there was some way to save it? Marquesses didn't just go bankrupt! There must be some secret funds somewhere.

'And what is Lysander going to do then?' Oriana hoped her voice was neutral.

'Join the army, I believe.' Lady Helena noted that Oriana's concern didn't extend to either herself or Arabella. 'He should have enough left to purchase a commission in some line regiment.'

'I ... I am very sorry,' said Oriana, remembering her manners at last. What an escape, she thought. Why, he must be nearly £20,000 in debt, possibly more. Oriana might find Lysander attractive, but the attractions of a man with no income were minimal compared with the same man with an estate and a proper income. Straitened means she could put up with – for a while and think herself generous – penury was another matter altogether.

Lady Helena saw, with satisfaction, that her companion was looking quite sullen with resentment. She had always enjoyed in the family the reputation of being capable of uttering unpalatable truths with devastating effect and, having scored a hit, she smiled quite composedly at her victim and said, 'Ah! Here we are at the vicarage. What a pleasant little trip!'

Clemency and Mrs Stoneham sat in the pretty parlour and looked at the notice in the Lost and Found column of the *Morning Post*. Mrs Stoneham had noticed it at once and put it aside for Clemency when she came for her Sunday visit. But she was relieved to see her young cousin early, for although she knew the notice could have waited until Sunday it had nonetheless been on her mind. She was the sort of woman who likes to be up and doing and the uncertainty of this whole business preyed on her mind.

'You don't think it's a trick?' asked Clemency cautiously. So far as she could remember, Mr Jameson had been a dry stick of a man, not one to whom she could make an appeal.

'It is possible,' said her cousin, judiciously. 'But there is no reason that you should give him your address. You could ask him to reply to a box number. Or even to insert another notice.'

Clemency considered. It was odd, now that a possible reconciliation was on offer, to realize that she wasn't sure she wanted it. Apart from Mr Baverstock, whose attentions seemed to have stopped, she was enjoying her new position. She would never have thought it, but being a governess had given her a freedom she had never experienced before. At Candover Court, where nobody knew who she was, she was respected only as she was worthy of it. And she had won that respect: from Arabella, from Mrs Marlow, even, she believed, from the marquess.

She had learned something else, too, that a governess had rights as well as duties. At home she had had duties; to pay calls with her mother, to dust the Sèvres ornaments in the drawing-room, but she had had no rights. There was no time for herself, when her presence couldn't be demanded, her thoughts interrupted. She was on duty all the time at her mother's whim.

At Candover Court her contribution to Arabella's education or even organizing the picnic was understood and appreciated. She did not believe that the same was true in her mother's eyes.

'You know, Cousin Anne,' she said at last, 'it's very odd, but I don't think I *can* go home on the same old footing now. It's not that I want to be a governess all my life, but I *do* want the independence it has given me.'

Bessy was right, thought Mrs Stoneham, looking affectionately at her young cousin, the experience has done her good. There was a new assurance about her, a new spring in her step even.

Mrs Stoneham would have been considerably disturbed to

know the part the marquess was playing in Clemency's transformation, but having satisfied herself that Mr Baverstock appeared to have learnt his lesson, she looked no further.

'Perhaps, my dear,' she said, 'you could let Mr Jameson know that you are well and happy, in a respectable household and want for nothing. It is always better to negotiate from a strong position.'

'I suppose I could,' Clemency sighed.

'You do not sound very enthusiastic,' observed Mrs Stoneham.

Clemency sighed again. What could she say? That her objections to the proposed marriage had gone? How could the marquess be expected to swallow such an insult? Was she really imagining that he would come *again* to Russell Square?

'I shall think about it, Cousin Anne,' she said at last. 'We shall have more time to discuss it when I come on Sunday.'

A knock at the door heralded Bessy.

'Her ladyship's carriage is here to fetch Miss Clemency,' she announced. 'The coachman is just taking the empty hamper. There's such things in it, you wouldn't believe, madam! Cherries, nectarines, asparagus and I don't know what!'

'I must come out with you and thank her ladyship myself,' announced Mrs Stoneham, getting up.

'Oh no!' cried Clemency involuntarily.

'Naturally, I must,' said Mrs Stoneham severely. 'Where are your manners, Clemency?'

Clemency could say nothing, but in the event her anxieties were unnecessary. The dogs were taking exception to the inclusion of a third person in the carriage and it was obvious that Lady Helena was only listening with half an ear.

If Clemency's attitude to life was changing, so, too, was Arabella's. Was it only just over a week ago that she had tripped off to meet Josh Baldock with no thought for the consequences? It hardly seemed possible. That episode had brought Arabella up with a start and she began to see, with Diana's help, that the hoydenish exploits of the past could, now she was sixteen, have more serious consequences. When Mark Baverstock suggested a stolen trip to the village fair, Arabella was far more alarmed than pleased.

She thought about it constantly and in silence. She told neither Diana nor Clemency. Both, she knew, would give a flat veto and that was not what she wanted. What she wanted was to understand what Mr Baverstock was *about*. Arabella was aware, this time, that she was playing a dangerous game, and if she hadn't confided in her brother, she must have told either her cousin or her governess. But for the first time in her life she had an important secret to share with Lysander, her access to the adult world, and so long as she had the safety of him knowing, she was not going to share it with anybody else.

Accordingly, when Oriana and Clemency were with Lady Helena on Wednesday afternoon and Diana upstairs reading, Arabella agreed to Mark's suggestion that they take a walk in the shrubbery. Like Lysander, Arabella did not think that Mark had any designs on her virtue, but all the same she was pleased to see the white straw hat of Lady Fabian in the distance as she sat underneath the cedar tree with her embroidery.

Mark was on his best behaviour. He asked his fair companion to choose him a rose for his buttonhole, he appeared amused by various anecdotes of her childish exploits, he treated her with a mixture of playful homage and respect and in short made himself very agreeable. He did not make the mistake of mentioning Miss Stoneham – he did not want to make Arabella suspicious – but after ten minutes or so, when he judged that she was ready he said, 'I can see that you are far too lively a young lady to sit quietly at home sewing your sampler!'

'I *did* try to do a sampler when I was little, but I never finished it,' said Arabella, laughing. 'We found it the other day in a drawer in the schoolroom. It was covered in little drops of blood where I kept pricking my finger. Oh! How I hated the horrid thing!'

'So you played truant from the schoolroom, did you?'

'Oh yes. I escaped whenever I could. I was always climbing trees and falling into streams.'

'What about the village fair? Surely you must have gone there? Didn't the gingerbread stalls and all the games attract you? Now, confess!'

They had. For several years Arabella had sneaked down both during the day and, last year, for the evening jollifications which were considerably more rowdy. The villagers, of course, had known who she was, but nobody had ever betrayed her to her aunt.

She glanced up at Mark's face, dimpled, and said mendaciously, 'Good heavens, no! That was completely out of bounds, though, I admit I always wanted to.'

She wasn't quite sure why she was lying, but she sensed that it would be wiser to hide the extent to which she could look after herself. She was certain that Mr Baverstock had a hidden hand, and she saw no reason why she should show all hers either.

'Let me take you then! I promise I'll look after you very well. I'll bring you home safely before midnight, like Cinderella.'

Why does he want to, Arabella wondered. She was no self-deceiver and certainly didn't rate her charms so high that he would want to take risks to spend an evening in her company. Why should he, when he could do so with perfect propriety at Candover Court?

'I can't believe our poor village fair holds such an attraction for you, Mr Baverstock,' she said.

'But why not?' he protested. 'As a boy I always went to our local fair. I am an expert at the coconut shy and can guarantee to win you any number of pretty fairings.'

I suppose it's possible, thought Arabella. Aloud she said, 'How could it be managed?'

'Simple. You normally go up at nine o'clock, is that not so?' Arabella nodded. 'I will meet you here – it's away from the house and we can't be seen – at half past nine. I'll take one of my horses if you don't mind riding pillion and we'll be there in half an hour. How about it?'

Arabella clasped her hands and gave what she hoped was a suitable squeak of joy. 'Famous! And nobody will ever know.'

'It will be our little secret,' he promised.

He'd done it! The silly chit had agreed. All it needed now was for Oriana to play her part.

Arabella allowed herself to be led back to the lawn and sank down gracefully on the grass next to Lady Fabian. Mark exchanged a few words with them, gave Arabella a suspicion of a wink, and then left.

* * *

Arabella was unable to do more than exchange the briefest of words with her brother, and then not until the following day. She was in an agony of impatience, was inattentive at her lessons and short with poor Diana. Finally, she saw Lysander alone for a few minutes after lunch.

'Zander!' she tugged at his sleeve. 'He's asked me!'

'What's that, Bella?'

'Mr Baverstock,' hissed Arabella. 'We've made an arrangement to go to the fair on Saturday night.'

'Good God, Arabella, are you mad?'

His sister tossed her head. 'If you're going to be stuffy I shan't tell you,' she said. 'I don't care what you think, Zander, I don't like Mr Baverstock and I want to know *why* he's doing it.'

'Sorry, puss.' Lysander flicked her cheek gently with one finger. 'Look, I'm tied up with Frome today. We'll talk tomorrow about four. Come to the estate room.'

'Shall you come after us with pistols?' asked Arabella, her eyes shining.

Lysander put it to the back of his mind: he still only half-believed in the story, and in any case he had too much to do to worry about it. But on Friday something brought the whole thing very much to the forefront.

He had spent most of the morning riding round the estate with Frome. Various tenants had to be dealt with, the state of some cottages looked at. By noon he was tired and thirsty. Frome went back to his office and Lysander decided to stop off at the Crown for a drink and something to eat.

He handed his horse to the ostler and strode into the inn.

The landlord was behind the bar polishing some tankards.

'Why, my lord!'

'Hello, Barlow.'

'It is a pleasure to see you, my lord. If you wish for some quiet, there's nobody in the back parlour. Now what can I get you?'

'Thank you. A glass of beer and some of Polly's bread and cheese is all I want.'

'Certainly, my lord. This way.'

The back parlour was quiet and cool and Lysander sank down gratefully on to an old settle. 'Business good, Barlow?'

The landlord shook his head. 'Only a few people to stay, my lord. Well, we're out of the way here, of course. A Mr Jameson came a week or so ago to call on Mrs Stoneham, I understand. Asked a lot of questions, he did.' There was very little Barlow didn't know about everybody's business. 'And a young gentleman has booked a room for tomorrow night for his sister's *governess*.' He winked at Lysander. 'Name of Richmond. Would he be staying with your lordship, I wonder?'

There was an arrested look on Lysander's face but he shook his head. 'Richmond? No,' he said. 'Possibly he's been staying with the Maddoxes.'

'That'll be it, seemingly,' agreed Barlow.

'And this Jameson fellow,' said Lysander, idly. 'What did he want? You know, I'm sure, that Miss Stoneham is now Lady Arabella's governess. I hope it wasn't bad news for Mrs Stoneham?'

'It was a proper fairy-story, like,' said Barlow, laughing heartily at the memory. 'It seems some heiress is missing and Mr Jameson thought it might be Miss Stoneham! Not likely, is it, my lord? Why, what would an heiress want with being a governess? No disrespect, my lord.'

'Most unlikely,' agreed Lysander.

Later, staring out of the inn parlour window, Lysander tried to piece together two pieces of the jigsaw. One was the Mr Richmond who had booked a room for his sister's governess.

When Mark and Lysander were on some spree they had often used false names. Neither relished being pursued by over-amorous mistresses and young men who were taken up by the Watch if things became too riotous, gave false names to the magistrate the following day, paid the fine and got off. He, Lysander, had been Mr Abbott.

And Mark had been Mr Richmond.

The other piece of information was so astounding that Lysander couldn't credit it. It simply couldn't be possible that Miss Stoneham was the missing heiress, the one who had run away rather than receive his proposals.

No, it must be a fantastic coincidence. Miss Hastings-Whinborough must have fled to some schoolfriend, probably.

Young ladies worth £100,000 didn't hire themselves out as governesses for no more than £30 a year. Did they?

He wrenched his mind away from the missing Miss Hastings-Whinborough with an effort and tried to concentrate on Mark. It was plain now that Arabella had spoken no less than the truth, and, to a certain extent, Mark's motives were becoming clearer. He would hardly take an unwilling Arabella to the Crown. Not only did everybody in the village know her, but the resulting scandal could ruin him. Lysander might be hovering on the edge of bankruptcy, but he was perfectly capable of defending the honour of his sister. Lysander knew himself to be a very fine shot; Mark would not want to risk his skin, nor to face having to leave the country.

No, Mark had other game in mind, as the landlord had obviously realized. Who else could he be after but Miss Stoneham?

There was only one question of which Lysander remained somewhat in doubt: was this with the lady's connivance? Oriana had certainly hinted so. At the time he had not believed her, but could it be true? Miss Stoneham and Mark had been treating each other with civil indifference over the last few days, ever since the episode in the cloisters, in fact. Was this a front to disguise other feelings? Did Miss Stoneham *want* to go with his friend?

Suddenly, the bread and cheese seemed perfectly tasteless.

Mark Baverstock had spent a busy day on Friday. In the morning he had gone into Abbots Candover and booked a room for Miss Stoneham for the following night. There was always the risk, of course, that she would flee to her cousin's house, but Mark had every intention of cutting off that option. A ruined and disgraced girl would not risk further exposure and humiliation at the hands of a respectable relation. No, she would spend the night at the Crown (doubtless bewailing her lost virtue) and he didn't think she'd demur when he came to collect her the following morning.

If she was wise she'd learn to please him and by the time they returned from Paris he hoped that she'd be as pretty and tractable a piece as any man could desire.

He then returned to Candover Court and wrote himself a

letter demanding his return home. This took some thought as he certainly didn't want to travel with Oriana, who would be decidedly *de trop* for what he had in mind.

In the end he decided that his god-father's health was giving cause for concern. As he was known to be that gentleman's main beneficiary, his anxiety to be with him at his bedside would occasion no comment.

He finished the letter, sealed it, addressed it to himself in a disguised hand and rang for his valet.

'I want this brought to me tomorrow morning,' he said.

'Certainly, sir,' said his valet impassively. He was not surprised. This was not the sort of house he was used to, no proper provisions for a gentleman's gentleman, and he'd been wondering how long Mr Baverstock would put up with it as it didn't sound as if things were any livelier upstairs.

'Shall I inform Eliza, sir?'

'No. Miss Baverstock's staying, for a while, at least.'

'Oh!' The valet's brain seethed with conjecture.

'Just see that my things are packed. We leave early on Sunday morning.'

'Very good, sir.'

'And mind you keep your mouth shut.'

Mark flicked him half a crown and went in search of his sister. On Wednesday afternoon when she had returned with Lady Helena she had been in a foul temper and very disinclined to do anything. Mark devoutly hoped that a day's grace would have cooled her down somewhat. But when he eventually found her in the drawing-room she was not, initially, more amenable.

She was alone in the room, sitting on the window-seat, gazing morosely out of the window. There was, in fact, a charming view of the front lawn and gatehouse, but Oriana noticed none of this. All she could see was ruined hopes and selfishness on all sides. She was feeling extremely hard done by, and not even snubbing Miss Stoneham over the breakfast table that morning had served to raise her spirits.

She turned her head when her brother came in and then resumed her study of the lawn.

'Come on, Sis, what's the matter?' Mark strolled over and sat beside her. 'Aren't you pleased that pretty Miss Stoneham will soon be out of your way?'

Oriana shrugged.

'You did promise to help,' Mark reminded her.

'It's all very well for you,' snapped Oriana. 'You're planning to leave. But what about me? Do you think that *I* want to stay in this dreary place, where everything is falling to pieces, while you're off with your *inamorata*?'

'But I thought you had your eye on Lysander?'

'You thought wrong, then. He hasn't a groat. Lady Helena told me. The estate's being sold up. There'll be nothing left.'

Mark whistled. 'As bad as that, eh? Poor fellow. I've had my suspicions, mind. I knew things looked pretty bad after Alex died, but I supposed he'd be able to salvage something. You can't marry him then, Sis.'

'Naturally not. So I want to leave too.'

'You can't, Sis. Not until I've got Miss Stoneham away safe.'

'Why not? Surely *I* am more important than that trollop?'

Mark began to feel alarmed. How like a woman to throw everything into jeopardy with her whims. 'Look, Oriana,' he said placatingly, 'it's only for a few days. I'll tell you what, if you help me with this I'll see that you get that new mare, eh?'

Oriana considered it. She'd been teasing her father for another horse all last winter. The one she'd had her eye on was a hundred guineas, and even so indulgent a father as Sir Richard had balked at that. But if Mark stepped in, then she would get her way. Mark usually managed to get what he wanted.

'Promise?'

'Word of honour.'

'Very well. What do you want me to do?'

That evening at dinner the marquess's dark eyes scrutinized the company. Mark, his friend – so he thought – was he really so lost to feelings of honour that he wouldn't hesitate to seduce one of his dependents and bring shame on an innocent girl? Lysander thought back over the years he had known Mark. Usually his light-o'-loves had been women who had known the ropes, but there had been one or two episodes where Lysander had felt distinctly uncomfortable. There was a milliner's apprentice, he remembered, an innocent if ever there was one. Of course Mark hadn't left her penniless – he was a gentleman after all – but she had been distraught and weeping. No, Mark had not behaved very well there.

Then he turned his attention to Clemency. She was listening to Giles with an expression of kindly interest on her face. Giles was describing a trout he had caught and his misadventures with getting his line tangled up in a hazel bush. Lord Fabian was listening too, amusement on his face, as his heir inexpertly tried to be the man of the world in front of Miss Stoneham.

But Lysander was not interested in Giles's fish. It was Miss Stoneham he was considering. *Was* she playing a part? Surely she could not be the daughter of that appalling parvenu? It was true that they were both fair, but Mrs Hastings-Whinborough's hair owed everything to the bottle: Miss Stoneham's, he was certain, was quite natural.

Then there was the insistent feeling that they had met before. But that, Lysander knew, was nothing to do with the house in Russell Square. The memory was tantalizingly elusive, but he had the distinct impression that it had been outside. Furthermore, during that moment in the river, he had known that Miss Stoneham, too, remembered their meeting. Had she, or had she not, been about to tell him when they were so unfortunately interrupted by Arabella?

No, he decided, Miss Stoneham could not be Miss Hastings-Whinborough. If she were, Mr Jameson would hardly have failed to discover it. But how odd that the heiress was also a relation of Mrs Stoneham. Perhaps she and Miss Stoneham were cousins, which might account for the colouring. In any case, Miss Stoneham was plainly a lady. Lysander had a horror of what Lady Helena called the 'mushroom classes'. He would certainly be trusted to spot some upstart a mile off!

Whatever Miss Stoneham's background, she was plainly no vulgarian.

Lastly, his eye travelled to Oriana. Ever since that trip with his aunt she had been behaving differently. He had asked Lady Helena what she had said to bring about the change, but she had only laughed. 'We had a very agreeable drive, Storrington,' was all the reply he got. 'Don't sit there, there's a puppy somewhere on it.'

Oriana was being decidedly off-hand. Usually the evening passed in a pleasant flirtation, but no more. Oriana either stared, bored, out of the window, or else made malicious remarks to Miss Stoneham. At one time he'd even thought she was striking up a friendship with Adela, but that seemed to have faded.

Lysander found himself thinking that Oriana's behaviour was, in fact, somewhat ill-bred. She rarely bothered with Diana and Giles, was dotingly fond of Arabella when she remembered, was rude to Miss Stoneham, and the only people to whom she behaved with propriety were Lord and Lady Fabian and his aunt.

A true lady, thought Lysander, watching Clemency tactfully bring Diana into the conversation, is civil to all and gives everybody their due. He wondered why this hadn't struck him before.

Ever since her talk with Cousin Anne, Clemency had spent every evening in the quiet of her room struggling with the question of what to do about Mr Jameson's notice.

Cousin Anne would urge her to answer it, of course. Clemency wasn't sure how far her cousin's loyalty to her went. Would she feel it incumbent on her to answer if Clemency did not? But things had got so complicated since she'd run away that she found it difficult to work out exactly what she *did* want.

First of all, there was the marquess. She had, in fact, run *away* from him. Now she would give anything to be able to reverse that. She loved him, she liked and respected Lady Helena and was fond of Arabella. She believed she would be happy at Candover Court. There was certainly plenty for her to do and it was work she thought she'd enjoy and do well.

But if she were ever to be mistress of Candover Court then the marquess would have to know the truth. And how could she ever tell him? Furthermore, time was of the essence. Within a few months the estate would be sold. There was no use braving his wrath and hoping that time would soften his anger. By then it would be too late.

How duped he would feel, and rightly! Clemency shuddered. She hadn't meant to deceive anybody, but somehow one thing had led to another. Then she would have to recognize that it would be a marriage of convenience to him. Opulent brunettes were what he really went for. Could she cope with loving somebody who didn't love her, even if he was more civil than he had been at first? Clemency suspected that that would be a special sort of agony.

Perhaps, she thought wistfully, he'd come to love her, or at least, be fond of her, if he could ever forget how their marriage came about.

She sat down on her bed and carefully tore out a page from one of Arabella's exercise books. Somewhere she had a pencil. In the end, after several drafts she achieved something.

Jameson. Box 240.

Miss C. H-W is with family of utmost respectability, she wrote. It was, of course, quite untrue. Lady Helena was eccentric and the marquess's respectability somewhat in doubt. *She intends to remain unless she is allowed to manage her own future without interference.* Was that too strong? She was a minor after all. Perhaps she should soften it a bit, especially as she wanted Mr Jameson to renegotiate the marriage. What about: *She wishes her future to be a matter of mutual agreement.* Yes, that sounded better. How should she finish? What about: *Respectful compliments to all.* Mr Jameson would understand that she meant her mother. Then a box number.

She wrote out a fair copy with several minor adjustments and looked at it.

Jameson. Box 240
Miss C H-W is safely with a family of the utmost respectability. She wishes her future to be a matter of mutual agreement. Respectful compliments to all. Box No....

Yes, it would do. And, unaware that one of the guests had very different plans for her Sunday, she decided that she would take it to Cousin Anne's after church and see what she thought.

Eight

Clemency came down to the breakfast parlour on Saturday morning just in time to hear Mark tell the assembled company that he was going to have to cut short his visit.

'It's m'god-father,' he said, looking down at his letter. 'Poor chap. He was a military man, y'know. Never been right since he got a ball in his shoulder at Badajoz.'

There were general commiserations. Clemency couldn't help feeling that they were more for Major Armstrong than for the loss of Mr Baverstock. Her own feeling was one of profound relief. She hadn't realized how much his presence oppressed her until she knew she was going to be relieved of it.

'I hope we shall not be losing you as well, Miss Baverstock,' said Lady Fabian politely, though privately she felt that that lady would be no loss.

Lysander said very little. When Mark broke the news he'd given his friend one swift, sceptical glance and then returned to his kedgeree. He had realized that some excuse would come and had only wondered in what form. It would obviously have to exclude Oriana so Mark's solution was, he thought, quite neat.

'You cannot mean to travel on a *Sunday*, Mr Baverstock!' cried Adela.

Mark's eyelids drooped. 'Alas, Miss Fabian,' he said, 'I must. But "the Sabbath was made for man", you know, and I could not reconcile it with my conscience to be away from my god-father at such a time,' he added piously.

Humbug, thought Clemency.

The conversation turned to the events planned for the day. Lady Helena announced that she must put in an appearance at the village fair that afternoon and would be happy to take

133

anybody up in her carriage who wished to go.

'I shall not stay very long,' she finished. 'Would it amuse you, Maria? Lord Fabian?' Both professed themselves at her service. 'What about you, Adela?'

'I do not think I care for such things, Cousin Helena,' said Adela.

'I am sure Diana would like to go, wouldn't you, Diana?' said the marquess. He'd rather revised his early opinion of his young cousin; under that shyness and awkwardness was a very engaging little soul.

Diana nodded, her eyes shining, and looked at Arabella. Arabella glanced at her brother.

'I'll take the girls in my curricle, if they don't mind a bit of a squash. Oriana, what about you? Will you go with my aunt?'

Oriana stifled a yawn and said she thought not. She didn't see that she owed the marquess more than the minimum politeness as he had so selfishly decided to sell his patrimony. 'I do not find the antics of yokels amusing,' she said. 'I shall stay with Miss Fabian.'

'Giles,' said Lady Fabian, 'what about you?'

Giles was in something of a quandary. He was young enough to enjoy a village fair but, on the other hand, he wanted to be where Clemency was. And it seemed as if she wouldn't be going.

Lord Fabian looked across at his son. 'I think you'd better come with us, Giles,' he said. The young cub had been hovering around Miss Stoneham long enough. Doubtless she'd welcome a respite.

Clemency excused herself and went up to the schoolroom. Nobody had even considered that she might want to go and, stupidly, she felt upset. She was the *governess*, she told herself firmly; governesses were not normally included in parties of pleasure. If she'd wanted that, she should have stayed in Russell Square. She would be foolish to allow it to oppress her. She had plenty to occupy her, let her get on with that. There were no lessons on Saturday mornings, but she had some work to do pasting Arabella's flower drawings on to card and making a mount.

She did not relish the idea of staying with Miss Fabian and the Baverstocks, but she would take care to keep out of their way. She couldn't help noticing, though, that Miss Baverstock appeared to have ceased her pursuit of the marquess. What did she mean by it? Was she really grown tired of him – preposterous thought – or was she now so sure of him that she could afford to seem indifferent?

In the event, however, Clemency had her afternoon in peace: Mark and Oriana were in Oriana's room composing the letter that would bring Clemency running after Arabella.

Oriana was taking a keen, and somewhat voyeuristic, interest in Clemency's fate.

'What are you planning to do?' she asked curiously.

'I shall lose Arabella the moment I spot Miss Stoneham, and take the lady into the bushes somewhere. After that, I don't imagine she'll be much trouble.'

'It won't work,' said Oriana decidedly. 'The bushes will be full of other couples, have you thought of that? Besides, people know who she is.'

Mark looked annoyed.

'No,' went on Oriana, warming to Miss Stoneham's ruin, 'you'll have to take her to the Crown.'

'She wouldn't go. Don't be stupid, Sis.'

'She would if she thought Arabella was there.'

'I believe you're right,' said Mark slowly, having turned it over in his mind. And to have his way with her in the comfort of a bedroom would undoubtedly enhance *his* pleasure, if not hers.

'Of course I'm right! Now, supposing I write that having shown Arabella the sights you're going to give her supper in a private room at the Crown?'

Mark began to laugh. 'Brilliant, Sis. Nobody will be able to say she was *forced* to come. She'll come running!' He patted her hand. 'You deserve that little mare.'

Oriana had extracted one of Arabella's compositions from the schoolroom the previous evening and now sat down at the rosewood desk to imitate the writing.

'How about this?' she asked. ' "Dear Miss Stoneham, you are not to worry that I am not in bed. I have gone to the fair with Mr Baverstock" – or should I write "Mark"? Yes, that would be more alarming. "He's going to give me supper at the Crown – it's a private room, so you needn't fear for my reputation – and bring me home safely. Arabella." Something along those lines?'

'Perfect, Sis.'

Oriana looked down at the letter. She thought she had imitated Arabella's wild scrawl rather well.

The village fair party returned having had an agreeable afternoon. Lady Helena had judged the marrows, the pigs and the babies and spent most of the money in her reticule on various useless trifles. Lord and Lady Fabian had done their bit and spent generously and Lord Fabian had even had a go or two at the coconut shy. Arabella and Diana, given two shillings apiece by Lord Fabian, proceeded to spend it on seeing Zabine, the gipsy fortune-teller, who promised them both handsome husbands and, in a giggling Arabella's case, twins. Arabella then went to watch Josh Baldock who was attempting to outdo his fellows climbing the greasy pole. He was wearing his oldest clothes and was already liberally spattered with dirt, but he grinned at Arabella when he saw her and Arabella, after a moment's hesitation, waved.

Lysander, too, was watching Josh, and when the contest was over and the contestants had dowsed themselves under the pump, he saw Josh heading for the beer tent and beckoned.

Somewhat nervously Josh went over. He had not forgotten their last encounter. But the marquess was not there to upbraid him.

'Can you keep your mouth shut?' he asked.

Josh goggled at him, but nodded.

'Good. I want you to do something for me.'

Josh nodded again, more warily this time.

'Lady Arabella will be coming down this evening with one of my guests. I want you to keep an eye on her. See that she's all right. Can you do that?'

Josh shuffled his feet. 'Aye,' he said without looking up. Then he took a gulp and added, 'Always been fond of Bella. If it gets a bit rough later on, I'll see that she's all right.' He didn't like to ask why Arabella's escort couldn't look after her – perhaps he was one of those London fops who'd turn tail if things got a bit out of hand.

'I shall be down myself, later, but I don't want you to take any notice of me, unless I call. Is that clear?'

'Yes, sir.'

'Good.' Lysander reached in his pocket and handed him half-a-crown. 'Don't drink too much. You may need your wits about you.'

Josh took the coin and pocketed it. 'Thank you, sir. You can rely on me to look after Bella. Lady Arabella, I mean,' he added belatedly.

'I know,' said Lysander. 'If I'd have thought otherwise I'd have broken your neck the other week.'

Unaware of the storm about to break over her head, Clemency had a pleasant and quiet afternoon. She marked some work, though one of Arabella's compositions had unaccountably gone missing, prepared a passage of French to be done on Monday and wondered whether they might tackle some Cowper. Diana, almost certainly, would like his romantic melancholy, she wasn't sure about Arabella.

She then sat down for a quiet hour with Mrs Inchbald's *A Simple Story* and attempted to become absorbed in Miss Milner's trials and tribulations. But she found the heroine's habit of forever falling on her knees in front of her guardian somewhat irritating and couldn't help wishing that she'd exercise her brain sometimes instead of her joints.

She then went upstairs to change into her black silk dress for dinner. She had learnt by now that Miss Fabian and certainly Miss Baverstock considered it far too well made and the bodice too low for a mere governess and she couldn't help smiling at what they would think of her other dresses in her cupboard at home; that frosted net over a hyacinth blue slip, for example, or that primrose satin with the quilled lace. She sighed. Governessing was all very well, but sometimes she longed for a little feminine frivolity!

At dinner that evening the conversation was animated. Mark and Oriana professed themselves all ears about the fair. What fun it sounded! Mark, especially, regretted missing it. Never mind, perhaps another year. Only Arabella was silent.

'Are you all right, Arabella?' asked Clemency anxiously.

'Only a little tired.' Arabella gave a weary smile. 'It was *so* hot.' She glanced under her lashes at Mark. Mark shot a triumphant look at Oriana.

Eventually, after two yawns, Lady Helena ordered Arabella

up to bed. Diana, unusually bold, begged to be allowed to stay up a little and her mother said, smiling, 'Just until half past nine, darling. Then you must go up.'

Soon after Arabella left Mark got up. He was sorry, he told the company, but he had a lot to do before his departure the following morning. He was sure Lady Helena would understand. He bowed and left them. Lady Helena was, in fact, mildly affronted, surely that's what servants were for? But as Lysander said nothing to stop him and as she herself did not care overmuch for either of the Baverstocks, she merely inclined her head and resumed her conversation with Lord Fabian.

In fact, the party broke up fairly early. Perhaps everyone was tired. It had, as Lady Helena confirmed, been a particularly hot day. At any rate, Lady Helena rang for tea shortly after Diana went upstairs and by ten the company broke up.

Clemency went up to the schoolroom for a few moments to check on the nature tray and then took the candle Mrs Marlow always left on the top landing, lit it from the wall sconce and went upstairs.

It was always a pleasure to come up to her little room. She hardly noticed its shabbiness now, only that it was quiet and peaceful and she had it all to herself. There was a full moon and pale streams of light came in the window and filled the room with a cool glow. It lit up the miniature of her father on the bedside table – and a small white triangle lying on the counterpane. Puzzled, Clemency put down the candlestick and picked it up.

What she read was so horrific that for a moment the words danced before her eyes and she had to take up the candle and hold it closer to read it properly.

Arabella gone to the fair with Mark Baverstock. Surely she could not be so lost to all sense of propriety as that! And she was going to supper with him at the Crown. For a moment Clemency felt faint with horror. Such an action would ruin her: she must be stopped!

She sank down on the bed desperately trying to think what best to do. She discarded any idea of telling Lady Helena: that way lay disgrace, she was sure. Nor did she feel she could tell the marquess. He was fond of Arabella she knew, but after the episode with Josh Baldock – and Clemency had not forgotten his anger there – she felt that to tell him would only serve to humiliate Arabella further. And this was quite apart from any awkwardness on her own account in consulting the marquess.

No, she must deal with it herself. First, she must check that Arabella was indeed not in her room and then she must somehow intercept Arabella before she got to the Crown. If the worst came to the worst she must take them both to Cousin Anne's, but she sincerely hoped that that would not be necessary. Her cousin was not happy about her position at Candover Court, she knew. She did not want to do anything which might precipitate Mrs Stoneham into writing to Mr Jameson and telling him of her whereabouts.

Frantically, she tugged at the buttons of her dress. This was no occasion for her black silk. She must put on something old, the dress she had worn to go mushrooming in and some stout boots. Somewhere she had her old grey cloak. She pulled the small jet comb out of her hair and hastily tied her unruly golden curls with a black ribbon.

Ten minutes later she crept out of her room, cloak over her arm and tiptoed to Arabella's bedroom. It was empty.

She would go out the back door, she decided. She knew where Timson left the key. Quietly she made her way downstairs, every creak of the old wooden staircase sounding unnaturally loud. She did not see, along the guest corridor, a door slowly shut. Oriana, with a satisfied smile, watched her go. That would be the last of Miss Prunes and Prisms, she thought. Serve her right.

While Clemency was tiptoeing downstairs, Arabella and Mark had arrived at the fair. Mark had handed his horse to the ostler at the Crown, bade him rub it down, see it was all right, handed Arabella an old loo mask, put his own on, and guided her back towards the village green.

During the day it had been noisy but respectable. At night it was another matter. The green, which that afternoon had seen the children's sack race and the greasy pole, was now cleared for dancing. And if the dancing was unrestrained, it was not improper, which was more than could be said for the behaviour of various couples already fumbling in the bushes. A fiddler wearing a battered three-cornered hat and a tattered waistcoat was playing energetically, a tankard of beer on a barrel beside him. Several ancient horn lanterns hung from trees and sent wild shadows of the fiddler and dancers over the green, so that it looked as if the devil himself were playing.

The beer tent was full with some of the rowdier elements already well on the way to becoming fighting drunk. Mark and Arabella were not the only two to come masked, there were others, young bloods from the nearby town on the look-out for compliant village girls. Already there were shrieks and giggles as wandering hands found their way into bodices: in short, Lady Helena could be forgiven for thinking that it was a most unsuitable place for her niece.

Mark glanced up at the village clock, just after ten. He'd amuse Arabella for forty minutes or so and then he'd be off to the Crown to await the delectable Miss Stoneham. Oriana was right, it was a much better plan. Miss Stoneham wouldn't want to be seen amongst this rabble.

From beside the beer tent Josh saw the new arrivals and recognized Arabella at once. Good, he thought, now he knew she was here, he could allow himself a drink. He ducked his head and went inside the tent.

Arabella was looking around her wide-eyed. Last year, when she'd come down it had been nothing like this. But then she and Josh had sat on a hay-bale in a corner and held hands. She'd been home before eleven, she recalled, perhaps she'd missed it. She clutched at Mark's arm. Even though she knew Lysander would be down as soon as he could, she still didn't feel comfortable.

Mark patted her hand. 'Now don't worry,' he said, 'you'll be all right with me. Here, let's take a look at the dancing. Do you want to join in?'

The dancers were surrounded by knots of older villagers, talking and laughing. Arabella recognized several and suddenly felt safer.

'Yes,' she said, 'let's dance.'

Mark helped her off with her cloak and dropped it with his on a tree stump. He held out his hand. 'Come on, then.'

*   *   *

The kitchen at Candover Court was not much altered from when it had originally been built. In the last century somebody had added movable bars to the fireplace, but the pot crane still hung over it as it always had done, and there was the spit and the basting pan still in the places allotted to them 200 years before. All Clemency could see, as she crept down with her candle shielded from the draught by one hand, was the faint glow from the fireplace where the coals were banked under the iron fire-cover. She did not see a still, dark figure in the shadows. She held the candle up and felt along the top of the back door for the key. Thank goodness! Quietly, she put it in the lock and was just about to turn it when a hand grabbed her shoulder. Clemency gave a shriek, which was muffled by the gentleman's other hand, and in her terror dropped the candle. The room was plunged into darkness.

'And just where do you think you're going?'

'Oh! My lord!' Clemency became aware that her heart was thudding wildly.

'Well?' Lysander bent down, releasing Clemency as he did so, picked up the candle and relit it with a spill from the mantelpiece. He was looking singularly forbidding. His sloe-dark eyes were stern and he was grim-lipped. He took her by the arm, pulled her towards him and held the candle up to her face. 'It wouldn't be to meet a certain gentleman, would it?'

'W ... what do you mean?'

'You don't fool me, Miss Stoneham. Miss Baverstock warned me that you were after her brother. He is leaving tomorrow and doubtless he has persuaded you that pretty Miss Stoneham would be better off under his protection than earning a paltry living as a governess. What has he promised you? Paris? Your own box at the opera?'

Clemency had been listening to the early part of this speech in bewilderment, but suddenly wrath overtook all else. 'Do you really imagine that I'd go with that ... that ... *louse*?' she cried. 'You must be off your head!'

'Shh!'

'Nothing, but nothing would induce me to exchange a single word with him if I didn't have to. I find him utterly contemptible!'

Lysander had put the candle down on the kitchen table and

he now leant back against the wall and folded his arms. 'Go on,' he said. 'Anger becomes you.'

White with rage Clemency reached in the pocket of her cloak and handed him Arabella's letter. 'Read that, my lord,' she demanded, 'and you will see that my sole aim is to prevent your sister's ruin.'

Lysander, frowning, took the note and scanned it. Arabella had not written the note, he was certain, but who had? It was certainly a clumsy attempt at her hand. He could not disguise from himself the inordinate relief he had felt at Clemency's repudiation of Mark, but could not rid himself of a lingering suspicion that she might yet be deceiving him.

'I think all is becoming clear,' he said, slowly.

'It may be clear to you, my lord,' said Clemency with asperity', but it is far from clear to me! In any case, we are wasting time.' She glanced at the kitchen clock. 'It is now a quarter past ten. Oh, do hurry.'

'Mark won't hurt Arabella,' said Lysander, folding up the note and putting it in his pocket. 'It's *you* he's after.'

'Me!'

'I should have thought that, at least, was obvious,' said the marquess grimly. 'Come, I have a horse outside. Let's be off.'

'But ... but, I don't understand.' Clemency was now as pale as her dress. 'I have no intention of going with Mr Baverstock. You are not meaning to force me?' Her voice broke slightly.

'Miss Stoneham,' said the marquess, 'please use your considerable intelligence. I am no pimp! Arabella told me of this escapade a few days ago. Mark has booked a room at the Crown and he intends *your* ruin, not Arabella's. My guess is that he will lose her at the fair and repair to the Crown in time for his rendezvous with you – who will come running to rescue her charge; wasn't that what you intended?'

'You intend to use me as a decoy?' Clemency took a deep breath. 'Lord Storrington, I may be only a governess and beneath your notice, but *I* have a regard for my reputation, even if you do not. If Arabella knows nothing of this, then I can see no reason why I should risk my good name at the hands of your vicious friend.'

'You won't risk anything,' retorted the marquess, 'because I shall put a stop to it long before. Now, come. You must at least see that Arabella is safe. Wasn't that your object?'

'If *you* are going, my lord, I cannot see that you need *me*.'

'Look girl, somebody has to deal with Mark. Do you think I'm going to let him get away with taking my sister where no lady should go and attempting to ruin a young lady who is in my care? I want to get to the bottom of this. I thought Mark was my friend. Do you think this is pleasant for me?'

There was something else at the back of his mind, a niggle that perhaps Oriana had been involved somehow. If Miss Stoneham was cunning, she might have written the note herself; if she was speaking the truth, then he would have to look elsewhere. Lysander was not used to looking at his feelings very clearly, but his present emotions were such a tangle of rage and jealousy that he was quite unable to sort out which emotion belonged where. And meanwhile time passed.

He opened the kitchen door and hurried Clemency out to where his horse was waiting, ready-saddled in one of the loose boxes. Lysander led the horse out, checked the girths and swung himself into the saddle.

'You'll have to sit behind me,' he said. 'Come on. Put your foot on mine and give me your hand.'

There was no help for it. In a minute Clemency found herself sitting astride, skirts immodestly bundled up, and feeling agonizingly conscious of his body against hers.

The ride through the night was both terrifying and exhilarating. They set off through the Home Wood as Lysander was anxious to avoid the road. He didn't want to risk being seen by Mark. He set off at a canter and Clemency had to cling tight, a feeling half-pleasurable, half-fearful.

'All right?' Lysander called over his shoulder. And was it her imagination, or did his voice sound a little constrained?

'Yes, my lord,' said Clemency breathlessly. Her hair had come loose and she was trying to stop it from blowing across her face.

Lysander reined in at the end of the wood. They were near where Clemency had been mushrooming and a field or two from the village green. Winking lights could be seen in the distance. Lysander guided the horse in the shadow of the hedgerow, then stopped.

'I think this'll do,' he said. 'I'll tie Strawberry to a tree. I doubt whether anybody will see him.' He jumped down and held out his arms for Clemency.

Without thinking, Clemency slid into them. For a moment he seemed to hold her close. She could feel his heart, his arms strongly about her. Then suddenly he released her as if nothing had happened. And nothing had, or had it?

Nervously, Clemency tucked her hair under the hood of her cloak and Lysander busied himself with loosening the girth.

'This way,' said the marquess, curtly.

Silently, Clemency followed him. As they got nearer, she could see that the green was crowded. Several hundred people were there, dancing, drinking, singing.

'However shall we find them?' she asked.

Lysander glanced up at the church clock. 'Nearly quarter to eleven,' he said. 'Mark should be going to the Crown now, if he isn't already there.'

They skirted the hedge and came out behind one of the booths.

'I asked Josh Baldock to keep an eye on Arabella,' he said. 'We may need him, so I hope he's managed to stay sober.'

At that moment one of the town lads reeled up and peered into Clemency's face and made a grab. 'P-pretty ... jush the kind I like.'

With a blow Lysander calmly floored him. He turned to look at Clemency. Her hood had fallen back and in the moonlight her loosened hair shone like burnished gold. A memory stirred and then vanished. 'For God's sake, put your hood up,' the marquess commanded. 'I don't want a riot.'

Clemency did so with trembling fingers.

'Now take my hand.'

'It wouldn't be proper, my lord,' whispered Clemency.

'Proper! Good God, girl, the whole thing is wildly improper!' Lysander seized her hand without more ado. 'But if you don't want to be accosted by these yokels, I suggest you put up with it. It's quite your own fault.'

'W ... why, my lord?'

'For being so beautiful.'

Clemency was silenced.

It did not take Arabella long to recover her composure and in a very short time she had forgotten her fears. She had always enjoyed dancing and Mark was attentive. There were several other young men who appeared to appreciate her charms and soon she was so absorbed in the dancing and giving coquettish glances as she passed down the line in Strip the Willow, that she lost all sense of time.

However, even she had her limits and after half an hour or so she begged Mark to stop.

'Oh, it's wonderful!' she cried. 'But I have such a stitch in my side.'

Mark glanced up at the clock. 'Are you thirsty?' he asked solicitously as he led her to one of the hay-bales which did duty for a bench and found a space for her next to two stalwart dames.

'Oh, yes!'

'If you'll wait here a moment I'll fetch you a drink. Some of the girls are drinking lemonade. Will that do?'

'Yes, please. But, Mr Baverstock, you won't be long will you?'

'I'll be as quick as I can,' he promised. He disappeared into the throng around the beer tent.

It wasn't until a quarter of an hour had passed that Arabella began to feel uneasy. The two women sitting next to her left and she began to feel uncomfortably exposed. She was also getting cold. She was only wearing a light cotton dress with short sleeves and she began to shiver. It had been a very hot day but now the wind had shifted to the east and a cool breeze had sprung up. Then she remembered that they had left their cloaks somewhere near. Now where? Glancing around she saw with relief that there was a bundle half-hidden by an old tree stump. After one last glance towards the beer tent she ran over.

Her cloak was there, but not Mark's. All at once the difficulties of her position rushed over her. Mark had left her. That did not admit of a doubt. What should she do? There were, of course, a number of villagers she recognized, but she was reluctant to ask for their help. It would be all round the village and doubtless would reach Aunt Helena's ears sooner or later – her escapades usually did. Lysander had said he would be here, but where was he?

She put the cloak on and held it round her, hiding her face as much as possible. Suddenly she saw him. He was standing at the edge of the green, half in shadow and there was a girl with him. Furthermore, he had his arm around her. Arabella got up and began to walk towards them. She would tell him her opinion of him coming to the fair to protect *her* and instead picking up some village wench! At that moment the girl turned and in the moonlight Arabella caught a glimpse of golden hair.

She ran over, forgetting everything else.

'Clemency!' she cried, and flung her arms around her. Now everything would be all right.

Lysander noted the name but made no comment. For a moment Clemency patted and soothed Arabella and attempted to control her own disordered feelings, for although she had been standing with the marquess for only a few moments before Arabella came, she had been acutely aware of his physical proximity and, from the constraint in his voice, couldn't doubt that this was mutual. Arabella gave a couple of small hiccups, raised her head from Clemency's shoulder and said, 'He left me, about a quarter of an hour ago. But, Miss Stoneham, why are *you* here?'

Lysander reached in his pocket and handed his sister the note, by now rather crumpled.

'But I didn't write this!' gasped Arabella. She looked carefully at it and added, 'But I think I know who did.'

'Yes?' said Lysander. He glanced at Clemency, who was looking stunned.

'Miss Baverstock,' said Arabella promptly. 'Look, Miss Stoneham, don't you remember, we had only a little of that good writing paper. We put some in Cousin Maria's room and the rest in Miss Baverstock's.'

Clemency said nothing. Her first reaction was one of relief, but then she thought, painfully, if the marquess *loved* Miss Baverstock, how would he take this?

'Is this true, Miss Stoneham?'

'Yes, my lord.'

Lysander gave a short laugh. 'Well, I cannot suspect Cousin Maria,' he said, 'but I didn't think....' His eye was scanning the crowd. He raised a hand and beckoned. To Arabella's amazement Josh Baldock came over. Lysander surveyed him; he was sober, so he judged.

'How did you come, this evening?' he asked.

'Pony and trap, sir. M'dad lent it.'

'I want you to take Lady Arabella home. Don't drive up to the house. Drop her at the gatehouse, understand?'

'Yes, sir.'

'But, Zander....'

'Listen, Bella. I've got to sort out Mark and you'll only be in the way. I want to know you're safely at home. Go in by the kitchen door. It's unlocked. Miss Stoneham and I shan't be long.'

'W ... what are you going to do? Miss Stoneham won't be hurt, will she?'

'It's not Miss Stoneham who'll get hurt,' said Lysander, grimly. 'Go *on*, Bella. We haven't much time. Take her, Josh.'

'I want to know all about it in the morning, mind.'

'I promise. Come along, Miss Stoneham.'

Some ten minutes after leaving Arabella, Mark was shown into a handsome room at the Crown, with dark oak beams and a fine four-poster. He was pleased to see that it looked out over the front of the inn so that he could see and be seen. Not long now, he thought. The landlady, having ascertained that he wanted nothing further, curtseyed and left. That one was up to no good, she thought. If her husband hadn't told her that his lordship knew she'd have been half-inclined to tell him to go elsewhere. This had always been a respectable house.

The moment the landlady had gone Mark flung open the leaded casement windows and sat himself on the window sill. It couldn't be better, he thought. There was plenty of noise coming up from the tap-room, so a few shrieks from upstairs would hardly be noticed. In any case, women usually protested when they really meant 'yes' and he'd no doubt that she'd be compliant enough before long. He allowed himself to drift into a highly stimulating reverie of all the things he intended to do to Miss Stoneham when she arrived.

Meanwhile Lysander and Clemency had reached the inn. They did not approach it directly, but skirted round by the stable yard.

'The room's at the front,' whispered Lysander. 'Now, do you know what to do?'

'I ... believe so.'

'Good girl. Now don't worry. Just do as I say and everything will be all right.'

The marquess was looking unusually grim and Clemency had not the courage to protest further. They went in the side door and the marquess beckoned to Barlow.

'The gentleman is upstairs, sir. Arrived about ten minutes ago,' said the landlord, staring at Clemency, who stood as much in the shadows as she could, her hood well over her face.

'And keep your mouth shut,' said Lysander. 'I believe I have a score to settle with *Mr Richmond* and I don't want to be interrupted.'

'Begging your pardon, my lord, I don't want no trouble with the law.'

'There won't be,' said Lysander shortly. He jerked his head at the landlord. Barlow, still muttering, went off.

Mark was sitting on the window sill staring out of the open window when there was an agitated knocking at the door and, scarcely waiting for an answer, a distraught Clemency rushed in.

'Lady Arabella!' she panted. 'Where's Lady Arabella?'

'Ah, Miss Stoneham!' Mark stepped back into the room. 'What a pleasant surprise.'

'Arabella! Where is she?'

'Allow me to take your cloak.'

'Mr Baverstock! I am come for Arabella. She left me a note ...' Clemency by this time was quite breathless. 'I have run almost all the way.'

'I have no notion where Arabella is. Nor, may I add, do I care.'

'But she said she was to meet you here!' cried Clemency, looking wildly round.

Mark stepped swiftly behind her, closed the door and locked it.

'W ... what are you doing?'

'Now you have come to pay me a visit, Miss Stoneham, I don't want us to be interrupted. Come, my sweet, the time for games is over.'

'G ... games, sir?' It was one thing to discuss a plan with the marquess outside, she realized suddenly, and quite another to find that her captor had locked the door. Her heart began to beat most unpleasantly and she stared at him with wide, frightened eyes. Surely the marquess would not leave her to her fate? 'What games?' she managed to say.

'The little game you have been playing with me. I could give you a far more amusing time, Miss Stoneham, believe me. So beautiful a charmer should not languish as a mere governess. I wonder Lysander hasn't had a try himself, but he's grown such a dull dog recently, positively Methodist.'

'But Arabella ...' cried Clemency, remembering her instructions.

'Let us forget that tiresome girl. So far as I know she's still at the fair. No, my love, it was Oriana who wrote that note. Clever, don't you think?'

'M ... Miss Baverstock?' So Arabella was right! That Miss Baverstock disliked her she knew, but that she would go so far as to plan her ruin was another thing entirely. 'Surely your sister would never....'

'Oriana found you very much *de trop*, sweetheart. You were poaching on her territory.'

Clemency was powerless to stop the colour flooding into her cheeks as the implications of this speech hit her. 'Mr Baverstock,' she managed to say, 'you have got me here under false pretences and it is imperative that I go and look for Lady Arabella. Will you please unlock that door at once.'

'Come, come, Miss Stoneham,' said Mark laughing, 'less of this outraged virtue, if you please.' With one swift movement he reached out and jerked her into his arms, cutting off her scream by kissing her brutally. He slid one hand down to her buttocks and held her to him. Clemency struggled to evade his kisses. At last he raised his head and said in a silken voice which chilled Clemency to the marrow, 'If you do not try to please me a little more, Miss Stoneham, I shall have to be rough with you.'

Suddenly a noise from the window made Mark turn round. Lysander had vaulted into the room.

'Well, well,' said Mark, 'what are you after, Zander, a slice of my cherry-pie? If I'd known she was your doxy, I'd have left her. Why didn't you say? As it is, I'm afraid finder's keepers.' One hand reached up and squeezed Clemency's breast.

Clemency, with all the force at her command, slapped his face. Mark flung her to one side and at the same moment Lysander leapt forward. In falling, Clemency had hit her head against a chest of drawers and it was a moment before she could pick herself up. When she did both men were fighting. Mark had an ugly bruise down the side of his face, Lysander's jaw was swollen, both men were panting. It seemed to Clemency's terrified eyes that they were intent on murder.

She glanced round. The shadows in the room were flickering wildly and at first she could see nothing. Then she caught sight of a heavy brass candlestick and picked it up.

Suddenly Mark reached out for the bed curtain, whipped it round the marquess's face and followed it with a tremendous punch. Lysander fell heavily. Mark, with an exultant laugh bent over him to deliver the final blow and at that moment Clemency brought down the candlestick.

There was a pause and, as if in slow motion, he fell.

Lysander rose slowly, fingering his bruised jaw.

Clemency rushed forward. 'My lord! Are you all right?'

'Just,' he said ruefully. 'He was in better shape than I thought.' He looked down at Mark who showed no signs of stirring.

'I ... I haven't killed him, have I?'

'No. Just concussed.' Lysander felt Mark's pulse for a moment then straightened himself. He limped to the desk, found some paper and a wafer, wrote a brief note and sealed it. He propped the note up on the desk and signalled to Clemency that they leave. Clemency unlocked the door.

'You haven't done anything foolish, my lord, like calling him out?'

'No,' said the marquess, shortly. 'I've told him to expect his sister in the morning.'

'I ... I'm sorry, my lord. If you were fond of her.'

'Yes, I was fond of her.' Lysander said no more and Clemency's heart sank.

They went downstairs. Barlow came out of the tap-room.

'My lord!'

'It's nothing, Barlow.'

'Let me get you some brandy, my lord.' He disappeared. Lysander leant wearily against the wall and Clemency looked at him with concern. When the landlord reappeared it was with two glasses. 'I daresay you could do with some too, miss.'

Clemency looked at Lysander.

'Drink it,' he said. 'It's only a small glass and we've got some way to go.'

By common consent they avoided the road through the village and took to the fields. At first Lysander seemed to show no ill effects, but gradually he slowed down.

'You'd better put your arm over my shoulders, my lord,' said Clemency. She was feeling suddenly light-hearted, almost happy. Whether it was the brandy, or being alone with the man she loved in the moonlight she didn't know, but when Lysander put his arm over her shoulders she put her own round his waist and tried not to feel as though she hadn't a care in the world.

Lysander was feeling slightly sick and dizzy, compounded by the sudden chill of the night air and the after effects of the fight and the brandy. Perhaps it was this that made him drop his guard.

'You know,' he said quietly, 'I love every inch of Candover. I hadn't realized until it became mine.'

'Yes,' said Clemency, 'I know.' What else could she say?

'I even thought of marrying money to save it.'

'A very sensible idea, my lord,' said Clemency, breathlessly.

'You think so?'

'Yes.'

They had now reached the patient horse who was quietly cropping grass in the moonlight. Lysander let go of Clemency and went to adjust the bridle and tighten the girths. As he did so the moon came out from behind a small cloud. Clemency was standing, her hood fallen back and her hair – she had lost her ribbon long ago – cascading over her shoulders like spun gold.

Lysander looked up and all at once everything fell into place. Immediately Clemency knew that he had recognized her. 'No,' she whispered, but it was too late.

Lysander pulled her into his arms and began kissing her desperately and hungrily, with no thought for his bruising. 'So sweet, so soft,' he murmured. 'How could I have forgotten?'

When he released her it was only to look down at her with softened face and whisper, stroking her face tenderly, 'My beautiful angel. Kiss me again.'

Clemency, her heart thudding against his, did so. She was now in a far more alarming situation than she had been with Mark, but the impropriety of it did not occur to her. All she felt was delight in being able to kiss and be kissed by the man she loved.

Suddenly Lysander swayed and would have fallen if Clemency had not held him. 'We'd better get home, my lord,' she said, striving for normality. 'You are hurt.'

For a moment more Lysander held her then he pulled himself away and said in a voice drained of all feeling, 'You are right.'

The journey home was accomplished in silence.

Nine

Clemency awoke the next morning to hear rain beating against the window. The sky was low and grey and the temperature had dropped. She sighed and closed her eyes again. There was a bruise on her head which throbbed painfully and her thoughts were tangled and alarming.

Eventually she staggered out of bed and splashed her face with cold water before hurrying to get dressed. Summer was suddenly over, it seemed, and she was glad she'd had the foresight to bring her long-sleeved grey kerseymere dress with her. The neck was edged with a vandyked ruff and the skirt with multiple flounces. Doubtless Miss Baverstock would think it very unsuitable.

Then she remembered. Hadn't the marquess said something about Miss Baverstock leaving? She pressed her hand to her aching head and tried to remember. If so, would he act on it? Then she began thinking about the rest of the evening, particularly its denouement. The cold light of morning brought no comfort. However could she have allowed that kiss? Worse, responded! However was she going to face him? It was too much to expect that his lordship forget *two* kisses!

Pressing her hands to her scarlet cheeks, Clemency sank down on the narrow bed and tried to think. Arabella, she knew, was safe, for she'd looked in on her last night. Her clothes were all over the floor, but she was deeply asleep and doubtless would not mention anything. Clemency devoutly hoped that when Molly picked up her clothes in the morning she would not suspect anything.

And the marquess? How was he going to account for the effects of the fight? A fall downstairs? And his behaviour to herself? Could he possibly love *her*? Or was it just the aftermath of the fight and the brandy? He had expressed the strongest condemnation of Mr Baverstock's advances towards her, so possibly (lowering thought) he would view his own as reprehensible. Clemency began to see that whatever his lordship decided to do, for her part she would do well to seem to have forgotten it.

If she could manage it, a calm, friendly unconsciousness was what was needed. Any show of agitation on her part would only serve to embarrass them both and raise the suspicions of the rest of the party. Clemency hoped, despondently, that she was capable of the exertion.

Thank God it was Sunday and she would be seeing Cousin Anne after church. Perhaps it *was* time she got in touch with Mr Jameson and attempted a reconciliation with her mother. At any rate, to open negotiations would not commit her and she could at least see where the land lay.

Oriana awoke somewhat later than Clemency to the same grey day, but her thoughts were positively sparkling. She'd got rid of Miss Goody-two-shoes and although she was condemned to stay in this ramshackle house a while longer, at least she had the pleasant prospect of a pretty little mare for the winter's hunting to look forward to. It would be amusing to see the horror-struck faces at breakfast when Miss Stoneham's 'flight' became known. Miss Fabian's moral indignation would be particularly diverting.

There was a knock at the door and Eliza came in with her early morning chocolate. 'Not a nice day, Miss Oriana.' She opened the curtains, set a couple of pillows behind her mistress's head and offered her a shawl.

When Oriana was settled Eliza gave her a tray on which was her chocolate in a covered bowl, and a letter.

'You may go,' she said curtly to Eliza. 'I'll ring when I want you.'

Eliza curtseyed and left.

Oriana tore open the letter, scanned it briefly and blanched. The letter was short and to the point.

Dear Miss Baverstock, I'm sure you know why I can no longer offer you hospitality at Candover. Your brother is at the Crown with instructions to await your arrival. I have ordered your coachman to bring your travelling carriage round at eleven o'clock. I shall make your excuses to my aunt and the Fabians. Yours etc. Storrington.

Oriana pushed the chocolate to one side so impatiently that it spilt on to the sheets. She ignored it. Whatever had gone wrong? How did Lysander come to know that Mark was at the Crown and what gave him the clue as to her own involvement? For a moment she toyed with the thought of accosting him with injured innocence, but then rejected it. What was the point? It wasn't as if she *wanted* to stay.

Had Miss Stoneham not turned up after all? But she had seen her creep downstairs, cloak over her arm. It would be like Miss Prunes and Prisms to turn tail at the last minute. Oriana reached out for the bellpull and jerked it so hard that the whole thing came away in her hands.

Eliza, who'd been downstairs flirting with Mark's valet, came running. The moment she entered the room she saw that her mistress was in a filthy temper. She looked at the bellpull which had come away and pulled out the fittings with it.

'This damned hovel!' cried Oriana. 'I'm not staying here another day. Eliza, I want you to pack.'

'But ... but....'

'Do as I bid,' snapped Oriana. She swung her feet out of bed, reached for her slippers, went to the desk and grabbed a sheet of paper. Behind her Eliza took a swift glance at the discarded letter on the bed and her eyes widened.

My lord, wrote Oriana, *I have the greatest pleasure in obeying your behest. In my view, this house isn't fit for pigs to live in and I wish you joy of your insipid little prude. O. Baverstock.*

She folded, sealed and addressed it. 'See that that's delivered to his lordship,' she said.

She felt better. They would be off by mid-morning; that

evening they'd be home. So what if the marquess hadn't fulfilled her expectations, there were others. She was handsome, well dowered, and there were plenty more fish in the sea. She and Mark would concoct some story for their father and nobody, but nobody, would ever know how she had been humiliated.

Clemency was just about to leave her room and go down to the breakfast-room, when there was a knock at her door and Molly entered.

'Excuse me, miss, a note from his lordship.' She gave a quick glance at Clemency's heightened colour and drew her own, perfectly correct, conclusions. Poor thing, she thought, if she's in love with his lordship; for they all knew he had to sell Candover Court and what then? He certainly couldn't marry a penniless governess and Molly doubted whether Miss Stoneham would consider anything else.

Downstairs was already buzzing with gossip that the Baverstocks had been turned out. Not that that stuck-up Eliza did more than hint, but they all knew that guests didn't suddenly pack up and go for no good reason. Good riddance, Molly thought. It suddenly occurred to her that Miss Stoneham might like to know; it was common knowledge downstairs that Miss Baverstock had had her claws into her.

'I understand that Miss Baverstock will be leaving today, miss,' she said.

Clemency was turning the note over and over in her hands, but she looked up at this. 'Oh?'

'Nobody's saying nothing, but that Eliza is rushing round demanding Miss Baverstock's trunk and their coach has been ordered for eleven.'

The two girls exchanged a look, then Clemency said, 'I can't say I'm sorry. You'll not mention that, I know.'

'All of us downstairs agree with you, miss,' said Molly hearteningly. She bobbed a curtsey and left. Molly liked a bit of drama in her life and in the last few weeks there hadn't been a dull moment.

Clemency sat down on the bed and with trembling fingers opened the note. It was quite short.

Dear Miss Stoneham, I trust that you are recovered from your exertions last night. Miss Baverstock will be leaving to join her brother this morning. I shall tell my aunt that you, very properly, brought me the note purporting to be from Arabella. I then went alone to the fair and dealt with Mr Baverstock. There will thus be no need for either you or Arabella to be involved at all. I would be grateful if you would show this to Arabella so that she understands her part. Yours etc Storrington.

Clemency sat quite still, head bowed. So this, she thought, is it. The tenderness of last night was to be erased, as though it had never been. Not one word to indicate any feeling, not even remorse. A note that anybody might read. It was all to be forgotten.

She sat up, blew her nose firmly, and tried to settle her thoughts. Lysander did not love her, could not. If he remembered their embrace last night at all, it was only to see it as an unfortunate result of his fight with Mr Baverstock and perhaps the Crown's brandy.

So be it. There was nothing she could do and she was certainly not going to put herself into the position of the love-lorn governess. Clemency hoped that she had more pride than that!

She put the letter firmly in her pocket and went down to see Arabella.

By the time the company was assembled in the breakfast-room practically everybody, except the young Fabians, knew the official version of last night's events, and those who knew the real version managed to play their parts so well that the surface was not disturbed.

The good breeding of all smoothed over any little awkwardnesses, such as Miss Fabian's asking if Miss Baverstock was quite well as she was not downstairs. When Lysander replied that Miss Baverstock felt that she ought to accompany her brother on his sad journey, only Miss Fabian felt any sorrow. Giles and Diana brightened up considerably, and Lord Fabian, after a sceptical glance at his host, said nothing. Lady Fabian had had a swift word with Lady Helena earlier and was able to give her husband a warning look perfected by nearly thirty years' experience. Lord Fabian, a diplomatic man, addressed himself to his kidneys and bacon.

Clemency had come downstairs with Arabella and was thus spared the ordeal of greeting the marquess alone. Her 'good-morning' was general and if she ate very little, nobody appeared to notice. She confined herself to a few commonplace remarks to Lord Fabian and Diana who were sitting on either side of her and was grateful for their undemanding company.

She had taken care to avoid looking at the marquess and tried not to listen for the sound of his voice. But, of course, it was the only one she heard and did she, or did she not, hear constraint in it? There was one moment only when she ventured to look at him, when he had risen to help himself from the sideboard. There was a bruise round his jaw and he looked pale. She noticed that he, too, ate very little, but perhaps that could be accounted for by his injuries. He excused himself from church and said that he thought he should spend the morning quietly at home.

Nobody demurred and it was a depleted party that set off for church.

Clemency heard very little of the sermon or indeed of the rest of the service, she sat, stood and knelt with the rest of the congregation and simply allowed her thoughts to drift. Her most important concern was what she should say to Cousin Anne. Her cousin would be expecting her to dictate an answer to Mr Jameson's notice in the *Morning Post*, but was that now obsolete? What should she do for the best? If she told Cousin Anne even an expurgated version of last night's events, what would she say? More importantly, what would she *do*? Would she feel obliged to write to Mr Jameson herself, feeling that her young cousin was in moral danger?

Clemency, by the second hymn, had to admit that she well might. Finally, (halfway through the sermon) she realized that Cousin Anne, like Lady Helena, would have to be told the official version and that she, Clemency, could not have the comfort of confiding in her.

'My dear Clemency,' cried Mrs Stoneham when they were sitting in the little dining-parlour, 'you look pale. Have you not been well?'

Clemency told her prepared story briefly and ended, 'As you may well imagine, I found it difficult to sleep and I stupidly knocked my head against the chest of drawers when I was taking off my stockings. I'm a little tired, that is all.'

Bessy, who had come in with the lunch, looked sceptical, but said nothing. From what she'd heard from old Mrs Carter in the village, Lady Arabella *had* been at the fair last night and she'd dropped a hint that his lordship had been there with an unknown female. Mrs Carter had paused hopefully, and on Bessy's not responding, had said, 'Doubtless his lordship knows best and I'm not one to chat about my betters.'

If his lordship had gone with Miss Clemency to the fair it would be quite a Romance, thought Bessy. But Clemency did not look like one who'd spent her evening wrapped in the arms of her lover.

'What a shocking thing that Miss Baverstock should try to embroil *you*, Clemency,' said Mrs Stoneham comfortably, now that she knew that everything was all right. 'Of course, you always had your doubts about Mr Baverstock, but that his sister, a lady, should.... Have another slice of lamb, my dear. You've hardly eaten anything.'

It wasn't until later, in the parlour, that Mrs Stoneham said, 'Before we discuss the reply to Mr Jameson's notice, I think you should know that I had a letter from Mr Jameson myself on Friday.'

Clemency turned a white face to her. Mrs Stoneham reached over and patted her hand. 'Now, don't take on so, Clemency. There's no need. He is not in the least threatening, but let me read you what he has to say.' She went over to her bureau and unlocked a little drawer. 'Ah, yes, here we are. The usual compliments, my great kindness in talking to him, hopes I wasn't inconvenienced etc.

It is doubly unfortunate that Miss Hastings is missing as I have some news that will materially affect her. Her mother has announced that she intends to accept the hand in marriage of Mr John Butler. At this auspicious time I feel sure that a proper letter of submission by her daughter would be most favourably received. Mrs Hastings' maternal feelings have been gravely hurt, but she is concerned only for her daughter's welfare.

Although Mr Butler has most generously offered Miss Hastings a home, I have taken it on myself to suggest that if a suitable respectable alternative can be found then a generous remuneration might be made to the friend or relative who agrees to shelter Miss Hastings during her maidenhood. Mrs Hastings has graciously approved.

If, therefore, dear Madam, you should hear aught of Miss Hastings, I am sure you will let her know the above and advise her accordingly.

'The rest is full of empty professions.'

Clemency sat stunned. 'Mama – marry!' was all she managed to say.

Mrs Stoneham rose and rang the bell. 'Bessy, some tea.' She handed Clemency the letter and quietly took up some sewing.

Clemency's first reaction was one of outrage. How *could* she? How could she even consider marrying again after her father? Papa who was so kind and affectionate to be supplanted? And by Mr Butler? Clemency had nothing against Mr Butler, he was well respected in the City and he had always been kind to herself, but he was not her father!

Mrs Stoneham had drunk her cup of tea and done two neat darns before she saw that Clemency had recovered somewhat. 'Do you know anything of this Mr Butler?' she asked. 'Mr Jameson obviously approves.'

'He's jolly and vulgar and wears stays so tight that he looks like a pouter pigeon. He dyes his whiskers.'

'Good Heavens!' cried Mrs Stoneham faintly.

'He's a fifty-year-old dandy. Apart from that I know no harm of him.' She sighed. 'I must be fair and say that he has always been kind to me.'

'You do not like it.'

'After Papa ...' began Clemency and choked.

'Now, Clemency, be sensible, my dear. Your mother is not the sort of woman to remain a widow. She is still young (though you may not think so!) attractive and wealthy. Naturally she will remarry and all the better if she marries a man of sense who is not just after her money, even if he does sport the dandy in his attire. After all, my dear, your mother is somewhat that way inclined herself.'

'I suppose so,' said Clemency despondently.

'When you have had time to reflect you'll see that it is so. And it's a godsend for *you*, Clemency. You can make your own terms.' She glanced out of the window. 'It's quite cleared up. Why don't you go over to Mrs Lamb's with some flowers I promised her for the church? Bessy should have the basket ready and a little fresh air will do you good. Don't let her keep you talking. She's very good-natured but somewhat inquisitive.'

She was pleased to see some colour in Clemency's cheeks on her return from the vicarage. She appeared to have recovered the tone of her mind and she was quite cheerful as she brought up the subject again. Yes, she could see that it was a good idea for her mother to remarry and now would be a good time to reopen negotiations. Did Cousin Anne have anything in mind?

'I wonder whether it might be best to allow me to negotiate on your behalf?' suggested Mrs Stoneham. Amelia Hastings was a hysterical woman, she thought, and given to emotional blackmail. It would be much easier to ensure a proper settlement for Clemency through a third party. 'I could say that you had communicated with me but that I was not at liberty to disclose your whereabouts. I have been considering your young friends, the Ramsgate girls. You know, my dear, this is *not* a suitable place for you. For a start, being so near Candover Court could prove awkward if you are suddenly to metamorphose into the rich Miss Hastings! I think you need young company and the opportunity for a proper social life.

'Would Mrs Ramsgate have you, do you think?'

'I imagine so,' said Clemency, trying to infuse a little enthusiasm into her voice.

On her return from Abbots Candover Clemency found that Lady Helena wished to see her.

'She is in her boudoir, Miss Stoneham,' said Timson, who gave her the message. 'She asked to see you as soon as you came in.'

'I'll go up at once,' said Clemency, her heart pounding. She couldn't help wondering whether, in spite of the marquess's best endeavours, somebody had caught sight of her at the fair and told Lady Helena. What should she do? Deny it? Refer her to the marquess?

In the event, neither option was necessary. Lady Helena merely wished to thank her for her good sense in the matter.

'Heaven knows what would have happened if Arabella had gone!' exclaimed Lady Helena. 'And although I cannot condone Storrington's method of dealing with Mr Baverstock, at least that tiresome couple have now gone and all's well that ends well.'

Clemency couldn't help reflecting that it had been herself who had dealt Mr Baverstock the *coup de grâce*. But she merely murmured that she was happy to have been of service.

'I should like to take this opportunity of saying, my dear Miss Stoneham, that I consider you to have shown great forebearance in your dealings with the Baverstocks. A very ill-bred pair in my opinion. I cannot imagine what Storrington ever saw in them.'

'I'm sure you are right, ma'am,' said Clemency demurely.

Her ladyship laughed and dismissed her.

Though Clemency rejoiced that the Baverstocks were gone, nevertheless, she couldn't help but realize that life had not gone back to the ease she had felt before their arrival. The marquess was now busier than ever and when he did appear Clemency noticed, with pain, that there was a coolness between them. He was perfectly polite, but the warmth and even the occasional sparring she had cherished was now wanting. He spoke more to Adela than herself.

She read and reread his letter as if by so doing she might find some words of comfort for her sore heart. But there was nothing. The letter remained, like his lordship, courteous and remote. The man who had put his arm around her, called her beautiful, kissed her, had vanished.

There was nothing she could do.

She tried hard to keep up a façade of normal behaviour; plan interesting lessons for the girls, help Lady Helena brush Millie, discuss the day's meals with Mrs Marlow, but it was uphill work. The pleasure had gone out of it and Clemency found herself feeling very down and disinclined to eat.

On Wednesday morning the marquess addressed her for the first time since the night of the fair.

'I am expecting Thornhill, my lawyer,' he said. 'Would you arrange with Mrs Marlow about a room for him, Miss Stoneham?'

'Certainly, my lord.'

And that was all.

'Mr Thornhill?' said Mrs Marlow. 'We'd best put him in Mr Baverstock's room, miss. A very nice, well-spoken gentleman and not one to forget the servants.' She spoke with some bitterness for Mr and Miss Baverstock had omitted any vails at all for the servants, which had caused much resentment downstairs.

'Is he here often?' asked Clemency.

'Every month or so, miss, since Lord Alexander died.'

'I see.'

Clemency wondered whether he knew of Lysander's abortive attempt to find a wife, and then dismissed it. He would certainly not bother to look twice at the governess.

The following morning Lysander and Mr Thornhill sat in the estate room. Mr Thornhill noted, with concern, that his noble employer looked even more haggard than when he had last seen him, and, not for the first time, cursed the 3rd Marquess who had been concerned only to squeeze every penny out of the estate without putting anything back, and who had allowed his heir to grow up selfish and vicious with no thought for anything save his own pleasure. What Lord Alexander had cost the estate, first and last, he hardly dared to think. If it had not been for him the estate, though run down, would have at least been solvent.

'I have had several offers for Candover, my lord,' he said, opening his leather case, 'and I think these two look the most promising. A Mr Cromer and a Mr Barnstaple.'

Lysander sighed and held out his hand for the letters. 'I've never heard of either of these gentlemen,' he said.

'No, my lord. Both new money, I gather. Mr Cromer is something in the Weardale coalfield and Mr Barnstaple is in wool.'

'Mr Cromer's offer is slightly better, I see.'

'Yes, my lord. Only I understand that he's unwilling to keep on any of the servants and I knew that that was a consideration for you.'

'Mr Barnstaple, on the other hand, is willing to take them on. What sort of man is he? Have you met him?'

'No, my lord. I've only met his man of business. Something of a rough diamond, I think. But his agent says that his benevolence is praised by his workforce.'

'Naturally,' said Lysander, dryly.

Mr Thornhill permitted himself a slight smile. 'Would you like me to follow up these two gentlemen, my lord?'

Lysander gazed out of the window for a moment before replying. The mellow stone of the gatehouse glowed golden in the morning sun. A few early autumn leaves scurried across the lawn. 'Yes please, Thornhill. Doubtless they will wish to come here to see the place. And I should certainly like a look at them.'

It wasn't until near the end of the conversation that Lysander said idly, 'By the by, Thornhill. Do you remember Miss Hastings-Whinborough?'

'Yes, my lord.'

'Do you recall her Christian name, by any chance?'

'No, my lord. I don't believe I ever heard it. One does not normally bandy about a young lady's first name.'

'No, of course not,' said Lysander in a dampened tone.

'Would you like me to find out?'

'No, no. It was just a passing thought.'

Mr Thornhill made a mental note but said nothing. The conversation turned back to financial matters. It was agreed that Mr Thornhill authorize Mr Cromer's and Mr Barnstaple's respective agents to come down and look over Candover.

'I'm afraid I don't have any good news about the family jewels, my lord.'

'Good God, are there any? I thought they'd been sold long ago.'

'There was a small box in Drummond's bank vault, but it contained nothing of any value except for Lady Storrington's pearls. The rest are mere copies.'

'Very likely,' said Lysander. 'I remember Mama saying something of the sort when I admired her tiara one evening.'

'However, she did manage to save her pearls, perhaps because she brought them with her on her marriage.'

'How much are they worth?'

'A hundred or so, my lord.'

'Let Lady Arabella have them. A hundred pounds is not going to make that much difference one way or the other and it is right that she should have her mother's jewellery.'

'Very well, my lord.'

Mr Thornhill stayed a couple of days, going over the ledgers with the marquess and Frome and approving their work. There were only a couple of small points outstanding, he said at last, beginning to tidy up his papers: the Hughetts' tenancy agreement, for example, but he rather thought he had the relevant papers somewhere in his office. If his lordship would excuse him he had promised to see Lady Helena at four o'clock.

Though several people had remarked on the marquess's haggard looks, Clemency's wan face and loss of appetite had not gone unnoticed, by Arabella at least.

Arabella had had several conversations with Clemency about the night of the fair. 'Zander won't talk about it,' she complained. 'He says I must try to forget the whole thing! Now, Miss Stoneham, that's quite impossible, don't you think?'

'Perhaps he's concerned lest you blurt it out in company,' suggested Clemency, though she couldn't help thinking that all the marquess wanted was to pretend it had never happened.

'I don't think it's at all good for my mental equilibrium not to talk about it,' announced Arabella, and when Clemency laughed, added, 'Look at Zander, he looks *dreadful*. Has he said anything to you?'

'No.' Clemency felt her colour rise.

'Well, there you are.' She looked carefully at Clemency who'd turned her head away and said, 'You don't look well either. Mr Baverstock didn't hurt you, did he?'

'No!' But Lysander did, she thought painfully.

'I don't believe you. Why, you are as white as a sheet.'

'Arabella! You *must* guard your tongue. I was not – er – assaulted by Mr Baverstock, if that's what you meant. I had a few unpleasant moments, that is all.'

'But something happened, didn't it?' she persisted. 'Why, Zander positively avoids you now. I shall tell him how upset you are.'

Clemency spun round at that. 'Arabella, if you *ever* mention one single word to the marquess, I shall leave,' she said, fiercely. 'I am serious, mind. If there are moments during that evening that I find painful, I prefer to keep them to myself. You have absolutely no right to intrude on my privacy.'

Arabella was so taken aback by this attack that she could say nothing. Never had anybody, and certainly not a governess, spoken to her in such a way. A month or so ago she would have made her resentment plain, but she had done a lot of growing-up since then. Instead, she kissed Clemency's pale cheek and said, 'I'm sorry. Truly, I did not mean to offend you.'

Afterwards, in her bedroom, Arabella thought about the incident. She remembered seeing Lysander and Clemency at the edge of the green, his arm around her. For a moment, before they saw her, they looked like a couple. Together. The thought suddenly struck her that they were in love.

Had they had a quarrel? Arabella had noticed (though Clemency had not) that Lysander sometimes watched her when nobody was looking. He was not at ease, certainly, for somehow, whenever he and Miss Stoneham were in the same room, Lysander was sure either to keep his distance or else to find an excuse to leave.

It said a lot for Arabella's new-found discretion that she said nothing of this, not even to Diana, but continued her silent observation of them both.

Mr Thornhill left on Saturday morning and Clemency had a peaceful afternoon with her cousin on Sunday. Mrs Stoneham had written to Mr Jameson, but so far, there had been no reply, certainly no irate Mrs Hastings had appeared.

'I would guess that your mama is taken up with preparations for her wedding,' said Mrs Stoneham soothingly. Privately she thought it extremely unlikely that Amelia Hastings would want a beautiful young daughter to share any of her limelight. 'I daresay we shall hear when Mr Jameson has had time to consult with the Ramsgates.'

And there the matter rested.

It wasn't until the middle of the following week that Lysander had a letter from Mr Thornhill and its contents exploded Lysander's fragile peace of mind. Mr Thornhill discussed the arrangements for Mr Cromer's and Mr Barnstaple's agents to come and view the property and then added, *You may be interested to know that Miss Hastings-Whinborough's Christian name is Clemency. Unusual, though pretty, I think.*

Unaware of the storm about to burst over her head, Clemency had decided that Arabella and Diana's nature diary was now in a fit state to be admired. They spent several mornings binding the separate leaves together, with Arabella's drawings prettily mounted on one side and Diana's descriptions of the flowers and their habitat on the other. Clemency herself wrote a brief introduction saying how delighted she was with their work and commending their diligence.

They spent most of Wednesday afternoon doing the final touches and Arabella brought it into the drawing-room that evening as they were all assembling for dinner and presented it to her aunt.

The little book was passed round from hand to hand and duly admired. Lady Fabian, naturally, was interested in Diana's work and Giles thought that the calligraphy of the introduction deserved his special admiration. Lady Helena, who had no idea that Arabella *had* any special talents beyond getting into mischief, was thunderstruck.

'These are your paintings, Arabella?'

'Yes, Aunt.'

'All your own work?'

'Of course,' said Arabella impatiently. She looked across at Clemency.

'Indeed they are, ma'am. Arabella has a very real talent in that direction.'

'I am amazed,' said Lady Helena, for once taking no notice of Muffin, who was chewing her shawl. 'Storrington, you must look at your sister's work. And Diana's too, of course.'

Lysander looked at it carefully, read the introduction (with a swift penetrating glance at Clemency) and then admired the rest. 'I congratulate you both,' he said smiling. 'You must have worked really hard.'

'Miss Stoneham showed us how to set it out and did the mounts,' said Diana, determined that Clemency's merits should not go unnoticed.

'And wrote the introduction, I see,' said the marquess.

There was something in his voice that made Clemency fear something. It was as if he *knew* she wasn't Miss Stoneham, but that was ridiculous. How could he possibly know?

The marquess, who had earlier been looking at the smoothed-out letter Clemency had left her mother, had just found the last piece of the jigsaw.

He said nothing, and a few moments later Timson announced that dinner was served.

It wasn't until the following afternoon that Clemency received a summons. She was up in the schoolroom preparing some French when Timson entered.

'His lordship would like a word with you in the estate room, miss, when convenient.'

Clemency dropped her pencil. 'Of ... of course,' she said. 'W ... where is he?'

'The estate room, miss,' repeated Timson patiently.

'Thank you. I shall be with him directly.'

Timson bowed and left. Clemency rushed to the looking-glass over the mantelpiece and smoothed her hair and twitched at her collar. Why did she feel so nervous? It was well over a week since the fair and he had made his indifference perfectly clear. Could he have found out something about her? Had that detestable Miss Baverstock written more lies?

She took a deep breath and went downstairs.

The marquess was standing by the window as she came in. Clemency curtseyed. 'You wished to see me, my lord?'

'Yes.' He did not ask her to sit down. He was looking, she noticed, unnaturally grim. 'Would you look at this, please. You may recognize it.' He handed her a letter.

Clemency did not need more than one horrified glance. Without waiting for permission she sank down on the nearest chair. For a moment she could say nothing; wild thoughts rushed through her mind of denying it, throwing herself at his feet, or precipitately fleeing the house. Her hands were trembling so much that she dropped the paper. Eventually she commanded herself enough to say, 'How did you come by this?'

'Is that *all* you can say, Miss *Hastings-Whinborough*? No apologies? No regrets at having duped us all? I see not! The person who wrote that letter, who was determined that I was *A*

Monster could scarcely have the proper feeling to acknowledge her deception!'

Clemency, white with shock, could only whisper, 'I thought you were your brother.'

The marquess scarcely heard her. 'God knows why you inveigled yourself into this house. Unless, of course, you planned to make me look ridiculous.' His voice was harsh and bitter.

'No! No!'

'Yes! Yes! What lady would even *think* of doing such a thing? Only someone with a low, ill-bred mind, dead to all shame, could have perpetrated so disgraceful a trick.'

Clemency was near tears, but as his words sank in, anger took over. 'How dare you!' she cried, her voice trembling with rage. 'Even the meanest felon is allowed to defend himself! But *you*, you have damned me as guilty without even bothering to check. Yes, I admit I am Clemency Hastings, but everything else I utterly deny. When I fled to Cousin Anne I had no idea she lived anywhere near you! If I had I would have starved rather!'

'A likely story! And I suppose you had *no idea* when you got yourself a position as Arabella's governess? Do you take me for a flat?'

'I cannot see that there is any point in my continuing,' said Clemency angrily, 'since anything I say is automatically disbelieved.'

'All I can see is that you planned, deliberately, to make me look a fool,' said the marquess bitterly. 'What were you doing? Seeing whether the marquessate was worth your money-bags?'

'What!' shrieked Clemency. 'If all you think I am is a callous little money-grubber, I'm surprised you didn't leave me to Mr Baverstock's tender mercies. All *I* have done, in very difficult personal circumstances – which you appear to think irrelevant – is use another name. And for *that* I have been insulted and condemned.'

'*You* been insulted!' cried the marquess. 'What about the insults *you* heaped on my aunt and myself by your absence! Your mother in hysterics and the only note we got was *that*!' He gestured disdainfully towards the letter. Lysander had not forgotten the humiliation of that afternoon and he did not intend to let Miss Hastings forget it either. 'And what am I now to tell my aunt?' He added sarcastically, 'That Miss Hastings-Whinborough, having insulted her once, has now been laughing at her behind her back?'

'You are twisting everything,' cried Clemency. 'You do not allow me to explain, you distort my words, I cannot see that there is any point in my staying.' Tears had started to run down her cheeks as she spoke. Stifling a sob with difficulty, she turned and ran out of the room.

Lysander was left facing an empty victory. For a moment he stared at the closed door, then he sank down at his desk and buried his face in his hands.

Ten

Clemency wandered blindly round her room trying to pack. She had pulled out her travelling valise from under her bed and opened it, but she felt incapable of doing anything more. She couldn't think straight, she found. Nothing seemed to make sense. She stood there, a pair of shoes in her hand, and couldn't think what she was meant to be doing with them.

It was all over. The marquess knew now who she was and he would never forgive her, never let her explain. Why had she ever embarked on so stupid a deception? Now, there was nothing to be done but go. Lady Helena would be shocked, perhaps she, too, would feel insulted; Arabella would be upset and the respect and even affection she thought she had gained would be lost.

Unable to see further than a blank future, Clemency dropped the shoes and sank down on the bed, staring unseeing, with tears spilling down her cheeks. She didn't even hear a knock at her door.

It was Arabella: she had run up to ask if Clemency would like to come for a walk. Diana had gone off with her mama and Arabella felt like company. She stopped in horror in the doorway as she took in the opened valise, clothes draped over the chair and lastly, Clemency's forlorn figure.

'Miss Stoneham! You're not *going*?' she wailed.

Clemency looked up, tried to speak, and failed. She made a little gesture, half-resignation, half-hopelessness.

'Zander!' said Arabella without hesitation. '*I'll* talk to him!'

'No!' shrieked Clemency. 'Wait!' Arabella turned. 'You don't understand. This is serious.'

Arabella came back and sat down beside her. 'If you tell me that you've been caught with the family silver,' she said, 'I shan't believe you. Besides, I doubt whether we have any left.'

Clemency managed a smile. 'I have done nothing wrong,' she said, 'but I *have* made a grave mistake.' She mopped her eyes and blew her nose firmly. 'If you promise not to run to your brother I will tell you what has happened.' She sighed. 'You will know soon enough, anyway.'

'I promise.'

'It's rather complicated ...' began Clemency.

Arabella listened wide-eyed. Clemency's tale was matter-of-fact and astonishing enough, but it did not escape her young listener that there was a hidden emotional undercurrent to all this: Clemency couldn't bear to say Lysander's name. It was always 'he' or 'your brother'. She had been pretty sure for some time that Zander was not indifferent to Miss Stoneham – Miss Hastings – either. Arabella knew how angry he could be if he felt slighted – especially by the woman who'd fled rather than receive his addresses. He would never believe that she was innocent of any malicious intent – at least, not whilst he was in a temper.

That Clemency was desperately upset, too, was certain. It seemed to Arabella that it was Lysander's injustice in not listening to her explanation that caused her to cry so bitterly, rather than dismay over her deception being discovered. It was the loss of Lysander's *good opinion* that hurt. With praiseworthy restraint she said nothing of this: she would think about it later.

'What shall you do?' she asked.

'Do? I shall have to go,' said Clemency in a flattened tone. 'I shall pack and leave as soon as I am ready. What else is there?'

'And Aunt Helena?'

Clemency sighed. 'Your brother will tell her soon enough.'

'I don't see why *your* side shouldn't be heard,' cried Arabella indignantly. 'I can see that what you did was wrong, but I'm also sure that my aunt made it very difficult for you to refuse to come here. I know what she can be like when she gets the bit between her teeth! Please, dear Miss Stoneham – dear Clemency – let *me* tell Aunt Helena your side. My aunt is fond of you: I'm sure she'll listen.'

'Very well,' said Clemency listlessly. If Lysander thought her scheming and malicious then nothing else seemed to matter. Let Arabella do her best: it could hardly be worse than it was now.

'Will it not be awkward for you, though, to go back to living with your cousin, so close to here, I mean?' asked Arabella next.

Clemency explained about the Ramsgates. 'In any event I can hardly remain in Abbots Candover, as you say. It would not be fair on Cousin Anne.'

'You will let me know your direction,' said Arabella anxiously, 'when you know where you'll be.'

'You will hardly be allowed to write to me!'

'Maybe not,' conceded Arabella. 'But I shall be in London next year and I could come and visit you, I am sure.'

Clemency promised. She knew it was wrong but the prospect of being able to hear about Lysander, even at second hand, would not be denied. Perhaps, she thought hopelessly, by next year this awful sensation of being amputated from part of herself would be dulled.

'Let me help you pack,' said Arabella.

Meanwhile, Lysander was telling an astounded Lady Helena his version of events. They were in the estate room, Lady Helena sitting in the leather armchair, her nephew pacing angrily up and down.

Once the first shock was over, however, Lady Helena was not inclined to accept the marquess's bitter denunciation of Miss Hastings' behaviour.

'Nonsense, Storrington,' she said firmly. 'There has never been the smallest hint of her laughing behind our backs. Indeed, if anybody should be laughing it is surely ourselves, having entrapped an heiress into so menial a position! Have you thought of that? Being Arabella's governess is no sinecure, you know!'

Lysander flung off her words with an angry gesture and resumed his pacing. 'She *said* she thought, when she wrote that letter, that I was Alexander!' he said scornfully.

'That is very possible,' conceded his aunt.

'What! You believe her? I suppose you think her coming here has got nothing to do with her having the temerity, upstart that she is, to insult the Candovers?'

'Storrington! Calm down!' commanded Lady Helena. 'This whole business is very unfortunate and your losing your temper will not improve matters. I should like to hear Miss Hastings' side of the story.' She put up her hand. 'She has one, you know. And I daresay the truth is somewhere in the middle.

'In any event, she cannot stay here and we must account for her sudden departure. Much though I like the Fabians, I think we should try and keep this to ourselves. They will be leaving soon, anyway. Giles's ordination, you know.'

'Why should we protect Miss Hastings' reputation?' snapped the marquess. 'She has taken precious little care of ours.'

'Do you really want your matrimonial affairs to become public property?' demanded his aunt. Sometimes she thought she was the only person in the family with any common sense at all! Lysander could be too tiresome sometimes, especially where his precious honour was concerned. First it was her brother, then Alexander and now Lysander! Lady Helena felt that she had soothed the male ego long enough and once this ridiculous affair was settled and Arabella safely with the Fabians then she would retire to Bath with her dogs, who were more congenial company and certainly didn't get themselves into idiotic emotional complications.

'She has been called away suddenly by her mother's illness, I think that will fit the bill,' she continued. 'Naturally, we have let her go. I shall express my sincere regret and so will you.'

The marquess had sat down heavily and did not appear to be listening. He was staring down at Clemency's letter. 'Do you really think she thought I was Alexander?' he asked.

Lady Helena saw that he had come out of his fury. 'I leave that to your knowledge of her,' she said calmly. 'And I shall speak to Arabella myself.'

Some fifteen minutes later Arabella was seated with her aunt in Lady Helena's boudoir. It was a room almost entirely devoted to dogs. Millie had had her puppies there and at least eight of the smaller dogs slept on carefully laid out cushions on various chairs. It was a measure of the seriousness of the occasion that Lady Helena had unceremoniously turfed Muffin off her favourite chair and sat on it herself.

She was astonished to learn that her niece already knew of Miss Hastings' deception, but as Arabella, wisely, told her story simply, she listened without comment. When Arabella had finished she said, 'I am pleased to hear Miss Hastings' side of things. It is much as I thought. Storrington has got on his high horse for no reason, so far as I can see. The girl was foolish, of course, to run away in that silly fashion, but since then her conduct has been exemplary.' She certainly had had enough to put up with from the Baverstocks, she thought.

Arabella took a deep breath. 'Now we know all about her,' she said, 'don't you think she'd make Zander a good wife?'

Lady Helena raised her lorgnette to survey her niece through it. 'Are you mad, Arabella? Why, Storrington would never hear of it after what has passed.'

It was *Lysander*'s disapproval she mentioned, Arabella noted, not her own. Encouraged, she added, 'Zander is not indifferent to her, though. Cousin Maria was convinced he had a *tendre* for her. Diana told me. It would explain his blind rage.'

Lady Helena looked at her niece carefully. 'And Miss Hastings?' she said at last.

'I am not in her confidence, Aunt Helena, but I think she feels the same. She's only been picking at her food, too, this last week or so. Surely you must have noticed? She's sorry about her deception, of course, but it's *Zander* misjudging her that has so upset her.'

Lady Helena shut her lorgnette with a snap. 'This puts an entirely different complexion on things!' she stated firmly. 'And we haven't much time if we are to sort things out before the place is sold. Do you know Miss Hastings' direction?'

A week later Clemency was in London. She had arrived at Mrs Stoneham's almost at the same time as a letter from Mr Jameson enclosing an invitation from Mrs Ramsgate and a draft for ten pounds for the journey. It seemed that he had lost no time on receiving Mrs Stoneham's letter. The truth was that Mrs Hastings was finding her daughter's continued absence an embarrassment and was anxious for her return. Now she was to become Mrs John Butler, Clemency's presence was no longer an irritant. The threat of Clemency staying with Aunt Whinborough was quietly dropped and she gave her gracious permission for her daughter to stay with the Ramsgates. Mr Jameson was to manage it discreetly – Mrs Hastings' own behaviour was, naturally, to be all sweetness and light – and Clemency would receive her mother's welcome.

Hard on the heels of Mr Jameson's letter came a note from Mrs Hastings herself, full of empty profusions, sending her dearest love to Anne for her care of her treasure, and an ecstatic scribbled note from Mary and Eleanor Ramsgate. *What fun we shall have!* wrote Mary. *Nell and I have vowed not to be jealous if you steal all our beaux. You are to have the top front bedroom and Mama has bought the prettiest chintz for the bed-curtains.*

Clemency looked at the notes. They seemed to belong to another world entirely and have nothing to do with herself. All she could feel was the ache of a bruised heart.

'I am delighted that everything is so happily settled,' declared Mrs Stoneham that evening as Bessy brushed her hair. 'It was becoming such a worry to me.'

Bessy pursed her lips. *She* wasn't pleased with the way things had turned out, not by a long chalk! Miss Clemency was a beautiful girl with lovely manners and rich too. She should have been swept off by the marquess, not arranging to go home by mail coach! Bessy had been looking forward to a romance with Miss Clemency going up the aisle of the little village church wearing a wedding dress and veil all of lace, and herself enjoying a good weep in the back pew. So far as she could see, this marquess needed his head examining! (Bessy would have been pleased to know that Lady Helena was in complete agreement with this last sentiment.)

Clemency took the mail coach from Aylesbury and arrived in London that evening. She was greeted rapturously by Mary and Eleanor Ramsgate.

'Famous!' cried Eleanor, kissing Clemency. 'We've been looking for you this half-hour at least. Come upstairs, Clemmie. You're in the pink room, you know. Your mother sent over *trunks*-full of your clothes, didn't she, Mary?'

'Quiet, Nell,' said Mary, kissing Clemency in her turn. 'The poor child's looking quite bewildered.' She turned to the butler who had opened the door. 'Dawlish, some tea for Miss Hastings, please. We'll have it up in her sitting-room. Come upstairs, Clemmie.'

Clemency went through the evening in a daze. It was strange to see her old clothes, to wear her hyacinth-blue silk with the tiny rosettes embroidered with seed pearls that evening, to carry a frosted fan and have her hair properly dressed by Mrs

Ramsgate's maid, instead of wearing her black dress and doing her hair herself in the speckled mirror in that little attic room. It was odd to be treated with deference by the servants, to take Mr Ramsgate's arm as chief guest into the dining-room and sit on his right.

The sense of unreality grew. She and Cousin Anne had decided that it would be best to avoid all reference to her position in Candover Court. Mary and Eleanor, though dear girls, were happily indiscreet and would doubtless think it a very good joke if they knew, but Mrs Stoneham felt that silence was the only safe option and Clemency agreed with her.

'You have been staying with me in Abbots Candover,' said Mrs Stoneham firmly that last evening. 'Nobody will question that.' What she did not know and Clemency had forgotten was that it was the Ramsgate girls who had looked up the Marquess of Storrington in the peerage and for whom 'Abbots Candover' might not be so unknown a name.

So when Clemency said that she had spent a month or so with dear Cousin Anne in the little village of Abbots Candover she was dismayed to see Mary shoot Eleanor a significant look. Neither girl was willing to say too much in front of Mama and Papa, but both promised themselves that they would get it out of Clemency later. However, they were foiled for that evening when Clemency excused herself early and went to bed soon after the tea tray had been brought in.

'Certainly, my dear,' said Mrs Ramsgate. 'All that horrid travelling! You look quite fagged out. Mary! Eleanor! Sit down! You've been chattering like a couple of starlings and I'm sure Clemency needs a rest from you both.'

Clemency smiled at her gratefully and left the room. But it was long before she got to sleep. She sat up in bed, her knees tucked up under her chin, staring at the fire. It was warm and cosy. The room had thick curtains at the windows and there were pretty rose-coloured chintz bed-curtains against any stray draughts. The carpet was warm under her feet. But all Clemency could see was her chilly attic bedroom with its narrow bed and plain coverlet where she had left behind her dreams.

The Fabians left Candover Court a few days after Clemency

amid many professions of thanks and regard. They were returning to Gloucestershire for Giles's ordination and to be with him when he took up his curacy in his god-father's parish and to hear his first sermon. At least, Adela was anxious about the sermon, Lady Fabian had the more prosaic wish to see that the respectable widow with whom her son was to lodge gave him plenty of good, wholesome food and to check that the sheets were not damp.

In the New Year Lady Fabian and her daughters would come up to London to organize Diana's wardrobe for her come-out and Arabella was invited to join them then.

Diana and Arabella hugged each other warmly and promised to write. 'You don't know how pleased I am that we are to come out together,' Diana cried. 'You won't forget me now, will you?'

'Of course not!'

Adela, watching them, sniffed. She was feeling somewhat hard-done-by. Miss Baverstock had left without asking for a correspondence and all she'd managed to do whilst at Candover was to distribute some tracts to the villagers – who had not been properly grateful for her efforts. She would be glad to go. Giles, for his part, had been very upset when Clemency had disappeared so suddenly. He had considered regarding her as a Snare and Temptation and foreswearing women for ever as a result. There were certain undoubted attractions in this rôle, but as his god-father had a number of pretty daughters he decided, sensibly, that he would regard Miss Stoneham as an Inspiration instead.

The house seemed very quiet when they'd gone; all three in the drawing-room that evening felt it. Arabella, watching her brother, noticed that he often looked at the chair where Clemency used to sit. He looked more haggard than ever, though he did his best to keep the conversation going.

Lady Helena, too, was withdrawn. In vain did Pongo lick her face or the Pekes yap for attention. Arabella had just begun to wonder how she was going to endure this until the New Year when Lady Helena snapped out of her reverie and said, 'Storrington, I think that we should all go up to Town.'

Lysander looked up, his eyes narrowed. 'Why?' he asked bluntly.

'We need it. Now the Fabians are gone things seem very flat. I have no wish to be here while these Cromers and Barnstaples poke their noses into everything and neither, I am sure, does Arabella.'

Arabella had perked up at this. Her aunt had something in mind, she was sure. 'Oh, do let's,' she cried. 'I should like to get some more water-colours and perhaps see a gallery.'

Lady Helena looked at her approvingly. Arabella had told her that she now had Miss Hastings' address from Mrs Stoneham. They might be able to do something if they were all in London and water-colours was an unexceptional excuse.

'That's settled then,' she said firmly before Lysander could raise any objections. 'We'll send Timson and one of the maids up to Town tomorrow to get things ready and we will go up on Friday.'

Lysander gave her a searching look but said nothing. He didn't entirely believe this tale of Arabella's water-colours, though it seemed plausible enough, and his aunt never set foot in London if she could avoid it, but he was feeling too depressed to argue.

The marquess, in fact, was suffering all the agonies of knowing that he had lost the girl he had come to love entirely through his own unguarded ill-temper. His moment of revelation had come, not during that second kiss, but earlier when he had taken Clemency's hand and they had waded up the stream together to look at the kingfisher.

He had endeavoured to stifle his feelings. Not for the world would he cause Clemency a moment's uneasiness, and it was impossible that he could ask her to be his wife when shortly he would not even have a home to offer her. Then, feelings of jealousy and mistrust would intrude. His reason told him that she was innocent of any encouragement towards Mark but his emotions, pricked on by Oriana, would not let him rest.

The thought of Mark enjoying those kisses and caresses that he longed for himself nearly drove him mad. He couldn't help seeing that Mark was so much more eligible. All Lysander could do was to push every tender wish down and offer Clemency the only courtesy he could: that of being a scrupulously correct employer. He had not enjoyed the experience.

When Thornhill's letter had finally revealed the truth to him his first reaction was wild, unreasoning anger. All he could see in Clemency's actions was a deliberate humiliation of him. It was as if she *must* know of his feelings for her and was mocking him for his pretensions. How could he now offer his hand in marriage to a woman he had insulted and traduced? If he could not, in honour, offer for her when he thought she was poor, still less could he do so now he knew she was rich. He would look like the worst sort of fortune-hunter. Whatever he might have said to the contrary in his rage, Lysander did not believe Clemency to be overly impressed by a mere title and what else had he to offer?

How could she possibly believe in his love after what he had hurled at her? No, he must resign himself to her loss and the bustle of Town would probably do as well as anywhere else. Better, in fact, for Candover Court was now so bound up with memories of her – carrying piles of linen upstairs, sitting on the window seat with Arabella – that everywhere he went held painful reminders of her loss. London, at least, was more neutral.

The afternoon of the day after Clemency's return Mr Jameson went to the Ramsgates' house in Tavistock Square for a meeting with Miss Hastings. He had expected a flustered and embarrassed girl, but he was soon to discover his mistake, for the young lady who greeted him was poised and collected. Mr Jameson, who had come prepared to play the avuncular lawyer confronted by a naughty schoolroom miss, found the role singularly inappropriate and was forced to abandon it.

Miss Hastings' blue eyes were steady, her colour unchanged. When told that her mother had been sadly afflicted by her daughter's undutiful behaviour, Miss Hastings merely raised one eyebrow in polite disbelief. A reference to Mrs Hastings-Whinborough's shattered nerves brought a cool, 'Then I am surprised that she felt able to entertain Mr Butler.'

Clemency listened civilly to Mr Jameson's prepared speech but it was plain that she was not impressed. Mr Jameson thought swiftly. Clemency's physical ressemblance to her mother, he saw, was misleading. She was more like her father, clear and incisive in her thinking. Furthermore, she would have £100,000 at her disposal when she was twenty-five. She would need a man of business on her own account then. The thought concentrated his mind wonderfully. He changed tack.

'Miss Hastings-Whinborough,' he began again.

'Hastings, please, Mr Jameson,' said Clemency. 'I find the Whinborough addition somewhat affected. My father was content with Hastings and so am I.'

'Miss Hastings, I come with proposals from your mother. She suggests raising your pin money to one hundred pounds a year and any bills in excess of that to be approved by her. She will also choose a new maid for you. However, I am not in entire agreement with her on this question. I think myself that you might prefer more autonomy in your affairs.'

For the first time Clemency offered him an approving smile.

'If you haven't any suggestions,' went on Mr Jameson, 'this is what I propose ...'

'I would like five hundred a year,' said Clemency firmly. 'And out of that I shall pay Mrs Ramsgate and have the choosing and paying of my own maid, as well as all my personal expenses. I prefer to deal directly with you.'

'Five hundred pounds! That is a lot of money.'

'I am a wealthy woman,' Clemency said calmly.

'I do not know whether your mother will countenance it ...' said Mr Jameson, playing for time.

'As you are one of the trustees, I imagine that you will be able to persuade her, sir. Or must I find myself another man of business?'

Mr Jameson knew when he was beaten. 'I think I may be able to reason with her.'

'I am sure you can.' Clemency sat back and offered him a smile. 'I should like you to do a couple more things for me, if you would, Mr Jameson.'

'Of course, Miss Hastings.'

'I should like to reimburse Cousin Anne for her hospitality. She is not wealthy and I would not like her to be out of pocket. Can you find a tactful way she could be sent, say, ten pounds?'

'Certainly, Miss Hastings. Your father did make provision for *ex-gratia* payments. It can come under that. And would you like me to include a consideration for her maid?'

'Yes please. Secondly, I would like you to find Sally Wilkins, my maid, for me. If she has no post, or is not suited, I should like her back. Here is her address.'

Mr Jameson opened his mouth and shut it again. Sally had been ignominiously dismissed following Clemency's flight and he was certain that this step would not have Mrs Hastings-Whinborough's approval. A moment's thought, however, convinced him that contact between mother and daughter would be slight. In all probability Mrs Hastings-Whinborough would never hear of it. In any event, Mr Jameson knew which side his bread was buttered on.

'It shall be done.'

'Thank you.' Clemency rose and Mr Jameson, realizing that his interview was over, took his leave with much bowing.

When he'd gone Clemency walked to the window and looked out. She had changed, she realized, in the last month or so. Before she'd run away she'd been obedient, even if occasionally resentful. She had still been a child in her old home. Now things were very different. Somehow she had found the confidence to organize her own life. She had embarked on her escape with no thought but to evade a hateful marriage and the threat of being sent to Aunt Whinborough. But she had gained far more.

The price, though, had been very heavy. Her thoughts, as always, came back to Lysander. Ever since she'd known him he'd been in mourning and that black coat, those black pantaloons and the black silk neckcloth seemed so much part of him that she could not imagine him wearing anything else. His coat was shabby too, and his linen frayed. Somehow, when she herself was a governess, this did not worry her, but *here*, amid all the opulence of Mrs Ramsgate's taste and with a knowledge of her own wealth, she couldn't help feeling upset that she had so much and he so little. She blinked back her tears.

And there was nothing that she could do about it. That was what hurt so much. He hated and reviled her, he had made that very clear! No, he would sell his birthright and join some second-rate regiment and she would just have to stand by.

She had, however, reckoned without Arabella and Lady Helena.

The next few days passed peacefully. The school term started again and the two elder Ramsgate boys took the coach back to Winchester. The youngest boy returned to his day school and soon there was only little Caroline up in the nursery. Mr Ramsgate took the ladies to the Theatre Royal to see Kean act. Mrs Ramsgate took Clemency and her daughters to the newly opened James Shoolbred Drapery Warehouse in Tottenham Court Road where Clemency bought a deep blue merino for a new winter pelisse and Mrs Ramsgate allowed her daughters to choose from Mr Shoolbred's tempting array some velvet for new spencers.

An ecstatic Sally arrived. Without a proper reference she'd found it difficult to get a job, she'd told Clemency, and had been helping her mother take in washing to make out. To her Clemency was far more open than to Mary and Eleanor, and Sally exclaimed over the bad luck which had led her to mistake Alexander for his brother. 'I should think this new marquess will come round, miss, never you worry,' she said. Indeed, Sally couldn't see that any man could resist her mistress's beauty. 'In the meantime I'll have these frills off that you don't like, shall I?'

Clemency agreed. She had little faith in Sally's optimism with regard to Lysander, but at least they could remove the overloaded frills and lace from her clothes!

On the following Monday Clemency was sitting with Mary and Eleanor in their sitting-room. They were discussing the fashions in the latest copy of *La Belle Assemblée*.

'Now, Clemmie, don't you think this is ravishingly pretty?' cried Eleanor. 'Evening dress of gossamer satin, body and Spanish slashed sleeves of pink satin and a cap with rosebuds.'

'It would suit you, Nell,' said Clemency, looking critically at the colour plate. 'Being fair I can't wear pink.'

'You're so beautiful you can wear anything,' cried Mary fondly. 'I don't know *why* you are removing all those frills!' Mary and Eleanor had a fondness for frills and always complained that their skirts were made too plain.

'Frills make me look like a dressed-up china doll,' answered Clemency. She had recovered something of her old spirits. Perhaps she was a trifle thin and there were shadows in those blue eyes for those who cared to look, but her friends found no fault in her. She was wearing a blue and white striped percale half-dress, embroidered with tiny blue cornflowers, which exactly matched her eyes. Sally had celebrated her return by giving her mistress's hair a wash in rosemary lotion and arranging it on top of her head in the antique Roman style with ringlets falling from a classic knot.

At this moment Dawlish entered with a card on a tray for Miss Hastings.

Clemency picked it up. 'Good Heavens!' she cried. 'Arabella! Yes please, Dawlish, ask Lady Arabella to come up.'

Mary and Eleanor exchanged glances. Clemency had not been in the house twenty-four hours before they had inveigled at least some of her story out of her. It was Eleanor who had found the marquess's name in the peerage and she had picked up at once that Abbots Candover must have something to do with her friend's rejected suitor.

Clemency did not tell them that she had been governess to Lady Arabella Candover, but she was forced to admit to an acquaintance. She contrived to make it sound distant. The sisters were fortunately too in awe of a Lady Arabella visiting their house to ask awkward questions just then, but both of them fully intended to before the day was out.

'Clemency!' Arabella almost ran into the room and embraced Clemency with fervour. She was hugged, kissed and looked over critically. 'That's better!' she cried, surveying Clemency's dress with approval. Lysander would be mad not to fall for so beautiful a girl, she thought.

Clemency laughed and introduced Mary and Eleanor. After a few moments conversation Mary said, 'Lady Arabella must have a lot to say to you, Clemency. I'm sure Nell and I will excuse you if you wish to take her up to your own room.'

'Thank you,' said Clemency. 'Come upstairs, Arabella. I have my own sitting-room where we may have a comfortable *coze*.'

'Well!' exclaimed Eleanor as the door closed behind them. 'I think you'll agree, Mary, that Clemmie has some explaining to do!'

Upstairs, with one accord, the girls made for the window seat. Arabella took off her bonnet and pelisse and flung them over a chair.

'But what are you doing in London, Arabella?' asked Clemency when the first greetings were over.

'Aunt Helena and I have come up with a Mission!' announced Arabella.

'A mission?' echoed Clemency. Vague thoughts of one of Adela's missions flashed through her mind. But that didn't sound like Arabella, still less like Lady Helena.

'Yes,' said Arabella, plunging in. She fully meant to carry all before her, by force if necessary. 'We are quite determined. It's Zander. He's going round like a bear with a sore head and he's eating nothing. His valet says he's lost weight and he's looking *awful.*'

'Oh!' Clemency had turned quite pale.

'We think it's high time he settled down. He's the last of the family, you know. Aunt Helena and I both think it's obvious that he's in love with you. The Fabians thought so too,' she added, in case one broadside was not enough. She then sat back and watched the effect of her bombshell with satisfaction.

Clemency's colour had risen. She pressed her hands to her cheeks. 'Oh,' she managed to say faintly. 'He can't ... I mean, he doesn't....'

'The only question is,' went on Arabella unheeding, 'are *you* in love with *him*?' Clemency was now quite scarlet. 'Do say yes,' pleaded Arabella, 'I should so much like you for a sister.'

'But ... your brother ... are you sure?' stammered Clemency. Could it possibly be true? Had the tenderness of those kisses really meant something to him? There had been times when Clemency had detected some warmth in him towards herself, but she had never dared to trust it. Could it really be so? Were Arabella and Lady Helena right? 'Lady Helena,' she said hesitantly, 'does she really approve? You are not inventing this, Arabella?'

'See if I am!' Arabella reached into her reticule and brought out a note. It was written in Lady Helena's spiky hand.

My dear Clemency,
    Arabella and I hope that you will be able to take tea with us this afternoon. We shall expect you about four o'clock.

It was signed simply, *Helena Candover.*

Clemency looked again at the letter and then at Arabella. Lady Helena had called her 'Clemency', had forgiven her her deception. Perhaps ... but here her courage failed.

'Oh, Arabella!' she cried and burst into tears of joy.

Arabella left some twenty minutes later having achieved her objective. True, her methods had been somewhat akin to the rack and thumbscrew, but she didn't think that gentle persuasion would have worked. Clemency had eventually admitted to an affection for Lysander. Naturally, this had been hedged about by various ladylike circumlocutions, but Arabella was easily able to ignore those.

She hoped that her aunt would be as successful in dealing with her brother.

Mrs Ramsgate, much impressed by a visit from Lady Arabella Candover, told Clemency that the carriage would be ordered for her at twenty to four and no, she was certainly not to *think* of taking a hired cab.

Clemency put on a Spanish pelisse of shot sarcenet in her favourite deep blue and Sally tenderly fitted a tall-crowned bonnet decorated with ostrich feathers over her mistress's golden curls.

Clemency entered the carriage with as much the same feeling of doom as if she was entering a tumbril. She clutched her reticule in one hand and stared unseeing out of the window. Sally, who was with her, had no such qualms. Of course everything would be all right! And wouldn't she have something to tell her mum when she was maid to a markiss's lady!

When they arrived at Berkeley Square Clemency found that she was trembling so much that she could hardly step down from the carriage. Apprehensively she followed the coachman who had knocked on the door for her. It was Timson who opened the door.

'Good afternoon, Miss Hastings,' he said. 'May I say how delighted I am to see you again?' Rumour had spread like wildfire downstairs and Timson and Mrs Marlow were in agreement that Clemency would 'do'.

'They say she has a fortune, Mr Timson,' said Mrs Marlow. She had always liked Clemency and now felt that the sudden acquisition of a fortune reflected very well on her judgement.

'Thank you, Timson.' Clemency noted that he'd used her real name.

'Would you come this way, please?' He walked purposefully across the hall, flung open a door and announced, 'Miss Hastings, my lord.'

'Oh! But ...' stammered Clemency, turning bright pink. 'This is dreadful! I thought ... I mean....'

Timson gave her a smile of fatherly encouragement and closed the door behind her.

Earlier that afternoon Lady Helena had tackled the marquess. Her technique was masterly. First she reduced his conceited opinion of himself by reminding him of a number of foolish episodes when he had failed to take her advice as a scrubby schoolboy. Then, when she felt he was properly humble, she told him in no uncertain terms that this nonsense had gone on long enough. He would propose to Miss Hastings without delay – she was coming to tea that afternoon – and he would please see to it that he was properly betrothed before his guest left the house.

As Clemency had done with Arabella earlier, Lysander floundered in a morass of half-sentences. Lady Helena brushed all this aside. 'You're in love with the gel,' she announced, brooking no argument. 'From what Arabella tells me the sentiment is returned by the lady. God knows why, for you're not at all good-looking and you have the devil's own temper! What's this?'

Lady Helena had spied a piece of paper on the desk covered with figures.

'I had thought of asking her,' admitted Lysander, running one lean hand agitatedly through his hair. 'I've been trying to work out how soon I could repay money from her dowry. This column is for necessary improvements, here I have approximate yield. And of course, there are the debts.' He sighed. 'But it's hopeless, Aunt Helena. How can I ask her to marry me, when I need her money so desperately? She's never going to be impressed by this!' He gestured towards the paper.

Lady Helena picked up the paper, tore it in two and dropped it into the waste-paper basket. 'Really, Storrington, you put me out of all patience! The poor girl doesn't want to be *audited*, she wants to be made love to! Have you *no* sense?'

Shortly before four o'clock Lysander was in his book-room. He was impeccably dressed in a double-breasted tail coat of black superfine, with black dress breeches and top boots. He was looking pale, but collected. He rose to his feet as Timson opened the door.

Whatever speech he might have prepared was doomed to remain unuttered, for Lysander, suddenly bereft of words, could only stare. He had only ever seen Clemency as a governess, wearing black or sober grey, and to see her in her deep blue pelisse matching those cornflower blue eyes almost took his breath away. He came slowly across the room towards her, his eyes on her face. Then he reached out and untied the strings of her bonnet.

Clemency stood as if hypnotized. When he'd taken off her bonnet he gently ruffled her curls and began to undo the buttons of her pelisse. Clemency allowed him to remove the pelisse and throw it on to a chair after the bonnet.

Then he said, 'I hope you are going to agree to marry me, because I am about to behave extremely improperly.'

A smile lifted the corners of her mouth. 'Again, my lord?' she enquired demurely.

Lysander, his face suddenly lightened, laughed and pulled her into his arms. 'But this time,' he said, tilting up her head with one brown hand so that he could look down at her, 'I don't need anybody to hit me on the head first! Kiss me, my darling!'

They both then promptly forgot everything but each other. It was some time later that they emerged from their enchanted state enough to begin to talk coherently. Lysander picked her up and sat her down on his knee in a large leather armchair.

'You don't know what I've been through,' he said, stroking her soft cheek with one finger. 'It was one thing to ask an unknown girl to marry me, her dowry for a title, but quite another when I knew I loved you so. I couldn't feel that I had anything worthy to offer you.'

Clemency turned in his arm to kiss his cheek. 'You love me,' she said. 'Is that not something, my lord?'

'Lysander,' corrected the marquess. 'I agree it's an absurd name, but I'm damned if I'm putting up with *my lord*.'

'Lysander then,' said Clemency dimpling. 'It is most

improper to say so, I know, but I have been in love with you since that first meeting. Imagine my shock when I discovered who you were!'

Lysander laughed and tightened his arm. Clemency saw that his whole appearance was changed. He would never be handsome; his features were too thin and angular, he was too swarthy, his nose too much of a beak, but looking at him now, when he was laughing, his face quite softened, he seemed like another man. Those sloe-black eyes were no longer cold, but warm, those finely chiselled lips tender, not taut. To Clemency it was like seeing the real person for the first time.

For his part, Lysander was feeling as if he'd stepped into a new world. To be relieved of the huge burdens left him by his father and brother, to have his home saved and a future assured, and all this by the hand of the most beautiful girl he had ever met, who united all the perfections of mind and body in her slender frame, was so much like paradise that he could hardly take it in. All he could do was kiss those rose-petal lips and gaze into those impossibly blue eyes as if he could never have enough of them.

The lovers were, however, destined to be interrupted. Lady Helena and Arabella, sitting upstairs, had heard Clemency's carriage arrive. Arabella indeed had run to the window and peered out in time to see the top of Clemency's bonnet going up the steps to the front door. Time passed slowly. Lady Helena glanced once again at the clock on the mantelpiece.

'Half an hour,' she said. 'As we haven't heard Clemency slam out of the house or Storrington shoot himself, I think we may safely assume that they are betrothed. I shall Go and See.'

'But, Aunt Helena,' cried Arabella, 'they won't want to be disturbed.'

'They may not,' stated Lady Helena, majestically, 'but they will have to put up with it. Candover itself is At Stake.' She strode to the door and sailed out, quite ignoring the dogs, who looked as horrified as her niece.

She flung open the door of the book-room to be confronted by her nephew and Miss Hastings in considerable disarray, (Clemency's hairpins were by now scattered over the floor) locked in an embrace and quite lost to the world.

'Storrington!' she commanded. Lysander looked up. 'Am I to

take it that you are now engaged?'

'You are, Aunt Helena.' The marquess smiled down at his betrothed. 'Clemency has done me the honour of accepting my hand in marriage.'

'Splendid,' stated Lady Helena. 'That is all very satisfactory. When you have finished your spooning will you both come upstairs? Arabella and I are awaiting your arrival for tea.'